MORE PRAISE FOR
HOW TO KIDNAP THE RICH

"Rahul Raina's *How to Kidnap the Rich* has already been optioned by HBO: a Delhi-set, reality TV–based literary crime crossover, it will appeal to fans of *Parasite* and *Crazy Rich Asians*."
—*Daily Mail* (London)

"A satire, a love story, and a thriller, *How to Kidnap the Rich* by Rahul Raina has shades of *The Talented Mr. Ripley*. . . . [It] casts an unerring eye over the huge disparity in Indian society. A rollercoaster of a read, this is going to be big."
—*Stylist* (UK)

"Hugely entertaining."
—*Bookseller* (UK)

"Rahul Raina's voice crackles with wit and the affecting exuberance of youth. His ripping good story grabs you on page one and doesn't let go, taking you on a monstrously funny and unpredictable wild ride through a thousand different Delhis at top speed. *How to Kidnap the Rich* roars with brilliance, freshness, and so much heart."
—Kevin Kwan, *New York Times* bestselling author of the Crazy Rich Asians trilogy and *Sex and Vanity*

"Part crime novel, part satire on modern India and told with authenticity, razor-sharp wit and a biting turn of phrase, Rahul Raina's *How to Kidnap the Rich* is a book I've been waiting a long time for. I can't remember the last time I read such an assured debut. Raina writes like he's been doing this all his life. Ladies and gentlemen, it's time to welcome a new star to the world of international crime fiction."

—Abir Mukherjee, author of *A Rising Man*

"Brutally funny and fast-paced, this debut from Rahul Raina proves he is a star in the making."

—Nikesh Shukla, author of *Coconut Unlimited*

HOW TO KIDNAP THE RICH

HOW TO KIDNAP THE RICH

RAHUL RAINA

A NOVEL

HARPER ◗ PERENNIAL

NEW YORK • LONDON • TORONTO • SYDNEY • NEW DELHI • AUCKLAND

HARPER ● PERENNIAL

Also published in Great Britain in 2021 by Little, Brown.

HarperCollins books may be purchased for educational, business, or sales promotional use. For information, please email the Special Markets Department at SPsales@harpercollins.com.

FIRST U.S. EDITION

Library of Congress Cataloging-in-Publication Data has been applied for.

ISBN 978-0-06-302878-4 (pbk.)

21 22 23 24 25   LSC   10 9 8 7 6 5 4 3 2 1

For my family, who were terrified this
book was going to be about them.

HOW TO KIDNAP THE RICH

PART ONE

ONE

The first kidnapping wasn't my fault.

The others—those were definitely me.

I was lying in a haze of brown bottles. Rudi was on the floor, face streaked with a little vomit. I was meant to be looking after him. Rudi had been doing coke, a disgusting Western synthetic drug. What was wrong with our drugs, the genteel natural Oriental ones like opium or khat?

That posh shit.

The statue of Saraswati was watching us unkindly from the corner. I could smell the stink of the camphor incense I'd bought to cover up the stale funk of beer and sweat and turmeric-laced street food.

Rudi's flat was—how do our elites say it?—uber classy. Flat-screens, silk carpets, modern art on the walls. Tasteful recessed lighting. We were ten days from Diwali. The place was cluttered with presents from hangers-on, advertisers, politicians. Hampers of food, boxes of sweets, flower arrangements, Japanese electronics, greeting cards stuffed with money.

It was one of those wet, warm afternoons where everyone was scratching their backsides and our great nation's GDP was failing to hit the World Bank's targets.

I wasn't usually the one drinking. But hanging around Rudi as much as I had recently, trying to watch him, cover for him, keep the papers from seeing him like this, had taken its toll. I was feeling guilty about it all, feeling annoyed because I couldn't spend time with the woman I loved—well, that situation had had its effect. The one damn day I needed to be completely alert, and I wasn't.

It was one in the afternoon. Three hours until the car was supposed to turn up to take us to the studio. Four hours before Rudi would appear, glowing, made-up, before all of India, on the number one game show in the whole damn country, *Beat the Brain*.

I was trying to reach for another can of something to sharpen up. I had just found a drink as warm as cat piss when the door exploded inward. Arms reached into the apartment and tried to remove the one hinge clinging to its frame.

I heard uncouth shouting. I scrabbled around, trying to get to my feet. All I did was throw my arms and legs in the air like an upended buffalo.

"Rudi! Get up! Someone's try . . ." I whispered. My throat was dry, barren, useless.

The door finally gave up, groaned like a fifty-year-old at the gym. I tried to shout again. My lips flapped uselessly.

A man walked in, dressed like a hospital orderly, carrying two folding wheelchairs in his arms. He smiled at the mess of the two of us on the floor.

Whack, whack went the cosh.

I screamed, and again when I tasted blood. I had a surgical mask strapped around my face. I gurgled uselessly into it. I didn't fight back. I didn't do anything. I was grabbed up and strapped into a wheelchair.

I saw his yellow teeth, a necklace of black prayer beads like shrunken heads, and heard a voice say, "Quiet, or the fat one gets it."

Was that meant to be a threat? He had misunderstood our relationship.

Rudi never even woke up.

That was back when I had my finger. I miss that little thing. Later on, they had to show proof of life, and what better than the servant's little pinkie?

They hacked it off with the kind of knife used to cut vegetables at the dhabas; one of those blades used to trim great bunches of coriander at the market stalls. There was a lesson in this for me: you try to blackmail a kid into giving you a cut of his riches and you end up getting your bloody appendages cut off.

I miss that finger. It was a good one.

Fucking Delhi. Fucking India.

Now this isn't like one of those films, you understand, the ones that start out as comedies, where Shah Rukh and Preity are friends at university, and then after the intermission everyone starts getting cancer and mothers start weeping about family honor until finally there's a wedding where everyone dances their troubles away. There is no tragedy here. Just me getting my finger chopped off. And a series of kidnappings.

No mothers to guilt-trip you. No tears. No emotional business, ya? Just a total khichdi from beginning to end.

It had all started so innocently.

One million three hundred thousand rupees. That's all I got. Four weeks of frenzied, sweat-soaked studying, fourteen hours every day, so that spoiled little brat could get into the university of his parents' choice.

Now, you think, 1,300,000 rupees, Ramesh, that's a lot! You're earning more than 97 percent of Indians, at least according to the tax office; why are you complaining?

It's because I pay my taxes. I know, it's very stupid of me.

And because I live a mile-a-minute existence where every year could be my last, where I'm constantly on the edge of discovery, where every knock on the door might be the police, all for a gnat's-arse 1.3 million Gandhis—fine, fine, I'm complaining because I like complaining, it's a Delhi boy's birthright and I intend to honor it.

I met the kid thrice—no, three times, for thrice is not a word, never was a word, and never shall be, as Claire would have said.

I hated his name from the minute I heard it. Rudi. Rudraksh. Fucking Rudraksh. Who calls their kid that? White hippies from the sixties. It sounds like a movie star's offspring—one of those kids with a million followers on Instagram and a Louis Vuitton addiction. It sounds like a glue, or a floor cleaner: mighty, all-powerful, the housewife's friend, only forty-nine rupees.

Rudi's parents had a nice little flat in Green Park—not the most desirable neighborhood, but getting there. Aspirational location, the realtors would say, for those on the up. The cars were Hondas and Lexuses, no German ones yet.

For my first meeting, I carried a bag that said *DeliveryFast*—no questions at gates, no holdups, just waved through. I was pretending to deliver pizza. Very Continental. Very chic. I was getting above my station, as the Britishers say in those old films where they beat coolies for making eyes at their virgin daughters.

Rudi's father was fat and wore a shirt advertising his golf club. He was rich. Of course he was. If you're fat and Indian, you're rich; if you're fat and poor, you're lying. It's only the West where the rich are thin and vegan and moral. His wife wore the usual tight pink workout clothes. Their home was filled with lots of stone, medieval tapestries vaguely Mughal, ostentatious prayer room by the front door, Mediterranean porcelain statues, marble goddesses in rutting poses. Three bedrooms, four crore on the market.

I hated the boy immediately. Overbite, greasy face, piggy little eyes. Nothing like the real Rudraksh, the fearsome, all-knowing, all-beheading avatar of Shiva.

I'm being harsh on him. You know what my real issue was with him? Absolutely nothing. He was normal. Forgettable. Eighteen years old. I had seen a hundred of him in the five years up until that point.

"So," Rudi's father said. His eyes were rotating round his pig skull, full of masturbatory fantasies of how low a fee he could bargain me down to.

"So," said Rudi's mother, as if anything would be better than this: discussing the state of her marriage with her mother-in-law, or doing that yoga the whites do where you sweat out the Ganges (The *Ganges*? Such airs I've adopted), or worst of all, talking about my hopes, fears, and aspirations.

Thank God the foreplay was fucking brief. I went immediately into my spiel.

Ramesh Kumar—Educational Consultant. That is what my business card says.

You want your little darling to get 99.4 percent and become an IITian and lord it over the rest of us? You come to me. You want your little rasgulla to top the state boards, start his inevitable march to the corner office on Wall Street or in London or, God forbid, if everything goes wrong, Bangalore? I'm your man. Any examination, any subject, four weeks. Or your money back. And they all try to, every single one.

"You got 0.1 percent less than promised." "He only got into Vassar." "Rupa aunty's boy did better and he actually did his exams *himself*." I've heard it all.

I am one of the best exam-takers in Delhi, and so I must be one of the very best in the world. The Chinese are my only competition. There must be thousands of me over there, advancing the careers of the chubby children of communist officials, always fearing the bullet in the back of the head, or being packed off to one of those reeducation camps they've put the Muslims in, or worse, being sent to make iPhones in the Shenzhen factories with the suicide nets.

Fuck, those guys really know how to make people work. They really are the future. The Western rich, or the Indian, if their children fail, they become social entrepreneurs. The Chinese? Their children fail and become lunch.

We consultants, be we brown or black or yellow, are the side product of the Western arsehole meritocracy. We have to exist. We grease the wheels. We make this dog-eat-dog world work. We are where Fulbright scholarships and visiting fellowships and grants are born. We are the handmaidens of the brown takeover of the world.

I usually sit in my little second-floor office-cum-flat in New Delhi and sweat and sweat, and out of my balls giants of industry are born, future world leaders, presidents. I create them out of nothing, we all do, the armies of us all slaving away. Maybe one day we might have something too, kids of our own we can bribe to success, our own family name that inspires fear and kneeling and scraping.

Of course I do not tell my clients that. I tell them nothing of my dreams. They tell me what they want. I set out my rates. I tell them how little a few lakh rupees is against that future cushy job at McKinsey or BCG, and their pinprick eyes glaze over with lust and trembling, all very pornographic, and then they always lowball me, like I'm their village-born washerwoman who hasn't received a raise in fifteen years, rather than the man who holds their child's future in his hands.

They wouldn't fuck with me if I wore suits. But they would have to be Italian ones, or French. You wear an Indian suit, they'll smell it, and they'll fuck you even harder.

Suits. That's what I was thinking about as Rudraksh's dear father, Vishal Saxena (strong family name, manly name), eyed me and dreamed about how little he could get me for. The food courier thing was getting old. I was thinking of rebranding. I needed to talk to a tailor, soon.

"Rudraksh," Mr. Saxena said, and at that the boy snorted a little, woken from some daydream.

"Dad, you know I don't like that na—"

The father eyed him, silenced him, just like that. Indian parents, huh? Still got it, even if a generation ago he'd have been slapped for daring to open his mouth.

Mr. Saxena had fat lips, red lips, movie actress lips, very incongruous. His wife had none at all, and after being married to a man like her husband, who could blame her? Her lips had probably been pursed from the day she was married.

She butted in like she wanted me out quickly, so she could get the servants to fumigate the squeaky, plastic-covered couch I was sitting on. "Rudi wants Silicon Valley, a career in venture capital," she said, in the way that told you the kid didn't want that at all. "We want the All India Examinations Premium Package. Top Ten Thousand or your money back." She pronounced the words slowly, the syllables echoing one by one around all that tasteful marble and Khajuraho-inspired woodwork, like I was fucking illiterate.

I nodded, nice and slow. Let her think I was subservient if she wanted to.

She had the sort of face you'd expect. Condescending. The "We shop in malls now, not Palika Bazaar. Who goes there in this day and age, cousin, seriously? You and your husband? Oh" face. But you knew what she was capable of. Her face told a story of effortless upper-middle-class superiority. There was an honesty to her disdain. In this country, you should be very wary of faces that are one thing when they should be another. You ever see a concerned, kindly police inspector, or a helpful civil servant, you know you're in the shit.

The All Indias are the big one, the ones that everyone takes when they leave school. There are other entrance exams all year round for everything, one for law schools, one for the army, one for fucking toilet inspectors, but the All Indias are the cream of the crop, my biggest earner for the year. They are the gateway to the best universities, the brightest futures, the whitest lives. I had a complete All India package, the five component exams all done by me. I offered the common exams in English and Hindi, even though a duffer could pass them.

Beyond that, mathematics, economics, finance, the exams that helped you escape India, those were my speciality, but I also did whichever combination you requested, arts subjects, science subjects, no problem, all given whenever and wherever you wanted.

If you got Top Thousand, your future was assured. The McMansion in New Jersey awaited, along with the Chevrolet SUV and the kids' violin recitals you never attended.

Top Hundred finishers had their faces plastered on the buildings of the schools that had produced them. Their teachers got interviewed on TV, like they had overseen successful Siamese twin separations or Arab–Israeli peace talks. They'd jack up their prices and roll out their fucking educational apps.

Top Tens? They were instant celebrities.

You had to pick your clients carefully. If they were crooked and didn't pay, the whole year's take was ruined.

These guys, though, were too obviously greedy to be harmful. The people you need to be careful of are those who start talking about traditions and dharma and calling you beta and all that shit. They're the ones you run from. I had bitter memories of that assistant mayor's kid. Lots of screaming, very unpleasant. No more politicians.

My form was thorough. Social security number, Aadhaar details, income, legal and illegal, school history, who they'd been referred by. I paid a contact at the income tax office to run checks. All my clients had the usual background of middle-class petty larceny. A few bribes paid here and there for construction permits, to private schools for exam-less admission, to the government to pass off their kids as low caste for the quota admissions, the usual scum shit that makes this great country what it is, like the pesticides in the milk that give your children character, grit, and lifelong behavioral problems.

Everyone knows what makes India great. China has the communists in charge, Xi Dada and his cronies, Europe has piazzas and art galleries, America has beef and tits and money. We have democracy. We argue, endlessly. We speak eight thousand different kinds of shit, we insult each other, we make things happen. This is the country of deals. This is the country of talk. Every brick might be half-baked, every building might be missing the inside, held up more by belief than cement, but it gets done, at half the price, in half the time.

We signed the contract. I took a pile of the kid's textbooks. I was thrown out the back door. I went home, ready to spend a month filling my brain, eating junk food, and grinding my way to a better life for myself and the generations of Kumars to come, so that they'd build statues to me and call me their auspicious ancestor at the prayer services, the man who made the family fortune and brought luster to the family name.

In fact, to really explain how I got into this chaotic, fingerless mess, I have to go further back, even further than Rudi, to my origin story. My family was poor as long back as we could remember. There were the old rumors that every family has, that once we used to be poets, or that we were descended from conquerors, Greeks, or the British or the Russians, and that our poverty was merely temporary. Somehow it had become the sort of temporary that was extremely permanent.

Our business was tea. For generations we had sold that

beautiful fragrant herb, that bewitcher of men and moguls, to anyone who would—

All right, we did actually end up in the tea business, but it didn't begin that way. My father had been in road construction. His back had gone bad, and he'd burned his hands to hell before I'd been born, probably from falling dead drunk into the flaming buckets of tar they use. We don't have gloves in India. I remember the way he tried so lovingly to flex his fingers as he tucked me in at night ... Okay, he used to beat me, all right. He did the backhand slap that India is famous for all over the world, but his hand, stuck in a reverse claw with the fingers unable to curl, the muscles shot, the skin shiny with scar tissue, made the slap harder, caused me unimaginable pain, like it wasn't his hand at all, but a specially designed instrument he could summon at will.

A perfect start for a life of intermittent torture.

I never knew my mother. She died giving birth to me, and my father had nothing good to say about her. One day I had annoyed him somehow, lost a peppercorn, or the milk had boiled over, maybe, and he'd said, "He's stupid, he is, just like his mother. She had cow's eyes and long lashes. Should have known, shouldn't I?" and his customers had laughed and he'd hit me extra hard that night, so that it made his hand hurt even more than usual and then he could hate me with a little extra venom.

Usually the tea stalls had names, Singh's or Lalit's, but ours didn't, so I used to think that was what it was known for, The One Where The Guy Hates His Son, you know, bhai, the one by Kashmere Gate.

What else? Me?

There's no point even describing me. I was small and had big brown eyes. Today I'm larger and I have big brown eyes. Back then I wore seventh-hand jeans with holes in the crotch, and walked on plastic slippers around the edges of which my toes curled. Got it?

My father and I lived in a one-room concrete shell, down an alley, then down another, and another, from the place the Western tour guides said was the real India, the one with piles of spices, women in mango-colored saris, men who smelled of hair oil and incense and dragged cows behind them, stately and fat; the one where the whites got out of their AC jeeps and said how *overwhelmed* they were by the sights and the sounds.

This India, my India, smells like shit. It smells like a country that has gone off, all the dreams having curdled and clumped like rancid paneer. It smells like the inhabitants have drugged themselves with cannabis and alcohol and incense, and exist only to turn wheat and corn and rice into babies and shit. You drink, you gamble, you watch cricket and bet money you don't have, you lynch Muslims, you beat your kids, and they grow up and do the same.

Papa and I went to the temple every morning. I'll give the limp little lund that. Always very religious, one of the only things I've made sure to inherit from him—well, now I go as often as I can.

Every morning he rang the bell by the entrance of the temple (other parents would hoist their kids on their shoulders to do it—did mine?), and we removed our shoes and hoped they'd be there when we returned. Papa hawked a few paise into the collection box, a miserable amount even back then, before India was hit with inflation and McDonald's and kids with American accents at the malls. A quick bow before the goddess, dark and triumphant as her tigers crushed the life out of demons and men that tried to look at her tits. I prayed for a farewell to slaps, for money and escape. Papa prayed for chai-related success, that he wouldn't get syphilis, and that his only son might not be such a fucking dumbass when fully grown.

At least we prayed for something real, something tangible. Better than the tens of millions of rupees people spend every day wishing for their kids to be good people and TED Talkers and have fulfilling marriages or other rich-people shit.

Then the tea-selling began. Crack of dawn. Near the money-changers bilking the Western tourists by the Kashmere Gate. We wheeled our little tea stall, paint cracking and discolored, down narrow streets filled with polluted fog, distant night-watchmen and milkmen and washermen shouting out like ghosts, advertising, threatening, joking.

My father did the cycling, legs straining as we splashed across potholes, every muscle working in tandem, so he looked from skull to sole like one great machine that turned alcohol to money. I followed, trotting behind like a rabid dog chasing a bag of meat, looking up at the overhead power cables tangling and untwining, at the planes coming down to land at the airport. By the time we got to our designated place, worked out by my papa through subtle negotiation and some of those famous backhand slaps, I always had to scrape my legs of the muck that in a million years would be compressed to petroleum.

We were right on the edge of Old Delhi, where the medieval gave way to the modern. On the road, impatient moustachioed men taking shortcuts zoomed past on Hero Hondas held together by tape and prayers. Women watched their purses and held their keys like knives to scratch any man who got too close. Children my age, five to a rickshaw, were carted to their schools, uniforms blue and gray and green, noses snotty, hair slicked back with oil, clutching plastic lunchboxes filled with chapatis and vegetarian curries made by their loving parents.

That was their world, an India that seemed a century away from ours. That was all I saw of it, just a brief glimpse, twice a day. I would never be part of it.

I was lower lower middle class. My father owned a business, it's true, one I was set to inherit. We weren't starving, we weren't Dalits or homeless, but we were not going anywhere either. The great social movements passed us by. Independence, socialism, capitalism, everything was the same. My life was grinding spices for tea.

Even now, a decade after that last day, when I told my father to go fuck himself, I can still remember the mixture. Three parts green cardamom, three parts fennel, two parts clove, two parts cassia, half part peppercorn, half part black cardamom. Ground every day, every hour, every mind-melting minute, fresh to order, by yours truly. Heaven help you if you made a mistake. You should know by now what the reward for that was.

I had a stone that I used to pulverize my spices, far too big for a kid, fat and heavy and dark gray with little veins of white running through it like cellulite on a politician's thighs. I spent my days hunched over behind the stall and beat those spices into dust, my back in painful little knots by the end of the day. At night I had nightmares that I would turn into a hunchback and tried, in the pitch black before my father woke, to stretch my back straight, reaching with hands and feet to China and Pakistan, like Westerners doing dawn-light Bikram yoga to solve their lumbar issues.

"No shop-bought powders here, sir!" my father would shout. "All done fresh by my little runt of a boy down there. You, rat! Show the gentleman your muscles! Ha ha!" Sometimes a few insects, a little dirt, some spit found their way into the mixture, by accident, of course.

My hate could have made India the world's leader in renewable energy.

"Hot chai! Fresh chai! Ginger chai for the ill! Milk chai for the depressed! Garam! Garam! All day, every day!" Papa shouted for hours on end, his voice never growing hoarse, singing out movie songs when business was good, praising the gods, praising India, talking about how the People's Party would lose the next elections, how all our cricketers were fat and useless, doing his best to drown out his million competitors. I imagined they all had their own sons filled with hatred, and that one day we'd gang together and cut our fathers' throats, and turn the buffalo milk red and drink deep of the patricide chai.

Every day Papa stood behind his discolored copper pot, the Bunsen flame warming his balls, boiling the milk, watered down just enough that no one could tell. I still cannot stand the smell of scalded fat, nor the sight of milk froth erupting. I handed him bashed, broken, wretched spices at five-minute intervals. I carefully passed over the sealed jar of granulated sugar, clumped by moisture—*slap, slap*, too slow, "You dropped it, the bugs will get in now!"—sucralose for the newly corpulent rich, cups, mugs, jugs, the various tea mixtures . . .

We had six. Each jar had stuck on it a little newspaper picture of the god or goddess responsible for its auspices. One promised you wealth, another health, another many boys to be produced from your loins, another love, affection, womanly favors from that plump secretary at the front desk who you wanted to fuck on the side. You've already guessed they all came from the same pot. To the love chai we added some fake rose petals just for some color. We charged 50 percent extra. Fifteen rupees a cup! Can you imagine? Daylight robbery! Nobody ever ordered it, but even so! Better us, though, better our little harmless fraud, than the Chinese cutting up tigers to make Viagra tea or cutting up farmers to steal their corneas.

Every day, dawn to dusk, stuck behind the stall. I could have been out exploring Old Delhi, running through shadowed alleyways and abandoned havelis, thick walls no match for British cannon, stealing moldy books from the market, overhearing the plots of robbers and thieves and hijras, learning mystical secrets in verse from dehydrated-looking Sufis, betting grubby rupees on cat and dog and rooster and men fights, and instead there I was pounding spices all day long, and getting beaten.

At least my fingers smelled like the potpourri you get in all the finest houses nowadays, Fantasy Orient or Ethnic Adventure they are always called. That was something.

Some days I had a holiday. Not one of our government-mandated multicultural holidays, but one of the days Papa got drunk and I failed to rouse him. You had to shove him hard, try as hard as you could—a whole day of work missed because you couldn't wake him up? Oh you would get it extra hard then.

On those days, I went to school. I learned about the world

outside Delhi. I learned to read and write. I was a good little boy. I lost myself in books. A charity could have taken a photo of me and put me on their posters, the ones where knock-kneed children have their problems disappear and are "utterly transported from their miserable lives" because they read four pages of *The Very Hungry Caterpillar*.

Business was good, but where the money went to, I don't know. I never had a pot to piss in, and my papa certainly didn't. The front doors of his enemies' or loan sharks' houses were his preferred commode, or on their faces, he said, when at night he was drunk and the boasting began, about women charmed and necks broken in his glorious youth.

He did plenty of womanizing. He did nothing around the house. Who did my laundry? Where did we get soap from? Food? I rarely saw my father cook. Which housewife was charmed? Which working girl gave her evening meal to us?

Where was he born? I don't know.

What's become of him? You'll see.

No television. Every two-paisa family had something black and white, at least, but not him. Just a radio that squawked cricket scores so he could bet. Tendulkar gets out, Ramesh gets beaten. Sehwag gets out, Ramesh gets beaten. Dravid, he never got out. I liked him.

No kitchen. Just a little gas burner, on which my father would deign to cook chapatis when the feeling took him, which mostly happened to be when a woman was around.

The cheapest, meanest room he could find.

It was 2005, but we could have been living a century earlier. In 2005, the Americans would have been sitting in their Floridian subprime housing masturbating to Jessica Alba, not realizing the future was going to be black and brown and yellow. Even a few kilometers from where we lived, idiot Indian teenagers would have had iPods and listened to Blink-182, but what did we do?

Nothing. We had no money. Not starving, no, but . . . What a life that was. Never an idle moment. Always doing something: buying tea, selling tea, moping, crying, pounding, living a life that would never lead anywhere—my nightmare was that I would literally become my father, my hand clawing up like his, my chest sprouting with dark hairs like his, my eyes and face and brain turning into his. Maybe I would have. I would be like him today, angry and nothing and poor . . .

But this isn't a story about poverty. This is a story about wealth.

TWO

Where were we? Oh yes, I was committing yet another year of examinations fraud. Little did I know Rudi was going to be the client who changed my life.

The second meeting with the kid was no better. He was pissed off that I had not brought pizza. I was pissed off that I was getting so little money. (One point three million Gandhis and I was annoyed! My God, you could buy whole Bihari villages for that, mothers and fathers and little boys and girls, and do whatever you wanted with them, and there were probably people who did.)

Ten years before, I would have been the kid's tutor. We would have matured with each other, grown to recognize each other's strengths and weaknesses and all sorts of Western nonsense. I would have ruffled his hair when he brought me news of his academic exploits. He would have given me flowers and chocolates.

Now I was pretending to be him. That's what they mean by progress, I think.

We started with his wardrobe. Just a little con, telling the parents that every detail mattered: "Do you want a minor thing like wearing the wrong clothes at the exam to cause trouble?" It got you a few more thousand rupees at the end of the day in expenses, clothes, shoes. Nobody ever checked clothes, but the parents would swallow anything. All my clothes had memories, of a job well done, of a child sent on to a better life, of another set of greedy parents conned out of a few precious paise. When the results came out, the family were so grateful that for a few days you could make them sign off on any receipt, and you had maybe a week before they started getting avaricious again, for the car, the house, the summer internship at Google.

Rudraksh. Rudi. How do I describe him? Before the money, before the Armani suits, before the whitening-cream adverts and the diet advisers straining against the junk food and coke bloat?

Totally unremarkable face. Very north Indian face. Uttar Pradesh face. Hundred-million-of-you-in-villages face. No-matches-on-Tinder face. Rejected-for-arranged-marriage-after-first-meeting face. Oily in the T-zone. Probably sticky hands, but thankfully I always avoided touching them. Only sport played—table tennis. Badminton too athletic. Street snacks after school, stomach and testicles and blood full of golgappas and raj kachoris. Parents buying diet books for Diwali.

His hair was the usual long, greasy, unkempt mop of any self-disrespecting rich teenager. If I had still been doing wigs, it would have been easy. I kept a dozen of them in different lengths, all real hair, never shampooed or treated with soap, fifteen thousand rupees each. I had never asked where the seller, a worried-looking man in a flea-bitten shop in east Delhi, got them from.

But these days I kept the disguises for the exams simple. I'd stopped hamming it up. I had gotten a reputation. People thought I was being dramatic, pretending to be a film star. My fellow educational consultants rattled off dramatic seventies movie dialogues whenever I came near.

Rudi had spent his teenage years slacking off. Too much gaming. Too much frenzied midnight masturbation. When you asked him what he'd been studying, he'd sigh. If anything, he was even more annoying back then, before the fame, the money, the women, before he was Mister Number One, the Brain of Bharat, the Man Who Knows, the Nawab of Knowledge, because back then he was just another middle-class Indian kid, and they can drive you to suicide with one roll of their eyes.

First I had to spend three days with him, to figure out what he knew.

Those three days were torture. We went through his textbooks, barely opened, spines still uncracked, free of the usual Indian marks of virulent underlining and ink-run from tears and food stains from midnight cramming.

Every five minutes I had to tell him to pay attention to my questions about his work, about his syllabus, anything I didn't understand.

"Your parents are paying good money for this," I'd said, which had worked with kids five years ago, but he just moaned and kept flicking through his phone, the GIFs and YouTube dreck reflected against his grimy spectacles.

He had a guitar in the corner of his room that looked like it had never been touched, resting against the wall of the dark-colored wardrobe that you find in every Delhi bedroom, rich or poor, full of old shawls, moth-eaten wedding dresses, out-of-fashion salwar kameezes, and hard-shell suitcases from 1985 that no one wants to throw away, because however much money you have, Indian history has taught us that everything can turn to shit at any moment, and you might have to run away. Or maybe we're cheap. I don't know.

Piles of dusty Western DVDs crowded the shelves, crap some relative had probably hauled over from Canada back when that had been impressive, something you could show off to your neighbors, how life was so wonderful for our family in Amrika. That was before social media, when we could all see how stupid the Americans actually were, in real time.

Rudi was sweating heavily, and all he was doing was answering questions. There was a dark stain across his breasts. The fan, roaring above us at decapitation speed, did nothing but move hot air around. A new air conditioner rested on the ground, uninstalled no doubt due to some arcane labor dispute.

"Arrey yaar," he would say when my questioning became too much, or my displeasure showed. "Stop busting my balls, man. You know how much work this is? Dude, just give me a break."

Busting balls? Dude? He should show some respect to his elders. Only by about five years, but still. I was twenty-four and deserved respect. How our morals had eroded since the advent of smartphones.

Then he went back to nose-picking, muttering, surfing for music videos and girls he thought had shown too much skin on Instagram.

"Look at her," he'd say, in horror and delight, when he found some friend of a friend doing those duck lips on a Thai beach. "So immodest!"

It was extremely clear he had never touched or talked to a woman.

The Hanuman-sized mountain of work slowly came into focus. The little shit hadn't done any bloody studying at all. He couldn't tell me anything, couldn't give me any help whatsoever.

The parents had described him as "a good boy who needs help" and don't I know a lie the size of "the British are only setting up a trading post" when I see one. The prick was brain dead, a duffer, and whatever else Indian parents called their kids in films. He loafed around listening to Nirvana and emo music and didn't have the balls to take up marijuana or Marxism like any self-respecting kid would have in his situation. I had never felt the urge to smack one of my clients more.

I should have gone into yoga. Just spout mystic bullshit about chakras, book some rooms in a farmhouse outside of Delhi, hire a call-center type to be the receptionist, put up some just-bad-enough Web 1.0 site to lure in the suckers with my humility and lack of modern know-how, and away you go. White people's money up to here! They get diarrhea, you just tell them it's part of the process of enlightenment and letting go of the self.

After those first three days, the real work began. I got to studying. I had four weeks to prepare. Just enough time.

I lost myself in the books, as I always did. Hours went by. I remembered everything I read, as if it was burned into my eyes like the owner's brand into a street cow.

Back in my apartment, I'd lie back for a rest, let the fan whip dust and SO_2 across my face, sleep for three dreamless hours, and carry on, powered by coffee, Thums Up, and aloo parathas smeared with thunderously hot achaar from the stalls outside.

I fought an endless battle against mold and falling paint. I did the cleaning myself—just because I was a self-made middle-class businessman didn't mean I was going to lose my humility and get someone else to do it. The universal Indian floor, speckled stone, collected dirt like it was going out of fashion. The extractor fan in my bathroom was broken, so the whole place smelled of moisture and rot, mixed in with my cheap deodorant and weapons-grade bleaching toothpaste.

In my dreams, I thought of money and what I'd do with it. Kebabs. A blowout meal at Moti Mahal. Everything dripping with ghee. An air conditioner. A new motorbike. A few dates, splurging at some Connaught Place restaurant and failing to get into the sensible polyester underwear of a junior relationship manager at a multinational.

I saved my money. Sent it straight to the bank like an idiot, an A-grade vella. Saving for what? Could have made a fortune in construction or China or Bitcoin, said Sumit, "But I guess you just don't have it. So many of you don't."

What can I do? I am a follower of laws. I am careful. I plan for the future. Or I used to.

My life wasn't all work, though.

I went to the temple every day. Force of habit, force of slaps. Made sure to give twenty rupees; not much, but I had no ulterior motives and no greasy wishes, so it counted ten times extra. The metro ride into central Delhi was a dahi Bhalla of men leaking flop sweat and giving off looks of frustrated sexual longing for perfumed young women, even at five in the morning when you should be well girded against such thoughts by your wife's cooking.

I always went to the gurdwara too. Popped over, the British would say, as the late-dawn sun glinted off the golden dome of the Bangla Sahib, the smell of ghee and coriander making you choke as ten thousand servings of daal and gobi and chapatis were prepared by grunting Sardarjis dripping with effort.

Then a metro ride into Old Delhi, if I felt like it. I went past the Kabutar Market, where they sold thousands of multicolored budgerigars, cages stacked up, all shitting upon each other. Who bought them, where they ended up, no one had any idea. And not just birds, of course. Cows, goats, rows and rows of motorcycle helmets embalmed in plastic, a dozen shops selling the exact same Chinese suitcases, barks and ambers and potions and pastes from central Asia that could cure any ailment, girls in alleyways who beckoned you on to doom and destruction. Very close to what one finds in a mall, really.

I walked around a little, watched the Australian tourists counting their money in public—can you believe?—and then came to the church, the one by Chandni Chowk, quieter than anywhere else in Delhi. Most of the Christians had run away long ago, realized that they'd get less discrimination in the West. All that were left were the elderly, a superannuated wrinkled priest, the stink of mold hanging around him, a nun with thick glasses and worn rosary beads who reminded me of someone I had known long ago, the dream of the Christian Raj reduced to wasted muscle and worn bone.

I even did the Jama Masjid once a week. Educational consultants can do with all the goodwill they can get. Never on Fridays, when the place would be filled with twenty thousand wails to Allah about daughters and sons corrupted by modernity and whatever the saffrons were planning next (the young men who were the devout soldiers of our internationally popular government: maybe a pogrom, or a sterilization drive, or a lynching by those who thought every Muslim was trying to corrupt their sweet little girls through the love jihad). You'd go on a Monday or a Tuesday maybe, when little huddles of hungry-eyed men would fall silent if you passed within a dozen paces.

I'd say hello to my favorite beggar, Ram, who sat, legs and arms unmoving, just outside the Kasturba Hospital. I'd drop him a note of any denomination, and he'd say, in his beautiful deep voice, as if he had never seen me before, "Young man, you are going places! I was, too, when I was flying jet fighters in the '71 war," and then tell a long story of how he outclassed the Pakistanis in their American F-104s, and I always gave a little more, even though it was bullshit.

I'm not all charity and selfless do-gooding, of course. I needed him. I've lost my Old Delhi ways. I need my eye on the street now that I am middle class. This was how I kept in touch with things, the way I kept my feet on the ground. Home is home, I am who I am.

"Any information?" I'd ask, and his cunning eyes scanned the length of the road, watching the silvering on the veil of the young housewife, noticing the whisper of rust on the bottom of the coconut seller's bicycle, and the play of light on the faces of the passersby.

"Not a single bloody thing," he'd say.

I kept him on, for appearances. Maybe one day he'd be useful.

Then the street children clustered round him and pretended to be planes and they grabbed at my trousers for money and I gave it to them and tried to stop them fighting each other for it afterward.

Then breakfast, a mutton pastry in a café, and home to study for eighteen more hours.

Old Delhi seems real in a way that New Delhi doesn't. It is sedate, it is hidden, it is precapitalist. But it is all a sham. Depending on who you ask, Delhi is eight cities, each conqueror building on the corpse of the last; or two, the rich and the poor, as the Westerners say; or one, where all of us live arse cheek to arse cheek; or thirty million, once you factor in the underpass dwellers, victims of the famines in Bihar that the government says don't happen.

Me? I say Delhi doesn't exist at all, rich, poor, old, new, Mughal, British, Indian—it's all just money in, money out, buildings up, metro down, fingers off, fingers on. It's a mirage. It's a bundle of streets and blocks and enclaves that happen to exist next to each other.

The markets. The cafés. Chandni bloody Chowk. These were not the haunts of my youth. I only saw these places once I'd left the tea stall. I never had free time before. Get up, temple, haul the stall out, make the tea, listen to customers complaining about the wait, their weight, their marriages, their children, go home, sleep. On a free day, a blessed free day, maybe go to school, chase dogs, feel miserable. That was my life.

All because of tea.

I cannot stand the stuff. It gives me headaches and palpitations like Indian American parents get when they hear their kid is dating a black girl. I find it difficult to socialize with the colleagues I have in this wonderful business. They drink nothing but tea. Slurping it, spitting it, inhaling it as fast as possible, like it's a sport. Not that they're worth talking to about most things, sons of whoresons, but they leak exam papers like nobody's business, and you never know what else you'll find out: which policeman to avoid or which exam center is doing an anti-corruption drive. It is one of those thin spots in the earth's crust, where all the heat comes gushing out of the underworld.

So once in a while I ventured over there, to the alleys of teahouses in the warrens behind Karkardooma, where every scandal-fleeing ex-teacher in the world has congregated.

East Delhi: the place looks like a gray smear on Google Maps, with little sunburned parks where the fountains have run dry since 1994 and no cricket game ever follows the white man's laws, and it is no better from the ground.

East Delhi, most polluted place in the world, as the *New York Times* or the WHO will tell you, so polluted that it goes off their puny little three-figure scales and breaks their equipment. Pollution I can stand. It's the stink of spices and cow's milk boiled together, the smells of my childhood, that I hold my nose against so that I can barter and trade.

East Delhi, the place I call my home.

Let me describe the man there I knew best, if only because I got to beat him later.

He was one to watch out for, was Sumit. A shark. Thin, razor-sharp cheekbones, hungry eyes, an entrepreneur, a world-beater in waiting, one of him in every tea stall, in every back room in every shop in India.

You smelled the perfume first. Like grapefruit left too long in the heat, and starting to go soft and brown with rot.

"Still ordering wigs, huh, Ramesh?" he laughed when I came in, as he did every time.

I had ventured over that day to ask some questions about the government's new exam security proposals, and to keep my ear to the ground in the fast-moving world of educational impersonation. Western professionals go on hotel mini-breaks. I went to Sumit.

"Huh, Ramesh?" said one of Sumit's chamchas, his hangers-on. They wore muscle shirts with the sleeves cut off, just like their lord and master. They always had large transparent bottles in front of them, full of creatine or some other Western concoction. I'd seen Sumit's selfies. Working out in a mirror-walled gym in Vaishali built in some family's basement, where all the talk all the time was of Marvel actor workouts and hair-loss supplements. His social media was workout selfies and idiotic phrases: "Fail to Plan, You Plan to Fail," "A Journey of a Thousand Miles Begins with One Step," the stuff you start saying when you hit forty and the girls start calling you Uncle.

And they all smelled of that bloody perfume, like a giant preening cloud with hair-gelled edges.

Sumit noticed me sniffing. "Paco Rabanne. You want to buy some?" he said, and somebody pressed a bottle into his hand out of nowhere.

I rolled my eyes.

"Business doing well lately, brother?" he asked. "You should come work for me, Ramesh."

"Why? You in trouble? Need someone to run the organization for you? Not making enough money from counterfeit perfumes?"

"Ha! Ramesh, Ramesh, Ramesh," he said. "Always with the comedy."

Sumit looked exceedingly proud of himself, as always. He basked in self-satisfaction. He knew exactly who to grease, which sub-inspector wouldn't ask questions, which indebted civil servant would leak the syllabus, which exam marker could be gotten to. He faked driving exams, entrance exams, job interviews. He would probably start faking Tinder profiles next, for all the romantically uninclined of Delhi, the moped Romeos, the fuckless hair-oiled swathes of men who gathered in each coffee shop and street market.

He collected his hangers-on, the ones who'd failed their government exams, where ten thousand people apply to get one place as a clerk in the works department or a ticket inspector or a sewer cleaner, and drifted out into our world. They were clever, but one in ten thousand? So now they took exams for eighteen-year-olds, ones they could do in their sleep.

They modeled themselves on Sumit, doing all the outside things so the inside would follow, like how our government builds bullet trains in the hope that we'll become like Japan.

A phone call would come in and Sumit would too loudly answer, "Only twenty thousand, Uncle? I usually work in much larger quantities than that," and they would all whistle at his prowess and his imported cigarettes.

He continued to insult me at a breakneck pace. "I can never understand, Ramesh, how you run your little business. You are so stuck in the past. Do you even have a Twitter account? Join me, and you could make fifty thousand a month, easy."

"Fifty thousand!" said an underling.

I was a little annoyed at all this self-congratulation.

"Fifty thousand, ha! I've got these pricks in Green Park paying me one point three million. So you can take that and your jokes about wigs and stick them up your fucking lund."

"I know powerful men. Money men. Men who can snap their fingers and destroy your whole life." Sumit composed himself before he started to rant, like he'd been reading a black-market copy of a book on mindfulness.

"Sumit, a kebabchi could destroy my life with a rotten mutton galouti. I know thousands of *them*."

"I am trying to be nice here," Sumit said.

"I don't need your niceness, Sumit. How is it, I wonder, faking driver's licenses for thirty thousand Gandhis a go? But it's all these people to order about that you enjoy, isn't it?"

The underling winced. His little eyes took in Sumit's Casio, his jeans, his Samsung. He started to dream. Big trouble. Imagine surrounding yourself with so many desperate people. What a terrible business model.

"How many clients did you have last year? Two. Next? Two. You have no ambition, Ramesh. Here you are, year after year, doing the same thing. No matter the money you make, you'll always be small. All those brains God somehow gave you, and what have you done with them?"

"One point three million Gandhis. Pays better than all those fake ration cards you do. Now, Sumit," I said, adopting a more professional demeanor, "I came to ask about the new security checks the government has been talking about. Just tell me what to expect, O Grand and Mighty Assistant Undersecretary Knower."

"Only a fool like you would take the government seriously, Ramesh bhai. Security checks? Do you think they have the time to care?"

We spent a little more time insulting each other, trying to draw out information, deals. It was the only way we could communicate.

There were hundreds of thousands of men like us, young and carefree, old and broken, trying to make it, horse-trading, knifing, trying it on, in any one of ten thousand tea shops across east Delhi.

He was stupid, young Sumit. Thought having hundreds of clients was some genius move. Thought getting involved with gangsters and goondas was smart. I knew better. The more clients, the more trouble. The more young, hungry men around you, the more trouble. I was independent, I was high quality, and I was happy with my life.

Why I carried on living in Delhi, I didn't know. I spent my whole life complaining about it, the bitch heat, the bitch sweat, the bitch traffic, and never did anything about it. I should thank Rudi for changing that, at least.

Delhi isn't saffron. Delhi isn't spice. Delhi is sweat.

Eat. Work. Talk shit when I got bored. Those were my days before Rudi and I struck it rich, the days when I had all my fingers, and was not hated by every housewife and househusband for two thousand miles.

Until the exam day, I worked. I bled for that kid. I worked as hard as every Indian parent claims they did in the 1970s, when there was only one channel on TV, when they had to walk five hours each day to school, dodging landmines and pedophiles, when there were no snowflakes and millennials crowding the WhatsApp group chat of their imagination.

Every day I ate junk, chanas and bhel puris and golgappas from the hawkers outside, and didn't put on an ounce of weight. I argued at cafés about politics, the metro extension, traffic, the beggars from Bihar, exam questions, and, of course, the pollution. What other topic is there? Not even cricket gets talked about as much. I was mocked for my wigs and my affectations and my soft, gora, pampered clients.

I listened to film songs about moons and stars and destinies, and at night I bought imitation Levi's for fifteen hundred rupees from Alibaba. No more the polyester shit of my youth! No more cast-off Barcelona shirts from some spoiled kid in England or Spain! I was assured my clothes came from the same factory in Chongqing, the very same!

And then I took the exam, and my whole life changed.

THREE

I met the kid again, a week after our last meeting, to check in on some finer details, and this time the parents cornered me. They had been having second thoughts.

"You see ..." said Mr. Saxena, and tailed off. He stroked his hairless chin, trying to make his silence seem wise instead of pathetic.

"Oh God, Vishal, get on with it," said the wife. When she moved, I caught drifts of her perfume, expensive, roses and jasmine. She folded her arms and waited for her husband to do his socially ordained duty and tear into me.

His lips were fat like a Hollywood plastic surgeon's. His eyes furtive, red, like my father's, but without the yellow tinge to them. "So, uh, Rudr—Rudi, yes, sorry, thinks that you are not worth the money. We are thinking we are pay—yes, hum, yes, darling, I am getting to the—"

I stopped him right there.

"Sir," I said, most pleasantly, really rolling out the word, lots of R, "sir, you knew what you were doing when you hired me. You are a man of taste, of discernment." He was totally disarmed, like Pakistan after a war. "I was told about you by the Sharmas. Remember them? Their boy is in New York now. Thanks to me."

Vishal Saxena's resolve crumbled. Dreams of Manhattan filled his eyes. Hot dogs, Times Square, Gordon Gekko, women with enhanced breasts and reconstructed hymens. Mrs. Saxena, his wife, began to grumble.

"I know what I am doing," I continued. "I am as tough as your parents were with you, and look how you turned out. This beautiful house. Your charming wife. I am using tried and tested methods. You have paid a fair price."

I could have gone on. I could have extolled their interior furnishings. Their coffee table books of art and photography. The medieval temple carvings on their wall. How hard they both must have worked. How our children were becoming soft, no match for the Chinese. How they themselves had crawled to school, no doubt, for days, until their limbs had been stumps, how they had been beaten mercilessly and never made a sound, not like these children nowadays. But I'd done enough.

The husband deflated. Mrs. Saxena trembled, thunder before the rains, oh that look, how I knew it. "You bought a *Hyundai*? Your mother is staying for *how long*? Your bonus was *canceled*?"

"God fucking dammit, Vishal," she said.

"Namita, he says that he is very cost effect—"

"Rudi said—"

They started arguing with each other, about career and life decisions, and that time someone slept with someone, how could you, Vishal? For God's sake, Namita, it was only once, you were being a rea—

I slipped into the kid's room.

"Oh, it's you," he said, skin unwashed and dull with grease. "Have they fired you yet?"

"Not so fast, fat boy," I said.

He gulped.

He had those glazed, blinking eyes. We Indians are the horniest people on the internet, as any comment section on any video will tell you. We crowd around women, we beg for attention, we will even ask nymphs in sixteenth-century frescoes for their phone numbers. Maybe we're just needy. Maybe I'm just being overly negative about him, which is not uncommon for me.

But maybe, just maybe, we know that we desperately need our sperm to go into the waiting uteruses of our women, so that we may outbreed the Chinese, so we can swamp them with numbers, for gods help us, there is no other way we will win against them, and here is this feckless boy throwing his patriotic juices into tissues and toilets. Disgusting.

"Let us get this straight, Rudi," I said, and I had no idea how many times I'd be saying that phrase to him over the next few years. "I'm going to be doing this exam, and your parents are going to be paying me what we agreed. Got it? No more complaining."

My parents and grandparents and everyone back to the first generation—well, maybe not the spies or the Greeks—had been meek and mild and look where that had gotten them. I had an education, of sorts, and I was going to use it.

"Hey, sorry, man," he said, after a few seconds of silence. He would not look me in the eyes. Children these days. "It's just you've got to stop giving me so much shit."

"I am the person doing the exam."

"Well, yeah, huh, dude," he said, and added many things about his childhood and ADHD and school bullying and parental narcissism that I am sure were very sad. I just wanted my money, and some more jeans, and maybe a wife at some point.

I made my peace with him. I told him I'd never see him again after he answered some of my questions about his teachers' notes on Dutch diseases and market failures.

So dawned the day of the first exam. Hotter than a funeral pyre, sweatier than a third-class train compartment, one of those days when you think all the fires of hell have emptied into Delhi.

On my way to the test, I passed brick houses plastered in ever-present election posters, the whole year just one rolling vote. I walked past couples in parks hiding under jackets, trying to do that strange tongue-kissing, dirty kissing, firangi kissing they had seen in Western films.

The building was an ugly socialist compound from the sixties, from when Borlaug had delivered us from famine and we still had five-year plans. All around me were sweaty, terrified Indian youths, a few years younger than me, eyes betraying dreams of failure, of suicide notes telling their families they should have cared more, but also of success, unimaginable riches, of foreign lands where it rained all year round and everyone ate boiled vegetables and you could slowly stop ringing your family and forget all about them.

No checks at the door, whatsoever. It was just as Sumit had said. I needn't have let myself be insulted by him. Every guard and official turned his head and carried on Facebook-stalking the boys who had bullied them at school. No one looked at the doctored examinations card, at the boy called Rudraksh Saxena who had a face like mine. Life did not require further complications.

I remembered my first All India.

My first time, it was terrifying.

Now? Now it was boring.

The exam started off easy.

Little children around me sniffed with tears, victims of cramming and parental hard-luck stories, all their dreams going to shit, years of hard work turning to dust.

And I had had a month.

What deeds I had done!

Little prick Rudi was going for the economics stream, so I had been squeezing my head fuller than a three-child family on a motorbike with this year's assortment of equations, graphs, curves, calculus, and demand functions.

On the first day of preparation I had made microeconomics my servant. On the second, I had parted the waters of household accounts. On the sixth day, I had made the Black–Scholes equation dance for me, I had made a mockery of interest rate curves.

The first exam I took was the mathematics exam. Ninety minutes of multiple-choice questions. Children around me wept, sobbed as they realized they were fucked. I barely noticed. The kid was getting his future sorted. I was getting paid.

Then I did his other exams, day after day. The Americans have their puny SAT, all over in one day. The Indian way, that's the best. Five days, five exams, teach the kids that life is a relentless parade of fear.

I finished the last one, economics, and for another year, another client, the All Indias were over. A month later, the Saxenas would pick up the combined result. No worry, no problem.

I didn't think I even did that well. Top Thousand, definitely. Sumit would brag that he had to do badly on purpose so that he would not draw attention to himself. He used to be like that, telling tall tales, talking shit, but that was before he got beaten up.

I walked out of the hall at the end, looking at the faces of the kids around me, kids on floors, kids hugging pillars, like relatives after a train crash. I didn't think too much about it all. One month until the results. One month until the money arrived. One month until I could coast to the next job.

The day my life changed started out like any other. I was being casual, I was keeping to myself, as I usually did. Sumit, on the other hand, had been full of wig jokes on WhatsApp, but I could tell he was suffering. He was doing fifteen students at a time, subcontracting the impersonation out to his usual mix of druggie kids, dropout kids, kids who had run away from home, from poverty, indentured slavery, and molestation, and had found their only chance of steady work in committing fraud for him. Sumit took too many chances, too many jobs. He did politician kids, gangster kids, promised the earth to them. If even one of them had one bad exam, the kameena would be in a world of shit.

I would be getting the results after 12 p.m., when they would be emailed to the Saxenas. They would call, and then, much more importantly, wire me the money.

Midday came, midday went. No call. Nothing.

I went out and ate, as I usually do when I'm at a loose end. I went to my favorite haunt, a south Indian place that smelled of turmeric and bleach.

The results had definitely come out. Families sat all around me celebrating, decking their children's necks with garlands and stuffing their mouths with dosas. What were the Saxenas doing? Were they trying to cheat me?

The restaurant was filled with kids who had clearly spent the last few months constantly crying to their mummy and daddy, "I have failed, I know I have, I am a bad son, kill me now, I will do better in the next life!"—arrey, give me a break—and who were now crying tears of relief. A TV blared away in the corner, so family members could avoid conversations with each other—our restaurant owners know their customers inside out.

For my clients, my kids, there was none of that. No worry, no pain. They knew they would be fine, and their parents did too, because I was the best. Even on the off chance that things did go wrong, I'd be getting a thrashing and a request for a refund, all of which probably got my clients very excited because they would think they were hard-bitten go-getters who got their money's worth rather than meek chartered accountants with rapidly expanding waistlines.

If you were rich, your kid could always take the exams again. Live at home for a year, do some fake internship your golfing buddy arranged. It was the poor who needed everything now, whose seven hollow-bellied kids needed to leave the family home as soon as possible.

One family with a crying kid was discussing their plans to go to temple the next morning. Attendance always went up a hundredfold before and after the All Indias. All those prayers, offerings of ghee and spoiled milk! I really should have gone into the religious business. You never see a poor priest, do you, and they all seem to spend their days fucking their illiterate acolytes and posting the hidden camera footage on porn sites. That part I would skip, I promise.

In the very moment that my life changed, I was in that restaurant downing nimbu panis laced with chaat masala at a dangerous rate, waiting on tenterhooks.

I was angry. I was meant to be receiving 1,300,000 rupees! Wealth, fame, fortune! Jeans!

But no news at all.

I was getting very pissed off—march-over-to-Green-Park-and-burn-the-whole-charity-giving-NRI-infested-place-down pissed off, the Maoists in our eastern states level of pissed off—and then I saw it, in the corner, on the TV.

On the screen, I saw that prick Rudi. Fake lips Vishal. Namita in traditional sari, leisurewear discarded, namastes aplenty, fending off lusty embraces from local netas.

I shouted at the proprietor to turn the volume up.

It didn't take long to figure out what had happened. They were outside their flat, every TV company in the country jostling for space, cables snaking every which way, attractive reporters in Rudi's face, sweaty gentlemen shouting for calm, neighborhood mothers standing by, itching to marry off their daughters.

"What are you going to do now, Rudi?"

"Bill Gates is going to offer you a job, is that true?"

"How did you achieve this miraculous feat?"

The little fucker had come top.

I had come top.

Fucking top.

Of the whole country.

Well, not top. Actually second. But the first place was Iqbal somebody, and he sure as shit didn't count. No cameras for the Muslim.

First-place Vedic finisher.

Sisterfucker.

How?

You take an exam so many times, you get good. They barely change the questions from year to year.

Also, I'm extremely fucking clever.

On the TV, I could see Rudi's eyes were full of a new lust for life. No dreams of weed in sweaty bedrooms. Women, money, SUVs, that was what he wanted now. I could tell he wanted to eat the whole fucking world. His life had already changed completely. Top in the fucking All Indias. He did not have to do a day's work if he didn't want. He could coast for the rest of his life, become a member of an exclusive club, the best one possible, be in a better position than the prime minister's son or even his mistress; a club no doubt with secret ties and handshakes and a sex dungeon–cum– clubhouse on Golf Course Road, and riches, riches beyond all imagination.

He would be the answer to a quiz question now.

Who came top in the All Indias in 1974? Which All India

Topper is the CEO of Facebook? Which Topper married this Bollywood actress and gets to fuck her every night?

I checked my phone. I hadn't heard from Sumit. Usually he spent the day gloating, posting Instagram selfies with the kids he had "tutored," feeding them laddoos and handing them bouquets of flowers. Nothing today. Emptier than a eunuch's underwear. He must have been furious.

"Drinks for everyone," I shouted. There were maybe twenty people left in the little room, a cluster of sour-faced families and a few old men tutting at videos of twerking white girls on their phones. I was not exactly bankrupting myself, not with the money I would have now.

Rudi was my ticket to the big time.

I was going to be fucking rich. I had the bastard by the balls.

FOUR

And now, a little digression.

You must be wondering, how did he get to here from there? From well-beaten tea seller's slave son to charming, witty, urbane man-about-town? A metro-user, a bank-card-haver, a small-business owner, a taxpayer, an independent educational consultant. How did he make it? How did this urchin bloody learn English?

Well then, now I can tell you about Sister Claire, and how she saved me.

How young must I have been? I try not to do this bastard remembering very often, but I will to get the story straight.

I was eleven. There had been trouble with our stall. Papa had wandered in late one January night from one of those sharaab joints where they distilled the demon drink straight from antifreeze.

He was bleeding more than he usually did, and had two black eyes, but only kicked me a normal amount to scold me for letting the brazier run out, so he was basically fine.

The next day he left early without a word, in effect giving me the day off. Something was definitely wrong. I played "chase the rabid, frothing mongrel dogs," that beloved Indian pastime, now sadly lost to the iPhone generation, with some neighborhood children, and when Papa came back, he told me we were going to be getting up earlier in the mornings. No explanation.

I knew what must have done it.

He had given the wrong look to the wrong woman, for he just looked too much, my father, and his worst habit was the way his eyes never held just one thing, but all. He looked for watches, clothes, new people, waistlines, ways to make it, ways to get out.

Why hadn't that curiosity helped him to craft a life away from the tea stall? Maybe he'd looked and found there was no escape. Our life had continued without change from the first day I could remember.

As always seemed to happen with us, a slight alteration of our course came with a healthy dose of violence. At midnight just a few days later, our front door burst open. Nothing strange about that. Papa's drunk friends sometimes paid us visits, as did his bookmakers and loan sharks.

Papa woke quickly.

"So you fucked her, huh?" said the interloper, a man. His stance was unsteady. He had a knife, short and sharp.

Papa remained silent. It is always best to remain silent.

"My wife," said the man. Tall, muscular, knife-wielding. "My wife. I'll kill you. You haramzada."

They all seemed the same to me, Papa's women, like they were all one. They came to him, and he kissed them, once on each cheek. "One cheek is coffee," he said, "the other is chocolate. And then we will find out where is the sugar." That was his starting line, and my cue to leave.

"Do you know who I am?" the man said. "Do you?" Papa stayed silent. The man laughed. "I am the man who will kill you."

Papa thought quickly. He looked at me, and instantly saw what he could do. You had to give him that.

"In front of my son?" he said. "My only child?" His voice came out entirely differently. He put such emotion into the word "son." If I had shut my eyes, I would never have known who he was.

He got up, and held me in front of him. The tall man looked down at me. My father pinched me from behind, hard. I knew what I had to do. Deceit came easy. I began to cry. I held my hands together and said, "Not my papa, please."

My father edged forward, pushing me toward the man. I continued crying. I added a little dribble for effect.

"My only son. The last person I have left," my father kept saying, clawing at my shoulder.

I felt a sudden shove from behind. I fell forward, onto my knees. The man watched me with complete confusion. He reached down to pick me up. Then my father struck.

He punched the man, once, twice, kidney, gut. He kicked the knife out into the dark of the stairwell. He put a hand on the man's mouth to ensure he stayed silent. While punching, Papa caught a little of my head too, but I didn't care. I felt proud. I had played my part. I had helped him. Perhaps our relationship was changing, perhaps he had found new respect for me, perhaps he would fin—

He turned to me, his smile the widest I had ever seen it, and said, his words dripping with pleasure, "Remember the first rule. When you hit them, make sure they never get up."

He punched again. He was enjoying himself, right up to the point the man roused himself and started fighting back.

Papa fought on. He got a broken rib, and a black eye that he made sure was kissed away, but he didn't die.

What happened to the woman? I always wondered. Papa got off easy, but what did she get? Beaten? Worse? She got involved with the wrong man, a liar, thief, and cheat, and then she probably got hurt.

After Papa was beaten up, he continued to receive threats, so he decided to move our business to a place with more salubrious neighbors, to environs new, to horizons undreamt of by our family, by which I mean two miles away on the Bangla Sahib Road. Two miles! That was too much for him. It was clearly time for the younger generation to pull their weight. He made me do the cycling from that day on. Bhosdike.

Even though my legs ached every morning and night from that point on, my life changed from the day we moved. For one thing, we were in New Delhi, get-up-and-go New Delhi, center-of-the-world's-greatest-democracy New Delhi. None of that Old Delhi antiquated, snake-charming nonsense—just homicidal drivers, aggressively corrupt police, and choking, lung-throttling pollution.

Now we were surrounded by twenty-first-century people. None of the furtive looks of Old Delhi, secret plots, arsenic poisonings, jeweled daggers in the back. We were in the modern world.

We never went back to the Kashmere Gate together. I suppose that is why I used to go past it later on, when success had arrived, to show I could, that I would not feel the same fears he felt. That is a very stupid attitude, my friends. Never share it, for it's fear that keeps you from ending up dead or defingered.

That modern world ended up losing me my finger. And made me one tenth of very, very rich. There is a lesson there somewhere.

In New Delhi, the air reeked of gasoline and kerosene and CNG, the fumes of autos and buses and foreign cars, polished till gleaming. The smell of Old Delhi was there too, of charcoal braziers, fetid water, and undiagnosed mental problems, but hidden under construction dust and newly tarred roads and municipal gardeners spewing herbicide over grass verges.

We had set up our stall near a row of chaat and samosa sellers by the side of the road, near the public toilets. See! A place to eat, drink, and empty yourself, formed as if by nature itself, all without the nonsense of planning applications and zoning commissions. Our stall lived between a little stunted tree and a bench. Behind us was a wall, and beyond that, some planning ministry or governmental office, which would regularly belch out workers and hangers-on and small-business owners fresh from bribing their way to a better life, all of whom would descend on our stall.

But it is the noise I remember most of all. Noise, noise everywhere. Hooting cars, screaming children, masked motorcyclists, hawk-and-spit chauffeurs, businessmen screaming out deals at each other, perhaps in anger, or perhaps joy, girls being escorted by dowdy matrons to school, laughing at gawky teenage boys, white people of every stripe, backpackers, diplomats, groveling sadhus, straight-backed Sikhs, nuns.

I met her a month after we moved.

Her eyes were kind, like those of a mother or a sister—as far as I could imagine. They hit you like heat outside an air-conditioned store. She spoke Hindi nearly perfectly, but with a slight strangeness in her tongue from some foreign land.

She explained later that she had left her native France with a boy when she was twenty. He was greasy, untrustworthy, fond of the sound of his own voice, as all Frenchmen are, I am told, and had abandoned her, run off to transport drugs between Kashmir and the unwashed hippies in Goa, and, no doubt, to chase our chaste, innocent women. She had stayed in Delhi, lost and confused, got a job teaching English in language schools, found faith, and then joined the Sacred Heart Convent School.

Some of the sisters were lifers, who would have been totally lost back in Europe, brown souls underneath white skin, while the rest were just staying for a few years before being returned to the West, eager to see this country, just not the parts where they could not drink the water or had to travel a hundred miles to see a film.

They showed their pupils the true way of Christ, mass every morning, hymns sung to an organ groaning with rust and rot, Bible readings in staccato voices, but not often enough so that the parents would complain that their children were being converted.

Elocution lessons, deportment, English, French, music. Get them to university, five years of work, marriage, kids, tennis lessons, luxury cruises, death.

"That boy should be in school," were the first words I heard her say about me. A white woman speaking his language? Papa responded in English with "Tea?" He had recently extended his vocabulary to shouting the word at tour groups, and various cricket terms like "six," "boundary," and "jolly good shot."

The expansion of his vocabulary had occurred when we arrived in New Delhi. We couldn't be our simple selves anymore. We were dealing now with mobile phone users, metro riders, executives. We had to adapt. Papa acquired new skills—I found an English phrase book among his belongings, and soon enough English phrases among his speech. At least we got to double our prices.

"One chai," she said in response, in Hindi, and Papa had not known what to do.

I registered her accent immediately. I was even then on the lookout for life-changing opportunities. This was something different, something new, out of the ordinary. I was on alert.

She was looking over the stall at me, as if she was expecting me to be there. She watched me as I bashed away at the spices.

She was a nun. She was white, maybe fifty years old, with a few spare strands of white hair creeping out from beneath her hood. Her robes were dark gray, and there was a cross hanging around her neck.

She stared a little longer. She watched my movements. She nodded, as if I was someone she had known for a long time.

Then she repeated the fateful words, the ones that would change my life: that I should be in school.

Papa had not known how to respond: whether to call her a goat-fucker, or try to joke it off, play to the crowd by calling her a crazy woman, or say "These goras, huh?" She was white, she was a nun, and he had the slight deference toward religious figures that makes us Indians such marks for gurus, holy men, and messiahs, as well as every color of trade-promising conqueror.

"Would you like romance chai, madam? Increase your success in love life?"

The tea-drinkers laughed.

Claire's eyes moved from soft to hard in a second. "He should be in school," she said. "How old is he? Ten? Can he read? Write?"

Papa was out of ideas. He merely nodded his head. He didn't know anything about my education, so it came out faker than an Indo-Chinese friendship pact.

"Do you want me to call the Department of Education? There are laws against child labor, you know," Claire said, straightening the collar of her habit while Papa squirmed in front of her.

I remember the beatings and insults of my childhood, but the parts when Papa got humiliated? I remember those best.

He decided next on meek subservience, spineless prostration in front of the white woman, get her out of there, move the stall the next day if need be, for he could see in her eyes that she wouldn't give in quickly. He had that stomach-squeezing radar for trouble that all the poor have.

He lied and said I went to school every day—apart from this day, of course, but it was such a rarity he could not begin to tell her, but perhaps she could move out of the way, she was crowding his customers, a poor man had to earn a living. Claire didn't believe him. She looked down again at me, and nodded. I was at a loss. I nodded too.

I have to stress at this point that I was not totally academically deficient. I could read. I knew my letters. I had managed two years of school, if you added together all the hurried mornings and afternoons when I had annoyed my father enough that he had slapped me and sent me somewhere I couldn't displease him, or when I had been dragged there by neighborhood women who had gotten ideas from Western charities. In Delhi it seemed like your family's business was everyone else's, like your home was an alleyway that anyone could walk through. You would find yourself being taken by some unknown aunty to the vegetable market, for a haircut, another would take you for an eye test, and when you returned it was to see your father dead drunk on the floor, and you would wonder what exactly had just happened.

Papa had a reputation. Women were constantly trying to reform him, and me, for they feared I would go the same way. They must have had some effect, for I am a moral, upstanding citizen who, I must repeat, is stupid enough to pay his taxes in full. Social workers, lovers, teachers, distant relatives, a mixture of all of them sometimes, tried and failed to make him and me conform to Vedic practices, and if I got some time off the tea stall, so what?

I didn't go to school full-time, of course, not the Western way of nine to three, assembly, lunch, and poisonous feuds between social groups. The teachers marked everyone as present and let you run wild and free. The school authorities got their beloved literacy targets filled, received awards and money and garland ceremonies from the central government, and at the end of it all our education ministers got standing ovations from the UN and their faces on the cover of *Time*.

I learned Hindi from the school's comic books, the ones with all the gods from all the religions, the offspring of some faded "let's all get on together" initiative, a child of the "India is a pluralistic, multi-confessional democracy" bakwas believers. The comics were stored at the back of the class, where ceiling paint fell on them like ashirvads from heaven. I ate the stories up, sitting inside at break time while everyone else dirtied themselves outside. To me, the point of school was that it was a chance to stay indoors, away from the heat and noise, a place I could be clean and silent, but what do I know, huh?

"He knows his words. Education is dear to the hearts of the Indian people," Papa said, as if Claire was some tie-dyed hippie and not an educated woman whose Hindi was better than his. She watched him lie. Her lips curled slightly upward. He had decided to bullshit her with some Nehruvian nonsense about the eternal search for truth. That was from the newspapers he had begun reading. Our clientele wished to expound upon current affairs while they drank tea and pretended to be men of the world, or at least of the National Capital Region.

She was the first white person who'd ever talked to us.

"I'll be here tomorrow. With books. For him," she said.

Then Papa had started giving her a long speech on Saraswati, on the importance of reading: "We invented number zero, ma'am . . . My family has long history of loving books, we were poets, you know . . . I go to temple every day." She simply watched. He was sweating. His customers observed with amusement as my papa, the great talker, the great romancer, wriggled like a ferret in a sack in front of the white woman.

She said how things were going to be. And all he could do, out of ideas, out of theories and stories and sayings, was to say, "Yes, ma'am. Tomorrow, ma'am. Yes." He was ground down, and I knew I was in for slaps that night, big fat ones, alcohol-fueled ones, remembering-your-perfidious-dead-mother ones.

"Make sure you're here. I know the police. I teach their daughters," she said finally, and didn't bother to hear his reply before leaving, giving us all a sunny smile as she walked off.

Papa stayed stunned to the spot for five minutes, hands grabbing robotically for milk and tea leaves.

"Goras, huh?" he said when his face had unfrozen, for he had nothing else to say, and the fat self-employed businessmen at the stall had laughed at his humiliation.

He had recovered as the afternoon waned, and gone on as he did every day, speaking of bodily functions, of bowel movements, of liver imbalances, medicinal cures, miraculous pilgrimages, strange creatures found in the Yamuna, improbable lottery wins, of crotch rot, of talcum powder.

He slowly convinced himself that she would never come back. Just some white woman who had wanted to order him around, and a nun at that. He had had such respect for the Christians, but not after that, sirs, not after that.

The next morning, Papa and I were working industriously together, hand in hand, equal to equal, setting up our family business in an atmosphere of mutual respect, when Claire appeared, with books for me, with toys, plastic gods with lifeless eyes, a pair of shoes that lit up when I walked in them. My father had sworn, bug-eyed, when he saw her, and I had laughed involuntarily and been beaten very hard that night, the second night in succession, his shiny, whip-like hand getting plenty of use.

I understand why she chose a child to educate. She had not been serving the poor and the ignored as her books and sisters preached, but was merely teaching the daughters of the undeserving thick-necked rich at the Sacred Heart, and her faith was becoming hollow, meaningless. What I don't understand is why she chose me. Out of all the kids, the millions of them on every street corner and park bench and rubbish dump. I was not particularly angelic-looking. I did not have a good, toothy UNICEF-website smile, nor did inner light shine out of me.

Why?

She never spoke of any reasons or doubts. For me, everything would open up: learning, school, exams, college, a new life, something out of nothing.

Later she confessed that she had first seen me cycling to work in the mornings. I was only five minutes away from her school. She had walked by one day to hear my father complaining. And then she had seen me, and of course, that had been that.

A few years later, when she was ill, she would look at me as if she didn't see me at all, as if I was someone she had lost long ago. She would touch me and look on with surprise, as if it was a miracle that I was real and standing in front of her.

"We are going to make a life for you, little man," she would say, as if I did not have one already and she was some creator goddess breathing life into formless black Yamuna clay.

For the next few months, she came every day, at three in the afternoon, after her classes had finished. She had first come at midday, but "Please, madam!" my father begged, come when business is not so high, and around the back, please, madam, so that the businessmen will not be put off by a woman, a nun, who would interrupt their man-speak of actress-fucking and wife-slapping.

Every day, I worked extra hard in the hours before she arrived, pulverizing spices to the atomic level, putting tea strainers in a row, handling boxes and spoons with extreme care, placing each in easy reach of my father.

Then Claire came and we sat on the crumbling, pigeon-shit-encrusted concrete bench beside the stall, where I stumbled over English and Hindi, over numbers and letters and pictures of dogs and gods, and she ruffled my hair, gave me hugs and pats on the cheek when I did well, which was every fatherfucking time. I shooed away the inquiring eyes of little children more unfortunate than me. I was as status-conscious as any American suburbanite. They had BMWs and Jacuzzis. I had a nun.

In the first few weeks, I tried my very hardest. I was terrified that if I got even one answer incorrect, she would abandon me. Choose some other boy, one who had better prospects. My heart would beat as the appointed time approached, and I would always, always think that she would not come back tomorrow, that it would be the day she realized she was wasting her time. I am a great deal less worried about my meetings with white people today.

Of course she would not have abandoned me. But I had nightmares. Looking back, in the absence of a mother, the reasons for my fears were obvious, but it was painful to shake with terror at night, thinking she might find another pupil or project. (I have read *Psychotherapy for Dummies* exactly once, and that is what I gleaned from it.) But each day I saw her again, I felt safe. She would not leave. I made sure she never would. Whatever reason she had chosen me for, luck or fate or resemblance to someone long dead, I would keep her because of my intelligence.

Just being with her was something. I couldn't believe that she was white and she was talking to me and I was touching her and she me—how easily impressed I was in those days by Europeans! If I could advise my younger self, I would tell him to ask for money.

Over those months, she gave me little one-rupee sweets, bags of potato chips emblazoned with cricketers preaching victory, pencils, rubbers, sharpeners, bubble blowers. I thought that all whites must be something like gods. I know better today.

Finally someone was paying attention to me. Whether she was white or brown did not truly matter at the end of the day. She was spending time with me, and she never lost her patience, she let me ask unending questions, she never failed to laugh at my jokes.

"*Très bien*," she would say. "*Très bien, mon petit chou*, once again," and sometimes when we were done she would talk softly about France and films and folktales from her youth while my father looked anxiously back at us, fearful both of her sweet-scented retribution and of my head being filled with white-people ideas of secondary education and the inefficacy of corporal punishment. His usual trick of dealing with women, the seduction, was unavailable to him. She was educated. She knew more of the world. She was more experienced. She was also sworn to a lifelong vow of celibacy. He wilted in front of her.

If this was a biopic, I would have left Claire out. She would have made the whites uncomfortable. There would have been a montage of me growing up, stealing precious hours away from my abusive home, going to night classes, slowly crawling my way through the education system—until finally, after years of effort, I had mastered the letter A. It would have been purer, more Indian, more real. Everyone in the cinema would have cheered at the screen, at the boy who never gave up, who broke the system on his own, who made it under his own steam.

But that is not what happened. I do not care about what looks good. I care about the truth. Claire changed my life. I owe it to her memory to tell things as they really were.

Now perhaps I am misremembering things a little. No doubt I have softened the edges of my early life. I have created a narrative, like Americans do after hundreds of hours of therapy. Maybe Claire has become something in my memories that she never was, and her kindness has made my recollections of her rose-tinted. Maybe I have watched too many episodes of *Oprah*. But that is the way I remember things. When I think of Claire, I think of gentleness, of a woman who was tough with the rest of the world, but not with me, who ensured that my talent was not wasted, ensured that I did not become another faceless child who disappeared and never made his voice heard.

Maybe I am wrong. Maybe I could have risen as far and fast as I did without her. But I did not. I cannot lie. I have to tell the story of our time together. When it comes to Claire, I always tell the truth.

Over the next few months, I found a new sense of determination as a consequence of my time with Claire. She gave me a tin box with an engraving of Parisian landmarks on the outside, in which I kept my treasures, my pencils, my rulers, my books. I worked in the evenings, when my father was out, though our apartment building had a very unreliable, semi-illegal electric connection and we could not have afforded a generator in a lifetime of work, not with my father's skill at household accounts. We had a blackout across the city, cloaking in darkness the many families that roamed the streets, the cardboard-doored hovels that smelled of flour and fat and adulterated daal (which, I assure you, smells different than the real stuff), the little concrete roof where I worked under the stars. I ignored the spiders, the cockroaches that flew into my face, the screams and sighs, of men and women, of children being beaten, of weekly wages spent on alcohol.

I was never alone up there. That was the joy of our fecund Indian uteruses, supercharged by both ancient Vedic rituals and the poor's lack of televisions and Facebook (how the world has changed!)—never afforded a moment's peace!

I went up there in all weathers. When it was cold, I had a sweater Claire had knitted herself, of a dog named Snoopy. When it rained, I tried to stay out as long as I could, before running back inside clutching paper against my breast to save it from the rain. One night, a hoarse voice, soaked in decades of alcohol, said, "Get out of the rain, beta!" "He is reading! Reading!" A man laughed, and then another, and I had never known helplessness like those faceless people laughing at me.

When Claire asked me the next day what had happened to my sodden books, I could not explain. She ruffled my hair and I knew I had been forgiven. It was nice to feel that some of your problems had been solved simply because someone cared. Someone who wiped away your tears when you gave the wrong answer. Someone who gave you treats and sweets and attention, and shoes and a nice white shirt. It made you wonder what life would have been like if you'd had a mother from the start. How far you could have gone, the schools you could have gotten into, the life you could have led.

But then again, maybe I'd have been loved and nurtured and utterly useless anyway.

After a few months, Claire realized that there was only so much that could be done out of the backside of a tea stall on the Bangla Sahib Road. Not that that is such a bad place. Great commercial empires, multi-crore computer companies, have been built from it, as well as political careers groaning with corruption and virginity-taking and obesity. But it is a hard place to teach.

So much beauty! So much modern architecture! So much life! So much piss!

One day she told me that I would have to leave the stall, at least for a few hours every day. She would tell Papa tomorrow. I wept with joy and told her I loved her, and tried to keep my voice down so that Papa couldn't hear, even though the road was its usual ear-pounding self. I can be very stupid sometimes.

"I knew from the moment I saw you that you could do it," she said. She held me to her tight, her hands crossing my back as if she was scared to lose me.

She had changed my life. I had had nothing to do with it. All I had to do was work hard. Any idiot can do that.

For the rest of the afternoon, and the night, I bit my tongue. I clenched my fists tight and shook with joy. I looked around at the room, and knew, I just knew, that my life really would change from that day on.

When she told him, Papa exploded with rage. He could not hold his tongue any longer against this woman with these ideas, whoever she was, whoever she knew.

"You ... Ma'am, this boy, this is not our life, you are ... filling his head with such . . ." His child was being taken away, a child he owned. He had fed me and clothed me and wasted money on me that could have been spent elsewhere. Why else had he raised me? I could have been left to an orphanage, or on some rubbish heap to die, like a girl. I was his property, he wailed, I was being corrupted, I was being stolen and made white. He kept going until he had nothing else to say.

Claire stayed silent. She was an All India champion at that. "I'll be here for him tomorrow," she said.

The next day, when I woke, my father gave me an unpleasant smile as I started to pack my things, the pencil box, the nice smart shoes, the hopes and the dreams.

I knew that smile.

I never raised my voice to him, ever. I tried to avoid speaking against him at all costs, if I could. And yet that day, I did.

"No," I said, "No, Papa. No, you can't." I thumped my little fists against his chest.

You know what I got. He screamed. He raved. He beat me. And this time, a lecture too. I shall not bore you with the details. It was very histrionic.

"We will leave. She will never find us. If this white woman thinks she can steal my lifeblood, then she is mistaken. Pack up your things! No child of mine will ever be taken from me."

I wept throughout. My belongings must have been stained with tears by the end of it. Papa made sure to break my pencil case, just because he could. He marched me upstairs, knocked on the door, and made me donate the toys and exercise books to the family that lived there.

I kept the shoes. They would help me with cycling, and so I wheeled the stall that day, with eyes blood red, out past Paharganj, my father smiling all the while as he walked alongside. His smug expression held for three long days, just until the police jeep rolled up to him, and an assistant commissioner of police asked for his license.

My father almost laughed. The policeman pulled out his baton, raised it high, and gave him a crack across the face.

My father fell to the floor.

The policeman bent down close by his face, and said, "Don't go annoying the white woman again. That's a message from my boss. Understand?"

My father's previous enemies had been small. He had not known that. They had been men of violence, men of fists and blades, who would consider an opponent broken when he could no longer get up and fight. This enemy knew that the best weapon was the law.

I remember the first time I set foot inside Sacred Heart.

It was paradise. Grass as far as you could see. An army of groundskeepers. Red tiled roofs. A chapel. Trees, growing tall and strong. I had never seen anything like it. It did not even feel like the same country.

The only sign that I was still in India was the girls, the daughters of our elite, getting their nice Western civilized education so that they could leave and never, ever look back.

That day, and every other day that followed, they never looked at me unless it was to sneer. I was invisible. I had to get out of their way in the corridors, duck into classrooms and onto grass verges to avoid being pushed aside. Claire took me on a tour of the classrooms, and the teachers gave me their too-tight smiles, and as we turned to leave, I could see them sneering as well.

Some of the girls did look at me, though—the charity cases, the Dalit girls whose families had converted to get free places, and merely moved from the bottom of one caste system to the bottom of another.

You noticed little things. No concrete. Everything was wooden, but not our Indian wood, not cheap, not built to last for a summer or two. This was something different, nineteenth century, Claire told me, built by French businessmen trading calico and ivory, wood for the daughters of Europeans.

The staff watched me, the gardeners and the sweepers, not bothering to be secretive. They knew there was something wrong about me being there, my hand being held by one of the nuns, being spoiled, being coddled, being educated. They knew I was one of them.

In my second week, I didn't have Claire with me. I marched, proud and stupid, toward the gate.

A hand barred my way.

A tall man with beady eyes pulled me back, just inside the school gates.

"Inspection!" he laughed. "No dirt!"

I didn't know what to do. My lip began to quiver.

He shook his head at my uselessness and pulled my arms out in front of me.

I stood traffic-still while the sun cooked my neck red, my hands out, my back prickling with heat, men and boys passing me on the street, watching this strange ritual at the white man's gates.

The watchman rubbed my skin hard, until it turned red. He laughed. "Thought you were white under the brown, boy."

I hadn't known it then, but that was the start of it.

The whispering campaign. The solidification of hate.

"What's that urchin doing here?" a gardener said.

"He's going to make this whole place low class," a butt-scratching cook chimed in.

"These crazy goras, thinking they can change India," said an electrician.

The orchestrator of the whispering campaign against me was a man named Dharam Lal, the bursar's assistant.

The bursar himself was a septuagenarian father who spent his time gardening, handing out caramel sweets, and doing crosswords. But Dharam Lal controlled the purse strings; it was he who hired and fired. He was the most powerful Indian in the school, and he hated me. Isn't that always the way, friends?

I get nightmares about his thin, moustachioed hacksaw face even now.

The first time I saw him, I knew that Dharam Lal had bled. He had crawled up from the dirt, to a world where he could wear white shirts and sit in air-conditioned comfort and work with his mind. He had made it. I knew this in an instant. No one had to explain it to me. I did not have to deduce it. I just fucking knew.

About a month after I started studying at Sacred Heart, he visited Claire's little cell as my lesson was coming to an end. He knocked on the door, hard, then barged in without being asked, and glared at us without saying anything. Rather than reacting, Claire simply ignored him, and I could do nothing but continue to mouth out English even though my eyes itched to land on him.

"So this is the boy?" he said finally. I let myself look him up and down. His hands had marks on them, like my father's: rough, blistered, damaged skin. He had worked hard with those hands, as I had worked with mine. Nowadays my hands are soft. I have nearly forgotten myself.

"Say hello, Ramesh," Claire said.

"Hello, sir," I said, because it was important to be pleasant to everyone when you were educated, even when you could see they hated you. These Europeans and their morals!

Lal walked around the room, giving it an inspection: his gaze traveled across the little lace-lined pillows, the gauze curtains, the small pictures of St. Bernadette and Gandhi and Princess Diana. I could tell he disapproved of every detail.

"Do you think this is wise, Sister?"

"What are you referring to?" she replied.

"People are talking."

"Maybe you should stop them," Claire said, and turned back to the English grammar book in her hands.

She ignored his pacing, his desperate need to say something else. Many men in our culture want to be men of few words, men who are listened to without argument, and so Dharam Lal fought his need to get another word in, trying to remain quiet, lethal, deadly, which is not quite the same as having gravitas. He gave me a dirty look, ran his eyes over the white walls of the room to make sure I was not rubbing off on them, and left.

Those three years of daily lessons, from eleven to fourteen, were the happiest of my life. For other children in the neighborhood, fun was jumping in refuse puddles and being run over by trains. For me? History, English, mathematics, science, poetry. Claire and me, in her room, the one that smelled of sandalwood and vetiver and camphor, her attention focused solely on me, as if I was her whole world.

At the tea stall, my father beat me less and less. His hands stayed firmly on the copper pot. He started taking women more frequently to our room, the shy, penniless curvaceous women who queued up outside taxi ranks, their boyfriends-cum-pimps watching like hawks at every note that passed into their hands—this being the only work the men seemed to do in a day. My father spent his time with women who wore bright multicolored saris with easily unfastened hooks, women with ruby-red lips, large waists, faces that changed from seductive smiles to grimaces when the men weren't looking, and who could blame them.

On most nights, he took great pleasure in locking me out on the roof, whether or not he had a woman over. "Go and study," he would say, watching me scramble for ten seconds for books and paper before physically kicking me out.

Papa talked ever more to our customers. Usually, tea sellers do not have to ask after cousins and children and mistresses and every little detail of people's lives. They only have to make hot, strong, sweet tea quickly, and maybe talk a little about sport and how all politicians are corrupt. But something had changed: he had memorized entire biographies of his customers. Every second cousin's dog trainer would be remembered. Then the customer would leave and the light would go out of my father's eyes, like a temple statue that had turned into a real goddess for just a single moment, then back to lifeless stone. Seeing him take an interest in other people made me suddenly feel sorrow.

But he wouldn't even look at me. Maybe Claire had opened the floodgates. How I wished my father would give me even a quick look out of the side of his eye, just some acknowledgment, even if it was to show how little I meant to him, or how he had so much more to him than being my father, or how I was a worthless speck in his life and he didn't miss me. Anything was better than nothing. But for once, he was the model of self-control.

He had started treating his pots and burners and cups with such delicacy, with utmost care. Even they seemed to get more attention than me. Perhaps, somehow, my good example had inspired him to take better control of his own future, to expand his business, to look into the bright new horizon that the twenty-first century—Oh, of course he was doing it to show everyone that he was just as good as his boy with the fancy new convent education.

One day, a man, one of those newspaper-reading fellows fond of his own booming voice, took notice of my new shirt and shoes.

"Look at this man, this selfless chaiwallah," he said to everyone at the stall, letting out the poetry that had been strangled by a life of triplicate invoices, "who has saved up to give his son the life he never had. Look at his poverty, but look too at his son, who will never know want or hunger."

My father was enjoying himself. A crowd had gathered. How fortunate I was that high-data phone plans had not yet reached our land, for someone in that crowed could have posted the commotion to Instagram, preserving my image online forever, and my career of impersonation and examination consultancy would have been built on very unstable ground.

My father started to behave strangely. He started to bow and bat away the compliments from the crowd. He actually looked at me, for the first time in weeks. He took my hand in his and raised it to the skies. I was amazed he could touch me without beating or pushing or shoving me.

A few days later, he produced a black-and-white photo of a woman, to which he fixed plastic marigold flowers, and displayed it ostentatiously by the awning of the stall.

It was meant to be my mother, obviously. He would raise her specter at any opportune moment—her short, tragic existence—a reminder of the sacrifices we all make for the next generation.

The stall got a fresh coat of paint. The bicycle began to sparkle with polish. He was showing them all that his miserable life hadn't beaten him. Our stall finally got its name. The One Where the Man Gave His Son a Convent Education.

Of course, he did not actually talk to me in any meaningful way. We still went on for weeks without saying a single word to each other. His orders were impatient taps, half shouts, jerks of his head, never eye contact, never. He built a wall between us, thick and strong and invisible, like the one between poor countries and rich. We both knew that it was his fear of Claire that made him beat me less. I had some power over him, for the first time in my life, and he never forgot it.

Despite Sister Claire's love and attention, I had twin antagonists at that time: my father at home and Dharam Lal at school. The bursar's assistant watched and waited; his army of admin secretaries and dogsbodies always pretended they didn't know me at the gate when I came in. They made me sweat outside the entrance, never a glass of water given when I asked.

Aggressive cleaners passed me in the corridors, pushing dust onto the smart brown trousers Claire had bought me from Raymond, another of the Indian brands that our middle classes have abandoned recently, like multi-faith democracy.

Dharam Lal, he of the thin, long face, realized soon enough that the parents would have to get rid of me. A campaign would have to be started. He wrote the checks. He hired and fired the Indian workers, but to put pressure on a nun? He would have to work much harder to do that.

The other administrators were nuns and fathers, white and studious and useless, adrift in a country they didn't understand. They spent whole days smiling weakly. Dharam Lal understood what power was and how he could use it. But none of it mattered. Not to Claire. Not to me, in that light, cool room. She pushed me to breaking point. She took pride in my progress, smiled as my writing grew more confident, as I started to say

English words like they belonged on my tongue, as I became more polished, my confidence growing by the day.

We worked hard. Claire came from her lessons covered in a light sheen of sweat, strands of hair sticking out from under her habit, fresh from educating the daughters of the Indian elite, from teaching them tenses and directing them through yet another year of *The Sound of Music*, having to keep the peace when some crorepati's offspring wasn't cast as Maria.

Sometimes she took me along while she taught the girls, and I would watch from the back of the class as the students mastered bharatnatyam, or elocution, or Latin.

It was strange watching this white woman serving the needs of the brown. She was making these girls into her, so that they could escape their city and their country. She was doing the same to me. One time a girl turned around to look at me, then turned back to her desk and scribbled something on a piece of paper. She handed it to her friend, who passed it around, until eventually someone scrunched it up and threw it at me. I put it in my bag in order to prevent further drama, and only unraveled it later, when I discovered it said, *Are you her bastard?* I didn't understand the message entirely, but after that, I never looked at them again.

I didn't have friends. I didn't go out and play. I didn't talk to girls, either at the school or anywhere else. Claire worked me hard. If I did poorly, she gave me harsh words. "If you don't do as well as you can, you'll never leave here. You'll never have the life you should."

When I had failed her, her words would come out dull, and she would not look at me with love. She could keep this up for weeks. Then, the only words she would say to me, away from our lessons, were those over lunch, where she taught me manners and how to eat. "Back straight! Pepper mill! Elbows! Napkin!"

I was improving rapidly, devouring work, and "to support my development," as she wrote on the application form, she arranged for me to go to a charity school in New Delhi, an initiative that had been announced by the government—an initiative that had somehow been miraculously fulfilled. At the same time, my father replaced me with an electric spice grinder, and took great pleasure in it. Business was up. He would no doubt mention his absent son whose convent education was being paid for at every opportunity. Soon he would be a stop on the tourist trail. He no longer needed me. I had served my purpose. Twelve years old, and I had served my purpose.

Each day, Claire would look over every piece of work I completed, and every report I received from the new school. She would harangue my teachers when she disagreed. She knew every little detail about my education. She bought me books and clothes from her own salary, which was increasingly subject to delays by holdups in the bursary.

It was hard. When she thought I was being lazy, she wouldn't talk or look at me for days, and I would cry at night, when my father was safely tired out by female company; cry over the idea that she would abandon me, that I would go back to nothing, that I was nothing without her.

I worked like I was always going to fall backward and slide into sin, like there was something inside me that was corrupt and black that I needed to always keep under control.

I learned. My life got better.

And then, when I was fourteen, everything went to shit.

FIVE

Rudraksh Saxena's family was going to pay. If they were going to get rich, I wanted my cut too.

I did not do things delicately. I did not leave cryptic messages. I did not post letters through their door. I waited two days, put on my pizza delivery uniform, and marched straight in. Caught them unawares, no polite messages, no greeting card emblazoned with *Congratulations on the fraud!*

The Saxenas' flat was a beehive of activity. Journalists of all types—fat columnists and whisper-thin bloggers—neighbors giving jealous looks, several dozen school and tutorial college owners desperately trying to get Rudi's face on their billboards, advertisers, shop owners, brown-nosers from the People's Party, all of them crawling in the corridors and the stairwells, and me, skipping through like a film star in a Kashmiri meadow. Even a bunch of fucking priests had turned up, doing their Kali Pujas or whatever to wash away the sins of the world. The hijras would be here soon, cursing Rudi's unborn children to live with the blight of androgyny, but only if they weren't given a few thousand.

I held my breath.

I went in.

"Pizza here, sir, pizza, sir, watch out, watch out, sir!"

Invisible.

Unremarked.

Beautiful.

But no—my way was barred.

I was unfazed. Let it never be said I have panicked in unplanned situations.

A short, muscular man with graying hair, body gone to seed, no doubt many amateur impromptu wrestling championships in his past, held out a thick arm, and said, "ID, sir."

"Pizza delivery, sir."

"Show me app details and delivery code, sir."

So we were in that most Indian of situations, the passive-aggressive sir-off.

"What is your job, sir?" I asked.

"I am the independent security consultant hired by the happy family to ensure safety at this event, sir," he said.

There it was. Wonderful. Someone just like me. Someone you could do business with.

"How much?" I said. "Sir?" The ping of recognition went off in his brain.

He measured my worth, my desperation, and more important, how much of a cut he could get of whatever I was planning.

"Two thousand, sir," he said, with a knowing smile. I pulled out the money, and the arm was lowered.

"Sir," we both said, and nodded warmly at each other.

Inside the door there was a shoal of shoes, of worn Chinese trainers, of sweat-stained sandals. Strange, the Saxenas hadn't made me take mine off when I'd come before. They had suddenly become extremely pious.

Their living room was full of wires and surly cameramen. A harried female servant rushed from person to person, saving carpets from stains of imli sauce, sweeping up crumbs, picking up paper plates of samosa waste, admonishing middle-aged men for scuffing walnut side tables.

There were boxes of sweets, samosas, chocolates, and kebabs piled high on every flat surface, bunches of flowers covered in glitter, hundreds of cards, marriage proposals, advertising deals, dozens of little red envelopes of cash lying around, with the one-rupee coin studded on the outside for good luck. I helped myself to some, stuffing them inside the pizza box. The money was mine after all. No one noticed.

And in the center of it all, the man of the hour himself. Clad in a new gray suit, Armani I found out later, wearing chic leather loafers with those idiot tassels. He was being interviewed by some posh journalist, all beautiful vowels and Khan Market kurta and scarlet nail polish.

At least he had the sense to go pale when he saw me. Once in a while a man wants to be feared.

Mr. Saxena was stuck to him like a limpet. A producer was setting up a TV camera. Rudi kept looking at his father like a dying fish, and then at me. He tried to nod in my direction. He looked as if he was having a fit, the kind the rich fake to get out of jury duty. Mr. Saxena finally realized I was there. His first look was of total defeat. He did nothing, while his son kept jerking at him to get me out of there.

Mrs. Saxena was standing on the other side of the room, being asked questions from a hundred directions, busier than our civil servants are in January editing government websites to remove any mention of last year's targets, busier than the events planner for the billionaire's son's London statement wedding, the one where Mariah Carey gets paid a hundred million untaxed Gandhis to sing for fifteen minutes.

Her answers for one person dripped into another's. "Yes, he is thinking of Stanford, no, this dress is just a little something from Ritu Kumar, yes, his father has a master's from Western Kentucky State, no, I am not doing the 5:2, I am just naturally slim."

It looked exhausting.

Hauling bricks for a living, I can understand. Driving buses, making tea, yes. But telling lies, being pleasant, making false smiles, all day? I do not know how the rich do it.

The TV producer waved at Rudi, and the interview began. The woman asked him some questions about studying. Rudi twitched his way through them, never meeting the gaze of the camera.

"What about your parents?" the woman asked. "What part have they played in your success?"

And then something strange happened. His face took on a strange new look. He stopped slouching. He started to smile. On the TV monitor, behind the hair, the glasses, there was something new there.

He looked straight at the camera.

"I owe them everything," he said. "Everything I am today is because of them. I honor them every day, in all that I do. Our country is built on the strength of our parents." He smiled sugar sweet at the camera. "Am I speaking to the youth of India, Ashwini?" he asked.

"You're speaking to everyone," she said.

He nodded. He smiled again, but his eyes were still and unwavering. "Work as hard as you can. Then work harder. Listen to your elders. Never complain. They know best. Hold them close to you. They are wise beyond their years. Stand straight like your father, and be steadfast like your mother. That is all I have to say."

A lot of children were going to get beaten that night.

"Rudi, thank you," said the woman. "Who knew that someone so young had so much wisdom for our lost and disaffected youth?"

"Oh, Ashwini," Rudi said. "Isn't that always the way?"

Isn't that always the way?

They went on, discussing God knows what. I zoned out.

As the interview continued, Mr. Saxena edged toward me, dodging supplicants and wet handshakes. His wife watched his clubfooted, unsteady progress, and then noticed me, her gaze remaining adoring for her questioners while her mouth twitched in thin-lipped fury. She cut short her interviews and rushed in my direction.

They shared a look, a secret, unpleasant one. They might hate each other, but they were totally united in wanting to fuck me over. I would be better for their marriage than any overpaid therapist in Greater Kailash. Another string to my bloody bow.

I did not wait for them to start their blessed jugalbandi with whatever threat they were dreaming up.

"I get a cut of what your son earns. Or I fuck you. Understand?" Short and sharp. I'd been watching YouTube videos on negotiation by sharp-suited Americans with gelled hair and Italian names. (And watching my father's work over the years. But I didn't want to think about that. You can't say anything nice about your parents. That's the first commandment of being Indian. Unless you're on camera.)

Mr. Saxena gulped. "Oh God," he said.

He tried to explain things to me, but the words came out lacking fire. He knew people, he said. Policemen, politicians, civil servants, real big men, men who could snap their fingers and I would be in Tihar, beaten, buggered, and broken.

"If you knew people like that, I'd be dead already," I said.

Short and sweet! Thank you, Patrick DiMeo of New Jersey BMW Dealers.

Saxena opened his mouth and gasped in frustration. His wife kept blinking her eyes at him, hummingbird fast, to get rid of me somehow, to do something, anything. She kept quiet, trying to look elegant, unperturbed, classy, and hoped that finally her husband would prove himself to be the lion that five millennia of our dick-dominant society had told her she needed.

He realized her unspoken need. He reached back into the genetic memory of a thousand mighty generations of Saxenas, warlords, generals, peasant impregnators, gave his wife a look of total command, and dragged me past tapestries and newly discovered family members into his son's room. No coffee table books here, no waist-high statues of dancing girls in burnished bronze, no casually strewn copies of *The Economist*; just the usual detritus of the Indian teenage boy. Axe body spray. A Manchester United poster. General knowledge trophies he'd won when he was eleven. I much preferred it to the rest of the apartment.

Unfortunately, Vishal Saxena's negotiation technique was shit. He let me know too much.

"We have friends in high places," he started. He didn't look at me.

"Which friends, sir?" I said, speaking breathlessly, my tongue almost wagging in enthusiasm. Tell me more about your wonderful life, rich man! Impress me, amaze me, astound me!

"Oh, too many to count. I have friends in law, in accounting, my wife's relatives are in politics, and of course we have met so many new people through the foundation."

"Foundation, sir?" I said, my voice soft and sweet.

"It's my wife's baby. Did you think we were some small-time nobodies? We host fundraisers. We invite the high and the mighty. We know people."

"Artists, sir? Lawyers, sir? Writers? Journalists? Liberal civil society people?" I said, my voice full of lower-caste wonder.

"Of course," he laughed, and gave me a pitying look. "All the people who matter."

"All the people who look kindly on examination fraud, sir?" I said.

Never has a man broken faster.

"We were going to call you," he started babbling. "We don't want trouble, no trouble." He shivered. He looked like a small-town accountant who had been caught fiddling both the mayor's ledgers and his daughters. Blinking furiously, he sat on the bed, and started smoothing imaginary wrinkles on it.

His wife came in. "Jesus Christ, Vishal," she said, noticing at once his total defeat. The respect in her eyes vanished. She slammed the door shut behind us. She gave me a withering look, the type you'd give a street child trying to wash your car.

"How did you get to him?" she asked.

"Your foundation. All your do-gooding liberal friends."

She nodded. I thought I saw some respect in her eyes. "We'll make you a deal," she said.

"No deals. Ten percent. Or I talk. I wonder who came next top after your son. Maybe I'll give him a call. Or the government. Some investigator will want the kill of a lifetime. A Topper!"

That did it. Vishal Saxena collapsed completely and began to breathe deeply in and out. Oh, they would still try to hurt me, but it would have to be done later, when little Rudi had made some money, and then dacoits could be hired, guns could be brandished, limbs could be torn off, or, more likely, angry midnight emails about expenses and overspending would be written.

Mrs. Saxena moved out in a huff, cursing under her breath, making sure to check her sari in the mirror before she left.

I was lucky she hadn't conducted the negotiations herself from the start. If she had, I'd have been mincemeat. You could tell. She wouldn't have mentioned foundations. But your husband does the talking, he's the one in charge, forever and ever, that's what this country tells you, and her husband had failed completely. Thank God!

"So," said Mr. Saxena, picking himself up, as if this was a

business meeting with tea and namkeen, speaking with the deflated voice of a man who was going to be spending every waking moment at the golf club for a long time to come.

"I want to talk to the kid. I'm going to be his manager, aren't I?"

"Assistant," he babbled out.

I gave him a placid lower-caste look, like a cow or a nightclub toilet attendant.

"As long as I get paid. I want to get along with you. We all want the same thing, do we not?"

I held out my hand, filthy with invisible dirt. He went out and got his son without another word.

The kid took it well. He was far more concerned about women. He told me later that he'd got five hundred Tinder matches that week, probably four hundred and ninety-nine more than he'd ever had before. Hordes of beautiful girls, flirtatious, inquisitive, aroused, all of whom had their parents writing their chat-up lines. What they wouldn't do to have Rudraksh Saxena as their son-in-law!

Rudi did not care about a measly 10 percent. His mother shot her husband withering looks over the next few hours, while I introduced myself to everyone as Rudi's manager.

I asked the Saxenas for a hundred thousand for expenses, just for a joke, and Mr. Saxena paid it, no questions, just reached into a pocket and pulled it out. I got myself a taxi home, a deluxe Lexus SUV with AC and a hatted driver. Green Park, what a beautiful place. It was all mine for the taking. The air was better, the people more subservient, the police nicer, and the cars drove more carefully, not knowing which minister's son they might hit.

I began my managerial career. The Saxenas wired me the tutoring money without complaint, and suddenly I was richer than I had ever been before.

Sister Claire, I thought, Jesus, we made it. All our sacrifices weren't for nothing. Your death was not in vain. I made something out of myself. Sorry for the blasphemy!

We made it!

Wherever in heaven you are, we made it!

SIX

I tried to save her. That's why I got into this greasy business.

Dharam Lal weaved his campaign of hatred. I could not be allowed to contaminate the school further. To remove me, he would have to break her. And so he did.

I would finish my day at the charity school at three, and went straight to Sacred Heart to work with Claire. I was five years from the All Indias, and needed to do well to have any hope of a scholarship to a college. I had started a long way behind the other children my age. There was not a moment to lose.

I was becoming cultured. I was leaving behind Hindi, and settling into the mongrel Hinglish we all speak now.

After our work for the day had finished, I sat and ate, and Sister Claire spoke of her childhood. As she talked, her hair would twist free, a few locks of white sitting on her face, and she looked twenty years younger.

She had had a normal childhood: exams, fights with her sisters, boys, paddling in rock pools, spending hot summer days eating salted caramel ice cream.

"Boys—oh, how we would argue about them, all day long. How they would tease us! We would think of all the ways to entice them, to make them chase us, and then . . ."

"And then?"

"Nothing! We would run away!" she would say, with one of her wry smiles.

I had never known girls before, so I was very interested in anything I could find out about them. I knew men and women went together and made babies. But the girls I had known were noisy and annoying. I had no idea how or why they changed into things men wanted, fought for, bled for, how they became the women my father bought.

Claire taught me about how she saw the world.

"God is love"—that was her favorite saying. She would give money to the beggars who congregated by the school gates, and she would give food at local hospitals, and maybe save a tea seller's child in the afternoon, and would say all the while, "God is love."

Sometimes, of course, "God is love" meant blackmailing tea stall owners and twisting them into compliance. Such are the ways of the Christian God.

I would ask her for stories about her family. Those were my favorite. She would speak of long days spent sailing, of deserted coves and sandbars and sea foam, of cousins visiting at Christmas, of the sweat rising from the huddled crowds at midnight mass, of roasted chestnuts and steaming mugs of hot chocolate with brandy smuggled in, delivered by her parents when the skies were filled with summer lightning. She had grown up somewhere called Brittany. There everyone smiled and respected and liked each other—I found it totally unbelievable that a place like that should exist.

To me, her stories were fairy tales. It seemed impossible that someone could live like that, be so surrounded with love, to be without cares, to live a life that wasn't a struggle, day to stinking day. I knew I would never feel that.

But Dharam Lal made her life bitter. She would have to stop herself from crying around me. The nuns began to avoid her. Her classes were cut back. Parents came to her, not saying anything in words, but the message was clear. *Dump the boy. He is dirty and unclean. Why are you doing this? Our girls are your first responsibility. This is India, things cannot change here. You are giving him false dreams.*

Rumors had been spread, terrible stories, Claire said. She would not talk about them to me, but simply try not to cry. The room became dimmer every passing day. Her face became raw and lined and tired. She stopped talking of knitting and pastries.

I realized very quickly that I was the problem. I was always the problem.

"I can study at school," I said. "I don't need to come here every day."

My life would be limited to my father forever. I would turn into him. I knew it. For all the brains Claire said I had, for all the talent, I knew that I was him, and that in time, I would become him. That made me weep most of all.

But she refused to let me go. She held me tight whenever I so much as mentioned it. "Worse things have happened to me before. We shall beat them yet, *petit*," she said.

"Do you know how old I am?" she asked me one day.

"Young," I said, and she rubbed my hair.

"Not with this gray," she said. "Fifty-three. A year younger than my mother when she died. At long last, I have done some good in the world, no?" She looked at me, and took my hand as I sat eating my jam and toast, trying hard to keep it from falling on my school shirt. "I was stupid," she said. "I thought I had done the world good simply by putting on these clothes. But that is never enough. Never."

I nodded my head.

"I will do more good yet," she said. "This school, we cannot go on merely speaking about service and charity while we educate only the daughters of billionaires, of judges, of the police. It is not right. There must be more children like you here. I will not rest until it happens. All the others, they laugh, but I will make them see. You were the first, but you will not be the last. You are the future of this school."

I had never been the future of anything.

I would have sacrificed myself for her willingly. My life would be like it had been before the never-ending lawns, before books read lazily under banyan trees while girls played tennis, before the wonderful words, the history, and the poetry.

As I left, mad with thirst, I tried to drink at the water fountain just inside the school gates. A little drink after a long, dusty day. Not such a revolutionary act.

One second I was drinking water, and the next I was on the ground, and a gang of teenage boys stood over me, Dharam Lal's lackeys, workmen, lean, muscled, with growths of slug-like facial hair.

"Hey, look at this little prick," one of them shouted. I couldn't tell which one through my tears, and my pathetic scrambling to get up. "What is he carrying? Books?" They pushed me to the floor as I got up, kicked me, held me down, beat me, spat at me. They didn't have to urinate on the books. That was a new one.

As I ran from the school, I heard abuse, screams. I heard car horns. A motorbike screeched to a halt beside me, nearly running me over.

Actually, that may just have been Delhi.

I got home and was greeted with my father's laughter at my pretensions, my books, my big Western ideas. He would hound me for it until the day he died of alcoholism, probably, or, more likely, being shot by some unpaid gold-toothed pimp.

Usually he didn't say anything, but maybe my particularly pathetic condition that day spurred him to words.

He was lying in bed when I came back. He watched my face and weighed his words.

"She'll dump you one day, and find some other child to corrupt. See what she does when you have a moustache," he said. Maybe drink had made him loose-tongued, or losing some bet had made him shortchanged.

I did what I usually did. I picked up my books and went up to the roof.

Though that day, I almost believed him. I thought of what Claire had said, that I would not be the last. Would she look at some other child the same way she looked at me? What if I didn't do well enough, what if I failed her? Would I be the prototype, the failed first experiment? What was my future? No name, no connections, no money, wrong caste, wrong everything. I cursed her then, cursed her for her kindness, cursed her for all those countless afternoons when I had been taught to dream.

I would go back to making tea, ten rupees a cup (1.3 million rupees would be ten years of work, Papa, you prick). I would have a stall of my own. Maybe three or four generations in the future, someone would go to university and turn their nose up at the dirt and the grime. We would make it then.

I stopped my dreaming.

In the meantime, the stall was making more money than ever before. Of course none of it filtered through to me. Papa finally bought a television, which he hooked up to a noisy diesel generator. While he watched cricket matches and belched his way through kebabs, I curled in a ball and wept silently. At school, Claire was a woman on a mission. Papa was right, she wasn't happy with just me. She wanted to change things.

Claire started to bake. She appealed to the Indian sweet tooth. She made pastries, cakes, anything she could. She procured a table and sheets and cloths, and stood outside the gates every Friday and sold her cakes, and as the parents ate, she started, "Have you met Ramesh? Ramesh, tell them about your life, tell them where you came from, tell them what you have been learning." Slowly but surely, she thought, we would win the parents of the school around. Maybe there could be one child a year, maybe more, given an education, a new life.

I was charming. I told the parents everything. I let my brown eyes twinkle. I saw their spines soften and their smiles grow.

Dharam Lal did not like this development at all.

Always there was Dharam Lal, just out of sight, or his spies, everywhere, telling stories, trying to destroy my life before it had even started.

I would sit at the back of her class, and he would send a night-watchman to remove me. I would be heaved out with maximum drama, under her eyes. The girls laughed. Their minds had been poisoned against her by their parents. Crazy Claire, mad Claire, unclean Claire. There had always been something wrong with her, but no one had said anything, and now it was too late.

I fucking hated them, I fucking hated them, I fucking hated them all.

One day, Claire had been baking, cursing our Indian butter all the while in long streams of French, its taste, its texture, the accursed heat. I had been helping her as I usually did when Dharam Lal had suddenly appeared. I saw Claire turn gray, her hands shake.

"Who are you making these for?" he had asked. "The boy? Whose money are you spending on him?"

She had stood there, this woman of grand ideas and strong ideals, and taken it.

"Leave him, Sister. Leave him." Dharam Lal's words grew soft and dripped like honey. "He is not one of us. He never will be. Give me the word and he will be gone. Look what he has done to us, to you, to this school. He has infected you."

She stood and shook her head, first slowly, and then faster, as if to banish every word, every accusation.

"So be it," he said, watching us.

"Ramesh, come," Claire said. She started to leave the kitchen quietly. I began to follow, but a great hand grabbed me from behind. "Just leave," he said, his moustache so close I could feel it, his voice low and dark. "We don't want you here. See what you're doing to her. You must go. You must end this." I tried to run. I could not. I was useless, weak.

I tried to shout, "Claire!" but nothing came out. I could see her a few steps ahead of me. I turned. Dharam Lal was blazing with hatred, not only at me, but at what I stood for. I might be the first of many, and then what would happen to the world he had built?

Or maybe he did it because he could.

He slapped me hard, across the face.

He would have done more, he would have beaten me, but Claire, she stopped him. She pushed him away. She stood over me and picked me up.

Dharam Lal watched us both. That thin, thin face. That smile of triumph.

"The boy is cursed," he said. "He destroys everything. This is my world. No one gave it to me, not that the goras ever would. I took it. And no little boy is coming in here and turning it into a fucking charity school. I was nothing. Now I am something. No one is taking that away from me." He left as quickly as he had come.

He was a faceless man. He was a demon. He could have had any of a hundred different names. He wanted to destroy me, her, us, what we were building together.

He was every person I've ever hated, in one. He was history, he was culture, he was custom. I wanted to kill him.

There's always someone to drag you down in this country.

In the summer of my fourteenth year, it all ended.

They fired her. It was dressed up in the way the Westerners love. She was being promoted to head up a moth-eaten convent a mile or two away. She had further decided to dedicate her life to Jesus, it was announced. I moved her belongings one afternoon, small as they were, linens and pictures and books. No one helped.

That last day there was no hand inspection. They let me straight through.

I walked past Dharam Lal's office, my eyes blazing hatred. He saw me pass, skipped out into the cloistered hallway. He grabbed my shoulder and turned me around. "You must have been one hell of a fuck," he said, and smiled and barged past me. I had been disposed of. He had won. That was the last I ever saw of him.

I finished collecting up her belongings. Books, bedsheets, and pictures. So many pictures. Her family, her home, her early years in India, and a child. A brown-haired child. A white child. I never asked who it was. I packed them all away.

We caught a taxi, and that was the end of Claire's time at Sacred Heart.

Her new home was the Convent of the Blessed Mary, a small brick place built by a penitent Italian businessman who had reignited a speck of childhood faith on his deathbed. It was a retirement home for the forgotten, the crumbling, the dust-ridden, a small brick prison with a small brick courtyard where elderly sisters sat on three-legged plastic chairs and died their slow deaths.

She gave me a new life in exchange for hers.

I would lose her. I suppose it had nothing to do with being forced out. The cancer would have claimed her anyway. But it didn't feel like that back then. It felt like one long thread of misery, like Dharam Lal himself had poisoned her. I used to press parts of myself red looking for lumps of my own.

She didn't tell me until it was too far along. But I saw how she disappeared into herself, how her room became slowly darker as her inner light faded, how she started to lose her way in sentences, how her voice became cracked, like a smashed pot, how her eyes saw straight through me, how her past slowly, slowly became more real than her present, how the fainting spells she started to suffer were blamed on heat exhaustion, how she spent days in bed, weak in body and spirit.

I was sitting my All Indias two years early, not because I was clever, but for the usual reason the poor gave: desperation. I wanted my new life to begin—a scholarship at a college, a future, a life free from my father, as quickly as I could. All I did for a year was study. No friends to share japes with—not that I had any before, but perhaps I could have made some—no carefree childhood moments to recall when I was fat and arthritic. I helped at the stall, even though Papa didn't give a shit. Claire had told me that fathers and sons should be close.

I did well in the exams.

Oh, how I tore at the envelope when it came. I was about to go up in the world. My life was about to change.

I read the result.

Top Ten Thousand.

I gave Claire a smile. I pressed the paper into her hands.

Good.

Not good enough.

She hugged me tight. I started to cry.

No scholarships for me. They always go to the people who never need them, to people who don't know the fear of hunger, the fear of looking around at every adult you have ever known and seeing your every possible future, and every one of them being shit.

No college. It had been my dream for so many long years.

Every day with my father was a stinging rebuke. "Still here, Mr. Professor?" he would say. He would bring up my ridiculous notions of self-improvement to the lower-caste customers, mocking my pretensions and my intellectualism, and they would laugh their corpulent laughs at my temerity. To everyone else, the middle classes with their newly bought camera phones, he would hold up his educated boy. He had almost been annoyed by my failing to get a scholarship to college. What a story that would have made! The little prick had bought a phone. Old Delhi was entering the modern world. The white guidebooks say all the magic has gone. What they mean is that we have 4G data connections.

Sister Claire got me a job behind my back. One avenue had been barred to me. She would find another, by wearing out her shoes and the last stores of goodwill she had with her old girls and their husbands before the stories could spread to her former students of what she had supposedly done.

It was at a newspaper. I would be the stringer, slaloming around Delhi doing the investigative legwork for journalists, taking photos, getting coffees (a new Indian custom this, a modern form of libation for my elders and betters), running paperwork and legal releases, doing interviews with junior policemen and elderly neighbors who claimed to have seen wanted men. A good job, on my own for most of the day, a small salary, but plenty of opportunity.

I would work in the day, and at night I would study. Claire hadn't given up on the All Indias. I had one more chance, the next year, for a retake. I would spend the year working and studying, working and studying.

The boss, Mr. Prem, was a good man. A rotund man, with a gurgling, resonant chuckle that filled the room when he was happy. When he had caught some minister fucking his secretary, or a movie star cheating on his wife, his whole body vibrated with pleasure at another powerful man taken down. He would buy sweets for the office on Fridays, laddoos and besan and peda, and walk around tables pressing it into our mouths. His wife, one of Claire's old colleagues, would come and deliver his lunch, and she would always leave a little tiffin for me too, "Anything for Claire's young man," she'd say in a lilting laugh, and sometimes I'd only find it when I came back from long days out, and devour it even though it was long cold by then. That was what I had. Cold food and relentless studying. That's India for you.

Every Saturday, I went to the temple and offered my thanks. Thanks for what? For being born with nothing? For having to work every minute of every day? For having no life of my own?

Claire laughed when I told her about my temple visits. "Should go to church, young man!" Her face would be cloaked in the darkness of her room, beneath layers of swaddling, her voice leaking out of that shapeless white mass. She never sat in the courtyard—too much smoke, too many complaints, too many memories.

"I did my smoking when I was a young girl, cigarettes and all sorts of other things besides. And look where that led me. Here!"

She would try to ruffle my hair and press a crinkled hundred-rupee note in my hand, and just like the Indian grandmother you'd see in films, we would fight and fight about which sin was worse, taking the money or rejecting it, and I would exhaust her finally, and give it back, and would somehow find it in my pocket after I'd left.

She had wanted to change the world when she was younger. Revolution, anger, blood in the streets, paving stones thrown at police and politicians. She still could, with the little time she had left, but it would have to be through me. So that was what she did.

How long did I work in the normal world that people know? Six months? Six months of study and work, work and study, knowing that if I failed, this was it, but also living free of worry, having Claire to talk to, having some freedom of my own, for the first time in my life.

I went into the office, back out to make some C-grade actress pout into a camera, took metro rides to law offices, did interviews with computer millionaires, heard Mr. Prem's fatherly advice and devoured his wife's turmeric-laced daal while I suffered through my studying. How many months of happiness—well, near happiness—did I have before the cancer came in full force, before we understood why she was fading, feeling weak, and everything went wrong?

It was nice in the beginning. Papa looked like shit when I moved out, just him in that dark nothing room, just him and the plastic mattress I had slept on every day of my life, and the leak from upstairs that had turned the concrete soft. He would have no one to abuse, no one to brag to, no one to make jokes about, while I would be living the high life of the new metropolitan man in a grimy, windowless flat reeking of vegetable oil that I'd found in the back of a newspaper.

At first I thought he would let me go without saying anything, to show me how little I meant, but just as I went, out came the shiny hand to catch my wrist.

"Education will get you nowhere. I used to dream, don't you think I didn't? Fucking big man, you think you're the only person in this family who ever wanted to do better? Always thought I was an idiot, didn't you? You know where dreaming got me? It got me here, with you, in this hole, with a dead wife. She gave me an idiot child, and then he killed her." His eyes drilled into mine, his grip was iron hard, and you could tell it was hurting him to flex his fingers, the tendons straining the other way back to their natural curve.

"Your mother had such dreams. And I was a fool for believing in them. I did my school. I worked my government job. All I got for that was this hand. I should have left you to die. But instead I worked. I fed you. I clothed you. I made sure you lived."

So, he was playing the mother card. Was that all he had left? I let him have it, after all the years of resentment and frustration. I was never coming back. I would never go back to that room again. I'd make sure of it.

"She died because of you," I said. "She couldn't bear to be in the same world as you." I fell quiet. I had nothing else. I hated him too much to put into words. I could never have said anything near enough.

"All this education," he laughed, "and that is the worst you can do? You killed her. You destroy everything you touch. I heard about your nun. She must be so happy with her life, no money, no job, but at least she has her precious Ram—"

I hit him.

That was what he had taught me after all. I went for his rib, the one he'd almost broken before.

When he stopped moving, I knew I was done.

When you hit them, make sure they never get up. That was his gift to me.

So that was all he had, a nice little story with a nice little moral about knowing your place, all wrapped up in a bow after years of suffering in silence.

What a prick.

That was something I had already learned about in books, in all that useless studying about German architecture and Roman history.

I took my belongings, my books, my papers, and I left. That was all there was.

I turned a corner, and another. I looked at the people around me, sweeping the street outside their stalls, lying drunk in the corners of doors, watching the world go by through cigarette smoke. Their lives would never change.

I went to my new apartment, rent paid promptly at the end of every month, and I never looked back.

Finally I had money! I bought a motorbike. I could have gone to bars and clubs in five-star hotels, ordered a water just for show and stolen the branded napkins. I could have shoved my media badge in people's faces. I could have blackmailed junior politicians. But I didn't. I worked. I had a stupid dream of paying Claire back, of giving her a small something per month.

Hubris.

They could operate, I was told. But in a government hospital? Everyone had heard about those places. Uninterested nurses, overworked doctors, corridors full of angry relatives holding skeletal hands wasting away, everyone sitting on and in rags, broken tube lights that went *ping!* every five seconds, the smell of socialist promises turned to shit.

She was in a private room when I arrived. That was what being white got you. I spent a few minutes watching her sleep. A few weeks ago she had finally gone in for a test, had to wait a fortnight, and called me when she had heard, her voice far away and weak, her breath shallow between her sentences.

"Just a small nodule in the lungs," the surgeon said when he arrived. He was straight out of a film, Jackie Shroff down from the screen. Thick black hair with a streak of gray. Prosperous-looking moustache. I've always been jealous of that, having only a little neck and lip stubble to call my own. "How long you will wait, who knows? Six months? A year? It will grow a little in that time, no doubt." He looked down at Claire's sleeping body. I knew she didn't have that long. So did he. He saw the desperation on my face, and beckoned me into the corridor. I knew his look. Private rooms, clean rooms, did not need to be sullied by crookedness. That was for the corridors where the common people roamed. "Or I can do it privately," he said. "But it will cost you. Three lakh. There's nothing more valuable than health, beta."

He smiled when I cried out that I would never be able to afford it. He put a hand on my back and told me, in confidence, that I would be killing Claire if the operation happened in the government hospital, how scalpels slipped and arteries were nicked—he knew how close I was to her, and he might have a little proposition for me.

He was rich, but he had a conscience—I knew that because those were the first words out of his mouth, "I am rich, but I have a conscience." These richies always believe in self-advertising.

He was trying to do his part for the nation while running his private clinic for the housewives—the old India and the new, tradition and wealth, Vedic karma and Western capitalism, hand in hand. I imagine he has a charity now, with an Instagram page and many selfies with white-teethed children.

The devil always seems harmless when he appears. I knew that from long hours studying the Bible. He offers milk and honey and makes evildoing seem easy. He had been talking to Sister Claire. Claire had told him a little too much about her life, and about her charge and how special he was, how wonderful, how he had risen from nothing. Never do that, friends. It only leads to trouble.

He had looked into my eyes, red with tears, shirt collar stained yellow after a long day chasing leads, and said that he had the offer of a lifetime.

Sanjeev Verma had a problem, you see, and the problem was his son. A good boy, but lazy, soft in the head. He had the All Indias coming up. Maybe I could help somehow?

"Tutoring? I've never done it," I said, and he laughed, and for some reason I did too.

"Not tutoring," he said, and then he told me what he wanted me to do, his handsome face making it seem like the easiest, most rational thing in the world. "Just a little harmless play-acting. You only have to be my son for one morning. And the operation will be all paid for."

So I did it.

I sacrificed my retake of the All Indias. I can do many miraculous and inexplicable things, but even I cannot sit two exams at once.

I gave up my future for Claire, just like she had given up hers for me.

I had a whole new world of things to learn for the Vermas' idiot child. He was one of those arty children, and he was taking history, sociology, geography. So I had to take those too, on top of my sensible choices, economics and finance.

I started running late for my job assignments. Mr. Prem gave me long speeches about how I made him look like an idiot. His pride turned sour. No coming to my table to offer me extra kulfi on Fridays. The lunches from his wife stopped. The journalists became angry—their photos were never taken, their documents were full of mistakes, but I had so much to study. People looked at me and thought: How the fuck did he get hired? Bloody lower castes getting special treatment. My eyes were heavy-lidded from hours of work. I had a couple of hours' sleep a night. I fell off my bike a few times.

I cried fat tears, begged Mr. Prem for second, third, fifth chances. I was fired, of course. I couldn't even look him in the eyes as I collected my things.

I could imagine him in the future telling someone, "I once

took a chance on this lower-caste boy. My wife's idea. What a disaster!" and my mouth would taste of ashes and bile at having disappointed so many people.

I didn't tell Sister Claire. Of course I couldn't. She would never look at me again if she knew the truth. About the operation, about the money, about me giving up on the All Indias.

I cried into the night. I was stupid then, I thought the cancer had come because she had helped me, that she had sacrificed herself for me. Maybe I was right.

I did the All Indias.

I sat down at the desk each time and did the exams. I should have been at another center three miles away. But Ramesh Kumar was absent. Just another poor boy who never turned up.

I thought I'd be caught, that first time.

Did I leak sweat, that first illicit All India? Did I cry? I've pushed the memory down, like everything to do with those years, save Claire's broken smile, and "God is love."

Claire asked me how the exams had gone. Badly, I said. I must not have studied hard enough. I must not have been good enough. I wept. I held her hands and tried to make my face look honest.

"No, no, my child, at least you have your work," she said, too exhausted to do anything but sigh. "I know you did your best."

I came Top Thousand. That's how good I am. Verma did as he had promised. The operation didn't work. She got worse.

That's karma, as the whites say. That's how this country works, if you're poor.

She was never the same after. Veins shining through skin. The softness of her grip turned to the hardness of bone. No more beautiful stories. Just a low, whispered voice in a dark, airless room, skin turned to leather.

At night, I read her yellowed paperbacks of the Hardy Boys and Nancy Drew. I would think she was asleep, but when I finished, she would tell me to read another.

She spoke in bursts of one or two words. When I got her flowers, all she said was "You shouldn't." Croissants from the French bakery in Gole Market: "Sinful."

How right she was. I sold my soul for her, and it achieved nothing.

"She should be fine. I cannot tell what is wrong with her," Verma said at the one-month checkup. "You can never know with these things. Did I tell you? Rohit's doing well at Delhi University. Congratulations, young man!" He expected me to burst into a cheer. Did he mention that he had a close friend, a drinking buddy, with the same problem? Here was his phone number, just in case. He knew what a wonderful job I'd done.

I had no job, an apartment I was going to get kicked out of, and there was the future holding out its hand.

And so started my life of facts and names and arguments pouring like cement into my head, of illegally downloaded PDFs, of an unmade, sweat-soaked bed, of a room and a brain illuminated by the white-hot sear of a computer screen. Five years of it, and always in the back of my mind, wondering when I would be able to escape. Was I still going to be doing it at thirty-five? When would I start looking too old? Was I going to go back to a tea stall?

No one came to see Claire. Not her girls, not her colleagues, no one.

I fed her. I dragged her body from bed to wheelchair, so she could go outside and watch the nuns tend to their flowers. I wrapped her body with bandages. I held her head as she vomited blood. I watched her age twenty years in as many weeks. I cleaned the blood from her mattress. I rubbed lotion into her sores. I bathed her, and dried her afterward with a towel, rubbing it over her wet hair, and felt how small she had become, just skin and skull. I made her tea and dried her chin when the liquid fell from her mouth.

Sometimes she would be somewhere else entirely. She would call me by a name I had never heard before. She would call me "son." She would weep that she had not been able to save me, she would say that she wished I was alive and with her now. She cried that she had kept all the pictures, that she had never thrown out a single one. Then she would say sorry again and again and again.

Then I understood.

That's my fate. Always a bloody stand-in for someone else.

The last words Claire said to me, the most she had been able to say for months, like she traded those words for a day of life, were "God always was. God is. God will be. God is love."

What a load of shit.

She died in a government hospital, surrounded by bed upon bed of the poor she loved so much. She lasted three days after those last words, the worst days of my life.

She spent them shouting wordlessly. She would scream in the middle of the night and I would wake and hold her to me, and she would keep on screaming. I slept on a chair next to her.

I knew she was going to die when the screams turned to gasps. No need for a heart rate monitor, no sir.

Her last morning, she had a fever. There was nothing I could do to keep it down. No towel soaked in mineral water. No cold compress. She had vomited blood all over her bed, and I had run out into the corridor, searching for someone to come and help, but no one did. Then she was gone.

It's strange knowing that the only person who cares about you in the whole world is long dead, and that she would not be proud of what you've become, even if she was watching.

SEVEN

Rudi realized very quickly that I was the only person in the world whose fate was tied up with his own. Clever boy. I got 10 percent, and in return I did everything for him. All the signatures, the boring meetings, the food shopping, the transportation, and for that he got to abuse me in public. What a trade-off!

The paise came flooding in, from the usual suspects. Bournvita, asking Rudi to be the face of its "Drink Clever" campaign. Coca-Cola, with its "Onwards India!" ads, on whose sets I got to hang out with Alia Bhatt. Hero Honda—there we met half the cricket team, got some great Instagram shots, hashtag bharatrising. Rudi got rid of his glasses and wore contacts. Of course we made sure to turn that into a sponsorship opportunity too.

I controlled his official accounts, and spent hours every day posting on Snapchat and Instagram and YouTube and Twitter, delighting the people with Rudi's thoughts and bon mots and cultural commentary and cricket celebrations. I didn't try to be smooth, a manicured, polished celebrity. I just had to be a normal Indian teenager. I dialed my natural intelligence down about 75 percent, and there I was. Once in a while, just to remind them I was the Topper, I would have Rudi post some pictures of French chateaus or Mauryan temple complexes, and people would comment, *Such an intellectual, sir* below. I was twenty-four and had the world at my feet, even if it was someone else getting the praise.

All thought of Rudi going to university had gone out of the window. Why spend years grinding away when you could make money now, more than you'd need for a thousand lifetimes? The degrees could come later.

It was beautiful. The only problem was the hangers-on, the pitchmen, the certified investment opportunity people, but I got a driver-bodyguard for that, a cheerful ex-army soldier we paid a half lakh a month. He was called Pawan. He was short, thick with muscle, unremarkable, but a dependable driver. His wife seemed to do nothing but make achaar, so every Friday he offered us an oily jar each of mango or tomato or ginger, "Very Ayurvedic, sir, very good for leprosy and gout," or whatever combination of ailments his wife had googled that week. They piled up under my bed.

She called him as he drove us, hours of conversation a day. "How is my little pehelwan?" she'd ask him. "How is my shahenshah?" He gripped the wheel harder, fingers white, at every pet name. He would keep looking back. "Can I end the call, sir?" he'd whisper. "Can I talk to her without speaker?" but Rudi would shake his head. I realized he wanted to hear women say sweet things to their beloveds. He needed a girlfriend really badly, but that wasn't in the contract. I was many things, counselor, shepherd, guide, but I wasn't a sister-fucking pimp.

Most men want to hear how to get a woman, the combination of lies and bluster and magic and ritual, rather than how to keep her, but not Rudi. He wanted to know every detail, every joke, every tease about aches and pains and strange stains on the mattress. He loved it.

We had our driver. We had attention. We had money. What we needed was something to spend it on.

The first big thing he bought was a statement dwelling. An apartment in South Ex. I took a small box bedroom, intending to use it as an office, but I ended up staying there most of the time. I kept my own place, just in case. His parents had forbidden him from buying the place, and further forbidden me from moving in. Rudi told me about their fight, how his parents thought I was a lower-caste trickster who'd take all his money. Of course, I was the lower-caste trickster who'd made it for him in the first place. They stopped complaining when he bought them an Audi.

Rudi and I became flatmates without either of us even saying it out loud. I did the shopping and organized the cleaning and cooking. He littered rooms and hallways with drunken Amazon purchases and pizza boxes. It was quite perfect.

Rudi up close, you know, wasn't a bad person. He was more than a little fucked up, but then all Indian children are. We were a good team. He was fat, I was thin, he was light, I was dark, but one thing was just the same. The anger.

Not the usual teenager anger about not getting laid enough or not looking like Dwayne Johnson, but something deeper, much more visceral.

You move into a multimillionaire's penthouse apartment in a posh part of Delhi, and you think you'll be spending your time partying. No. You spend it cleaning up after a teenager.

Rudi would drown himself in meet-and-greets with fans, in interviews with press, Indian and foreign, in swanky parties, in European liquor and DJ sets in posh malls and perfumed, ochred girls called Ruby and Kitty and Sweety. They would surround him at the club. He would talk to one. They would take selfies. I would take them home with us. I would sleep. In the morning, I would pick up the bottles from his room. The girls would be gone. I didn't know how many there were. I thought he was enjoying himself.

Then one night, after dismissing another of his girls, he wandered into my room without knocking, holding a bottle of overpriced vodka, threw himself onto my bed, eyes vacant, and started talking. The search for true love hadn't gone well, again. You'd think he could just enjoy himself, but no—he wanted somebody who wanted him for him.

"I don't want kids, you know," he said. He looked up at the fan. "I'd fuck them up. Too many fucked-up kids already. My parents, dude, they always wanted more. Too much. Nothing was good enough. Easier to just hide everything from them."

He kept talking, about humiliation, about his feeling that he had never been enough, just him, an only child who had been too expensive to raise and hadn't given anything back, and I felt sorry for this eighteen-year-old who hid his sadness so well.

"Ramesh," he finished, "I don't just want women. I want true love, dude. I don't want to buy them. Fuck, sorry," he said, and wandered off with a sigh to phone out for Chinese, something else to hide from the celebrity nutritionist.

I understood. He wanted to look in a woman's eyes and see the one thing he could never have—that she would have wanted him when he was no one.

He wanted something real. When you're that rich, and that famous, you don't get real.

When he'd wake up in the mornings, he would go to one of his two bathrooms and have a shower, and it would take hours. The hot water tank would groan with overuse and I would knock to make sure something hadn't happened.

It would have been awful for me if it wasn't for the dump trucks of cash. Even the Saxenas tailed off on the whole fuck-me-over thing and let me get on with making them all money.

At least I was on Rudi's side. I had a stake in his career. Many people wanted him destroyed. The gossip stories started immediately. Rudi did act like a shit. Going to parties that became orgies of ostentation and alcohol, throwing around piles of Gandhis in crowds and watching the riot unfold, messing about at ad shoots, behaving like a little prick.

I went along to make sure he didn't get in trouble. I went to make sure he got back in one piece. I never indulged myself. I was in it for the money. No distractions, no women, no nothing. No getting addicted to drugs. No changing who I was. And certainly none of that falling-in-love, making-plans-for-the-future nonsense.

We were sitting in our flat when the call came, the big one, the one that changed everything. Rudi was watching TV. I was posting all the sponsored posts we'd agreed to on Instagram, all beautifully presented, all on time—I did a fantastic job for the money.

We were just minding ourselves, Rudi answering phone calls from long-lost friends and relatives—

Television. They wanted Rudi on television.

And that's how we became richer than God himself, or a reforming, business-friendly, Davos-attending chief minister of Bihar.

A call came in. A German accent.

"Am I talking to Mr. Rudraksh Saxena's manager?"

Yes, yes, you are.

The voice offered us more money than we thought even existed, the sort of money you see Indian cricket captains earning for sponsoring whisky, and suddenly everything changed.

I hired lawyers. I arranged meetings.

I went to Iqbal Tailors in Connaught Place and ordered a made-to-measure suit, and told them, "Something current, something stylish, something modern," but what I really meant was "I'm meeting white people, bhai, make me something they won't laugh at."

A few days later, we turned up to a glass-windowed office. The receptionists were white. That's how I knew I'd really made it.

We were on the thirtieth floor of a skyscraper, higher than I'd ever been before. I looked out of the window and saw the little people down below, straining, selling, sweating, and suddenly it finally hit me: from the moment I left this place, I would never, ever be like that again.

The lawyers with their Stanford degrees fought among each other. I sat beside one bored, angry Rudraksh Saxena for the next two hours, and drowned out everything but the money. The numbers kept getting larger. A hundred years of tea stall money, I counted, then a thousand, then ten thousand. Rudi wasn't just going to be a quiz show host. They wanted to make him into a brand, the face of the nation's youth, the boy who knew everything.

I celebrated with a glass of champagne, and looked at my own face in the bathroom mirror afterward, and was amazed I still looked the same.

One point five crores. Fifteen million blandly smiling Gandhis. That was my cut. (Take that, *Slumdog Millionaire*.)

I never met the men behind the scenes, the Swiss trying to get in on the biggest TV market in the world, a place where ten million people watched a normal evening program. Even their investment of several million dollars wasn't worth spending time in India for, it seemed.

I didn't care. I saw their cash and I saw what they built, and it was beautiful.

The car came to collect us in the morning. The driver even saluted.

The journey from our flat took an hour, but we didn't notice at all. Rudi and I didn't even talk. We just looked at each other and tried not to laugh at what had happened.

An executive met us at the gate, a suit I never saw again.

"Your corner of Delhi International Studios," he said. A corner? It looked like a palace.

He showed us the makeup room, the control room, a production room full of coffee, cigarettes, and the entrails of people's lives, all separated by a few corridors from the central studio commissary.

"All very impressive," said Rudi, acting very nonchalant-MBA-haver.

But even he gawped at the studio.

The suit knew it too. He paused outside the door, and turned to us and said, "Welcome to your new home, Mr. Saxena. I think you'll be very pleased by what we've made."

He opened the door. At first, all you saw was a dark cavern full of cords of wiring, a bank of seats for the restive, sweaty audience. A gush of air came out, so hot you felt like you were inside a tandoor.

We moved inside, closer to the stage, and everything revealed itself.

Pink lights, pillars, heavy drapes, faux marble, electricians, cameramen, running this way and that. A buzz of activity. They understood India, those Swiss men. They would have had dancers and item girls if they could, with the usual tasteful near-quasi-nudity, all in saris, just a little closer and lower cut than usual.

Beat the Brain.

What a fatherfucking joke.

Live on TV, live, live, live, for added masala, added pressure, the you-just-have-to-watch-it water-cooler conversation. Hundreds of starry-eyed contestants demographically selected from all over India appeared every month, and all they had to do to win the twelve-crore megaprize (chosen for numerological reasons; the Swiss had been told that twelve was a number with huge cultural importance to us) was to answer twelve questions and beat the Topper. And me and the production assistants in his ear telling him the answers.

We had two weeks of prep before the show actually started shooting. We had the money deposited in our account, fifteen crores a year, and Rudi was surrounded by an army of people panting to do his bidding. We spent the morning of the first show in the writing room, a bunch of arse-lickers and producer's assistants coming up with the jokes Rudi would tell that evening, and he had a photo shoot for coconut water in the afternoon with a bikini-clad starlet.

"Ramesh," he shouted, at any and all times of day. I would be finalizing questions, working out contracts for ads, perfecting every little detail of his life, and I would hear the screech from my walkie-talkie and I would go.

"Yes, sir, boss," I'd say when I reached him.

I'd started calling him boss in public. It was my cross to bear.

If the people around him, lund-lickers, makeup artists, Ayurvedic quacks, girls in sunglasses and pink lipgloss, enjoyed it, all the better.

Did he care that the only reason he was here was because of me? Did he thank me? Did he strew petals in my path?

His complaint this time was about tea, that filthy, life-quenching stuff.

"This chai is fucking cold!" he shouted.

"Okay, boss," I said quickly, "I'm on it. Whatever you want." I grabbed his tea, but he held his hand around the cup tight.

"Let it go, bewaqoof," I said quietly. He clutched it harder. The cup crumpled explosively as I snatched it out of his hand, dousing me with lukewarm liquid.

We stared at each other.

He smirked. I promised myself that the next time he came to me in the night and wept, I'd accidentally post it on Instagram. Let him become a poster child for mental health and watch his career implode.

He could do anything he wanted to me, he had realized. What could I do to punish him? If he fell, I would fall too, and no one would be offering me fifty million Gandhis to appear on *Bigg Boss* in two years' time when the scandal had died away.

I went to get his tea, as I did his French fries and condoms and whisky. I went out of the door without looking, trying to pat myself dry, and ran into a woman coming into the room.

She was carrying a bundle of papers and books, an earpiece thrown casually over her shoulder. I remember it so well.

"I'm, er . . ."

"I'm Priya. I'm the assistant producer. You're Mr. Kumar, right? Mr. Saxena's manager?"

Mr. Kumar? It was the first time anyone had ever called me that, apart from at restaurants and in taxis. I didn't know what to say for a few moments.

"Er, Ramesh, yes. Manager, yes. You're right. Not assistant. Never assistant. See anyone calling me an assistant, shoot him, okay?"

"I might do that anyway," she said, with a conspiratorial wink. She tucked a strand of her hair behind her ear and moved in closer. I tried to take a step back, and failed. "And I have so many other targets on my list too," she whispered.

"Bad day?" I said, and I didn't know why I was making conversation. Ramesh, I thought, you're here to make money and fetch chai and get out with your soul and your heart intact. Jesus, don't talk to this woman, she's much better than you, and my God, you're smiling. Why are you smiling like that, Ramesh? Because *she's* smiling?

"I'm just trying to avoid the boss. Like every day," she said. "Oh dear! Goodness, you're covered in tea! What happened? Can I help you?"

"No, er," I said. "You're busy. Please go. I'm fine."

"Are you sure? I'm going to be working on the show, so we should touch base. Here, take my number." She handed me a business card and then waltzed off, hair smelling like roses, balancing two books and a stack of paper in her arms.

Touch base? Who did she think I was? Some college boy with career aspirations? At least someone had given me their number. At least someone wanted to know who I was.

As soon as Priya started working with us, her biggest problem soon became my biggest problem too. We had a shithole boss.

His main issue was that he was a prick. Everything followed from that.

There wasn't anything that made Shashank "Shash" Oberoi happy, not his C Class Mercedes, not his ex-model wife, not trying to fuck the interns, not being surrounded by boot-lickers, nothing. Had he ever been happy, or had he started crying the moment he left his mother, and kept going?

At least Rudi could be pleasant when he wasn't drunk and abusive and chasing skirt. Oberoi was like an eternal conflagration of rage in a button-down shirt.

"Writing not funny enough, Rudi not charming enough, stupid, un-buzzy un-happening questions, camera angles unimaginative, lights wrong color, coffee not here, sound bad, Ramesh a fucking quasi-untouchable, bastarding unions, lazy Dravidians, sambar for lunch again, fucking Priya, fucking inflation, if only the Britishers were in charge again, fucking democracy."

He would say these things to us in production meetings while tearing strips from pieces of paper, rolling them into little cones, and picking his earwax with them, and saying things like "India is such a dirty country. Thankfully Modi is cleaning it up."

Whenever I said anything, he always gave me that look of surprise that all the rich lunds deploy when they realize I speak English.

Oberoi's favorite activity was putting Priya down in public. "Is that the best idea Ms. Bangalore University BComm graduate could come up with? Not very fucking good, is it?" he would say in meetings. "Are your parents dead? Because your inadequacy would kill them again if they were. Don't have kids, do you? So it's your uterus *and* your brain that are fucking barren."

She would sit and take it. It would require every ounce of strength she had not to stand up and walk out, but she would take it.

Oberoi was very proud of his master's from Southern Illinois University, "a very prestigious institution." We love that word. Prestigious. All American places are prestigious. It is very important that they are prestigious for the marriage ads and dating sites, otherwise how else do desperate parents sell their hairy, unwashed thirty-two-year-old sons who work in lower middle management? I think it's code for "Everyone's heard of it. You haven't? Fucking anpadh hick."

Oberoi made an easy job difficult. The show was a hit from the first day we aired. All we had to do was not fuck it up.

Every day we discussed each contestant, weeded out the frauds and the fakes, and picked the genetically noble, the truly deserving. It might be a washerwoman from Benares who'd lost her son in the Kargil war.

"How much do we give her?" a production assistant would ask.

"How many awards did her kid win?" Oberoi would say.

"None for gallantry," the boy would reply, facial hair failing to crawl up from his neck. "Er, just a second, sir, er, two for wounds. Died in a helicopter crash. Friendly fire."

"A hundred thousand," Oberoi would spit. A thousand US fucking dollars. Then he'd go back to posting Instagrams about his children and their prestigiousness, their school reports, their horse-riding lessons, their drama performances, although they never seemed to take a photo with him, along with shots of every five-star meal he ate, every cup of coffee, like it was 1995 and people were still impressed by that, every film ingenue he ever awkwardly posed for a photo with at a party and pretended was a close intimate. *Just catching up with*, he'd write, as if anyone believed him.

We would arrange for a camera team to go out and shoot our contestant in all their seeping filth, get clips of their hopeful little eyes reflecting dying fires, slow motion of their thin, gray-sweatered children covered in flies, get the audience weeping. Indian television doesn't do nuance. Neither does the West, though, does it?

We would go through a day of contestants, taking breaks so that Rudi, who was in the room in body if not in spirit, could take questions from reporters and gossipmongers calling on his phone, or take shots of the team at work, me in the background, just an obscured head popping out of a forest of arms and hair and MBAs, trying very hard to never be photographed, a hold-over from my former career.

Rudi took a million selfies, at the drop of a hat. He'd be talking, and then he'd say, "Ramesh! Selfie!" and I would hand him his phone, and run in the opposite direction. Never be photographed. Never be seen, ever.

When we came to film, a few weeks later, we finally saw our contestants, these denizens of middle India who'd just been hard-luck stories on our production notes.

I'd be in Rudi's ear, feeding him questions and biographical details.

"She was born on the night of the 1980 solar eclipse. Ask her about her star sign."

"You were born on the night of the 1980 solar eclipse. What is your star sign?"

Jesus. That was the first few weeks.

Thankfully he got better.

At least he never left any silences, and always, always he had that thick, cloying charm, the one he turned on in nightclubs and in front of TV cameras, the one I'd seen in his first interview the day he'd become the Topper.

He could pretend he was someone else now. He could perform. He was no longer Rudraksh Saxena, annoying Indian boy-child, but Rudi the Mental Maharaja, who bent knowledge to his will. He could behave however he liked, and someone would make a YouTube video about how it had contributed to his unlikely rise.

Of course he hadn't done anything at all. He knew that.

All *I* knew was that the audience loved him.

"Your son is a pilot? Ma'am, you are one very lucky mother. You know my own mother says to me, 'Rudi, why can't you be a pilot? Why do you just make these TV programs?' Ho ho, mothers, we can't live with or without them. Hail to the mothers of India!" Then he would flash his recently whitened teeth, and all over our great country, bosoms would heave.

Women over thirty, lower middle class and quickly rising, were his best demographic, the country's too. Some of them made up the studio audience; some of those were housewives, in bright makeup used to cover the strain of long, hard hours of work. They all strove to look and smell their best. Rudi wasn't an idiot. He turned up early and told them jokes. He stayed afterward and took selfies and signed pictures, and then disintegrated in the corridor outside, away from the cameras, and I pulled him together and sent him home. There he would swipe away on his phone for hours, text, and check his messages.

They bought shit, these women sitting at home watching the show, chapati flour, oil, washing machines, saris, back massagers, makeup, a deathtrap family car to replace the aging moped, the first Filipino computer, these wives of a hundred million office workers whose fathers had been farmers and who had been lifted from millennia of unchanging rural existence by American pension funds chasing high returns wherever they could get them.

These women wanted to give birth to him, to squeeze his little chubby cheeks, to pet him, all at once, probably.

These women had never had a competent man in their lives. Fathers who never talked to them, husbands who never listened.

Rudi listened. Oberoi would bark in my ear, scream for "tempo, tempo, tempo," and Rudi would stand and listen to the stories the contestants told him. He would ask for their opinions, their favorite shows, the movies they had seen.

You could sense their sighs as he genuflected to aged contestants, or did a speech about the new Indian millennium.

You can make a lot of money in this country by being the perfect fat little son.

Rudi played with the audience. He did these piercing looks to the camera when the contestants were talking about their wretched lives, and he was good at delivering our monologues about the strength of the nation, about parents and brotherhood and bloody Pakistan whenever we could.

Maybe other countries can produce quiz shows without bringing four thousand years of cultural tradition and seventy years of poisonous geopolitical rivalry into it, but we don't.

Rudi tried to sneak off during ad breaks. To do what exactly, I didn't want to know.

"This is so boring, yaar," he would say into my ear. "More boring than when my parents got obsessed with religion when I was ten, and I spent hours doing the musical accompaniment on the fucking tambourine to the Hanuman Chalisa."

After our first week's programs, we went out to celebrate at a pan-Asian bar-cum-restaurant in Khan Market. Rudi was stopped for autographs and selfies outside. Inside, all the sushi pizzas were covered in truffle oil, which I could not taste, and all I could say was "Divine!" Priya looked over at me and raised an eyebrow. She asked me if I wanted to get a drink at the bar. We left the table and elbowed our way through the wannabe film stars, lawyers, and oil executives. The VIP crowd congregated in places like this, which some in-flight magazines had deemed "Brooklyn chic." No one knew what it meant, but they showed up all the same.

We will do anything to impress foreigners. We have a story of Indian cooperation for any nationality. American? Isn't your President X just the best? Oh, you voted the other way? I preferred the last one too. Russian? We were such friends in the Soviet years, we've always been allies, look at our MiGs. British? Easy. Israeli? It's just you and us against the Muslims, huh?

Priya and I were ordering mojitos when behind us we overheard an accounts executive say to his associate, "You know, you Indians know how to keep your women under control. Not like the West. We've grown soft and decadent. The consequences of the sexual revolution have been a disaster for the human race."

I looked at Priya, my face breaking into embarrassment. I was about to say something, anything, when Rudi and Oberoi broke through the crowd and picked up our drinks. "Order another round," Rudi barked at me.

Rudi tried to hold court, but Shash Oberoi was not having it. He was the boss. Rudi was just the star. Neither knew who was more powerful, and they butted heads trying to find out, spent the last six months doing it every day.

"I was just thinking about buying a house in Defence Colony," Oberoi said, his voice dripping satisfaction as people clustered around him. The resemblance to Sumit, Mr. Paco Rabanne, Mr. "Ramesh you have no ambition," but with more fat and fewer steroids, was quite pronounced. The underlings would ooh and aah.

"Defence Colony? Yah, maybe if it was 1985. Ha ha. Only joking, Shashank," Rudi said.

Oberoi went red, tried to calm himself, put an arm around the back of a girl who suddenly appeared, a girl who'd been standing behind him the whole time. She looked around, anxious, uneasy.

This unfortunate competitiveness between Oberoi and my dear master would later prove, how do the Anglos say it, "problematic."

I wish I had paid more attention to it. I could have tried harder to broker peace.

But I didn't, for the only person I had eyes for, over Rudi's criticism of Oberoi's choices in clothes, houses, whisky, and women, was Priya.

Oh, I had it bad.

She controlled that first evening out, without saying anything at all. We ate where she wanted us to. We drank where she wanted to. These men thought they had the power, but they would have been nothing without her breaking her back for them.

She had to organize a birthday party for someone, a farewell party for someone else, anything and everything to keep the show and its staff going.

It was her confidence they were attracted to.

That evening, Oberoi tried it on first. He moved his arm from the woman next to him and edged closer to Priya. With just a casual movement, he placed his hand on the back of her stool.

I felt a shortness of breath usually only brought on by Diwali pollution. Jealousy? I was getting ahead of myself.

Priya shifted uncomfortably, shuffled the barstool forward, but Oberoi placed his hand on it again, and then he slammed it down insistently. Priya's gaze was calm, fixed on the new drink the waiter was making for her, when Oberoi started to paw upward, up toward her thigh.

I stay out of things. I stay quiet. I stay in the shadows. But with Priya, I couldn't help myself.

I wanted to hit him. I was going to hit him. I was going to sacrifice money, celebrity, everything I'd struggled for, Rudi's career, every—

And then we were saved by the bell.

A ringtone went off inside Priya's bag. She fished out a phone and pressed it to her head.

She began to smile. She'd been saved by who else? The blessed force that is the Indian wife, guardian of maidenheads, conservator of purity for countless millennia.

"Your wife, Mr. Oberoi," she said, and finally turned her eyes directly to his. "She's saying your card's been declined online?"

His arms retreated immediately to his sides. The little prick completely deflated.

He took the phone quickly and wandered off.

She picked her fresh drink up off the bar. We looked at each other, and I still wanted to say something, do something, but she just smiled and raised her glass, and I raised mine.

I should have done something to help her. Not only did she have to organize everything, keep us from slitting each other's throats, but this too?

"Priya," Rudi said, as he tried to clink his glass with hers. "Priya. Priya. Priya." He fell silent.

"Hey, boss," I shouted, "look over there, an image rights contract!" I grabbed his hand and pointed across the bar.

"What the hell are you talking about, Ramesh?"

So, not drunk enough for that. I changed tack.

"Is that your friend Shivansh?" I said.

"Where?" He looked around, and then wandered off in the direction in which I was pointing.

I saw him cross the room, confused, pawing at shoulders, grimacing at faces. His smile slowly turned sour. I even felt bad.

"Wasn't there," he said when he returned, his eyes clouded over. He went to sit on a sofa a few meters away and started chatting to a man in a suit. As soon as the man replied, he shut his eyes and started to doze off.

"Thank you," Priya mouthed.

"No problem." I smiled at her. We raised our glasses again.

And then Oberoi returned from his call.

"Priya," he said, "we were discussing something earlier, were we not? Something big."

This time I stepped in with a conversational grenade, "Why do these film stars earn so much money?," and Oberoi exploded with opinions, stories of being jumped in the line at a restaurant, of so-and-so's son buying an elephant, or of someone having Celine Dion perform at their wedding, and the tension died immediately.

Someone at the bar next to us objected to his comments, some educated nonsense about how Oberoi was part of the same system, and he got stuck in an argument, allowing us to retreat.

As we left, and Rudi began to slur out his commands to me, Priya took me to one side.

"Will you be okay getting home?" she asked. Her eyes were full of concern. Actual concern. I was momentarily nonplussed. She kept talking and I kept nodding.

"Coffee? Tomorrow?" she said. "I have some ideas I want to run past you."

"Er, yes," I said, stunned. "Thank you. Tomorrow. Touch base," I said, and she laughed.

I pulled Rudi up from the couch, tried to hold him up as we staggered out of the bar.

The next day, Priya and I had our first coffee date in the studio's canteen.

"This is nice," she said as we sat down.

"But we haven't said anything yet," I said. *Stupid, stupid, stupid* rang out in my head.

"No, just this, just being able to talk to someone without feeling hunted."

"Hunted?"

"You know. At the bar."

"Oh," I said. "I wanted to do something. I would have done. I'm sorry."

"I know," she said.

She gave me a smile and shuffled her chair closer, like we were co-conspirators.

I couldn't help but notice her hair smelled slightly of roses and her purple earrings caught the light as she laughed and propped her chin on her hand—here I am going on about her looks, but it was her intelligence, her determination, her drive, the way she made you feel as if you were the center of the room, that her mind was fixed on every word I said.

Oh God, Ramesh, I thought.

"I don't know much about you, Ramesh. Tell me something about yourself," she said.

"Born Old Delhi, moved New Delhi, lucky to go to charity school, then I went into precocious child genius management, you know how it is," I said. "What about you?"

"Born Ahmedabad, did my degree in Bangalore, and now I'm a TV producer." She laughed. "Much less interesting than yours."

Her parents wanted her married, she complained. "Darling, who is single at twenty-five nowadays? Can we introduce you to Group Captain Khurrana's son?" she imitated. "There's always some kid in finance or politics they want me to get married to," she added. Then she lowered her voice a little bit. "All a little like Rudi."

I laughed.

She held one of her purple earrings between her thumb and forefinger, and talked.

It was so damn nice, just listening to her slightly Gujarati-accented English, and then of course one of Oberoi's minions ran in and barked orders about buying flowers for some fat politico's nephew, and dealing with his credit card repayments or something, and Priya picked up her takeaway coffee cup and said, "Thanks for the drink, Ramesh."

Later on, I would get to knock out that bhosdike Oberoi, and it was one of the best moments of my life. But I won't get to that yet.

Hey, I was going to earn fifteen million Gandhis in one year.

I had something, I didn't know what exactly, with a beautiful girl.

I was happy.

EIGHT

Maybe at the beginning, things were good for Rudi too. Maybe there was a week, or a day, or an hour, where he was truly happy: rich, feted, a celebrity, an eighteen-year-old with the world at his feet.

Whatever his mental state, on the show he was good. Contestants were charmed. He never had a line, a hair out of place.

But he slowly got worse, a lot worse, and my ass-covering began.

On the show, his lines started to slip. Sometimes he looked at the camera with glazed eyes, just for a second, and I would see his face on the monitor and I could tell that he didn't know what he was doing or where he was, and a strange, illicit excitement would run through me, very much against my will.

One time we had a housewife from Amritsar, who had burned her arm in a boiling water accident when she was a kid, a usual Punjabi childhood incident it seemed, and Rudi just stared at her arm for ten seconds straight.

Her question had been "What's the fourth largest lake in Maharashtra?," one of the fuck-off-home-now questions Oberoi loved so much.

She stood there, unable to say anything, and watched as the counter clicked down, and the lights in the studio went red.

"Tough luck, tough luck," Rudi was meant to say, and read out the correct answer, ask about her family, usher her back into obscurity.

Instead he did nothing.

He just stared at her, at her furrowed, melted skin. Seconds passed, and still he said nothing.

"Get him to say something, Kumar!" screamed Oberoi.

"Rudi," I hissed in his ear. "Rudi, ask what she'll do with the money. Ask her about her husband. Rudi!" My eyes were clamped to the monitor while Oberoi spat at me from my side.

"Your husband loves you, even with your arm?" Rudi said robotically. The woman's lips started to quiver. Moisture appeared at the corners of her eyes, and I could imagine why, the tears of a woman who had tried hard to conquer her fear of being seen in public, who had told herself that she would never cry again.

"Y-yes," she said, "but sometimes . . ." She grabbed at her sleeve to dry her eyes.

Rudi looked totally trapped.

The audience was uneasy. Their boy was falling apart. We had to act bastard fast. If they started booing, his whole career would be done, the gossip rags would never let off. I understood the situation immediately, but Rudi, he just stood there looking terrified, his mouth ajar in surprise.

"Fucking tell the prick to say something," shouted Oberoi beside me, breath smelling of bourbon. "He fucks up now, the show goes down and I'm completely fucked, you hear?"

"Rudi," I said. "Say these words exactly: your husband loves you, even with your arm. No question. It's a statement."

Rudi said, "Say these words exactly: your husband loves you, even with your arm. No question. It's a statement."

Fuck.

The gods be praised, the altars be sanctified, the woman nodded. Put it down to caste-based deference, TV nerves, globalization, whatever, she nodded!

"My husband loves me, even with my arm," she said quietly.

"Because that's what love is, isn't it?" I said. Rudi repeated it. He had enough sense to smile to the camera. "We take the good days and the bad together. We take the good things and the bad. No love is perfect. We all have our problems. But we deserve to be loved. All of us. From the lowest of the low to the highest of the high. That's what makes this world go round." The woman was still crying, but they were happy tears now, son-has-returned-from-war tears. I let myself look around the control room. Priya was gazing at me in the darkness of the booth with admiration. She mouthed, "Thank you." I was totally lost in her, almost like Rudi had been moments before. Then Oberoi slapped me from behind and told me to get on with the bloody broadcast.

The audience had started clapping and hooting and stood in all their sari'd splendor.

"Rudi, go over and hug her," I hissed, and he did. He nearly squeezed the life out of the woman, lifted her off her feet.

"Thank you, India, and goodnight!" I said, and so did he.

Disaster averted.

It was spellbinding, snake-charming television in the end.

"Thank fuck," said Oberoi, but he'd use it for ammunition in his weekly debrief, when the table in front of him was stacked with whisky miniatures, the usual middle-aged cocktail of statins and beta blockers, and a miniaturized digital blood pressure monitor he'd begged some American relative to bring on their annual visit to India. Complaining about Rudi gave him a break from complaining about his bills, his mortgage, his wife's spending, all the nonsense that he preferred to ignore.

They would never go directly at each other at work, Rudi and Oberoi. They would insult me or Priya or another underling, and compete at how dismissive and cruel they could be.

And then Rudi would come to me at night and weep.

It had been one of Oberoi's genius ideas. He wanted to freshen things up, he wanted to avoid any more strange Rudi silences.

Challengers Week. Three kids a show, Rudi's age, who'd all taken the All Indias that year. They would come in, try to take Rudi's crown, and, obviously, lose.

The first four days went off without problems. The kids were all bespectacled and pure and from poorer families, and at the end of the show their parents came onstage and we gave them fridges and dishwashers. Very sweet.

But Oberoi had something quite different planned for the last day. He told us as we sat around the table for the production meeting: me, Priya, a few scriptwriters—Rudi was absent as usual.

"A real challenger," Oberoi had said, "someone the audience will hate."

"Hate?" said Priya. "But that isn't how this show works. Rudi wins, but we don't humili—"

"And that's where you're wrong, Priya. Our ratings have gotten soft. The people have tired of charity. They need humiliation. We need Rudraksh to crush someone. Someone rich and arrogant."

Someone like you, I thought. I didn't say anything. Maybe it wasn't a good idea. Maybe Rudi would look arrogant himself and out of touch. But at least Oberoi had ideas, at least he wanted to keep things fresh. Something to distract Rudi from his boredom, to change things up? It could work.

The kid's name was Abhi.

His introductory video was very swish. Expensive cars, fancy drinks, nightclubs, lots of young women showing flesh. The audience was visibly disgusted. So far so good.

On the screen, his interview began. "I love to party," he said. "I work hard and I play hard."

The audience began to boo.

"I'm going to put Rudi in his rightful place," he continued, his eyes darting from side to side. The little prick was reading. I looked over to Oberoi. He was smiling. "I'm going to dethrone Rudi Saxena, and then I'm going to be the Brain of Bharat."

He was not exactly endearing himself to the audience in the first place. Then he said the real dynamite line.

"I've studied abroad, but now I've come back to India to show people who the real champion is."

The audience began to boil with anger.

In the control room, Oberoi was beaming with delight.

"This is awful," said Priya. "He's just a child. They're going to rip him apart."

"Exactly," said Oberoi, pulling at the corners of his moustache. "Think how great Rudi will look."

I glanced at Oberoi. He was loving it. Maybe he was loving it a little too much, I thought. Probably loved getting Rudi riled up.

In the studio, out came Rudi, looking pissed.

Out came the kid, Abhi, waving shyly. T-shirt with a foreign label? Check. Designer trainers? Check. An expensively dressed sacrificial lamb.

He had a beautiful face. Youthful, toothsome, a milk advertisement face. His hair looked like it had been designed to be ruffled. His cheeks were red. His smile was innocent.

That smile didn't survive a second in the studio.

I had never heard anything like it. The audience was ready to riot. They were shouting, "Rudi, Rudi, Rudi!" The women were howling with rage. The men were making anatomically incorrect comments about mothers. Why always them? What have they done? It's un-Indian, I say.

Rudi had been watching the video, as always, from the green room.

He was in a rage.

He ripped into the kid, all the usual hits. You don't honor your mother and your father. You ran away from this country. You have too much money. You don't know what life is like for normal people. I didn't even have to prompt him. He was consumed with anger.

"And to top it all," he finished, stabbing his finger at the young kid stood behind his podium, "you insult all of the people watching this show. You insult their histories, their lives, and everything they have struggled against for generations. Young man, you are arrogant and uncouth and un-Indian, and Rudraksh Saxena is going to take you down!"

He was out of control. He was completely enraged. I had never seen him like this. The boy, his face, the situation, the video, everything came together just then.

"Rudi! Calm yourself!" I said. But he didn't listen.

The audience had gone straight to ecstasy. They clapped. They applauded. They stamped their feet and the seats shook to their rhythm.

Rudi was wide-eyed with rage, his breathing hard, a rich kid who wanted to usurp him right in front of his face. He was getting out of control. I had never seen him this angry. If Oberoi wanted to pump some life into the show, if he wanted to avoid frozen silences, then it was working, far, far too well.

Abhi tried to respond, but he was utterly drowned out. Anti-national, NRI, traitor, foreign-resident, bad at arcane general knowledge: all the choicest insults rang out from the audience. Men stood up and shouted, competing with each other to get a close-up shot from the audience cameras that they could use as their Twitter picture, just above the bio they'd update to read, *Media Commentator. Pro-India. Patriot.*

"We shall see," shouted Rudi, "after the break, who will be the real brain, and who will be the drain." He came up with that one himself. I hold myself in no way accountable.

We went to the ad break. The audience fell immediately silent.

Priya put down her headphones, shot Oberoi a look of hatred, and went out to the studio floor. She walked up to the kid, who'd gone totally white, and gave him a hug.

"Why did you even do that?" Oberoi asked when she returned. "He has to learn someday how the world is."

Priya bit her tongue.

We came back from the break. The audience began to scream with rage again, the dramatic shits. Oberoi tapped at his laptop, and up came Abhi's first question.

What is the tallest mountain on planet earth?

Mauna Kea. Everest. K2. Elbrus.

"You have thirty seconds," said Rudi. Abhi had regained some of his color. A simple question. He could do this, you saw the kid thinking. He was giving himself a little silent pep talk, full of positive thinking and the other coping strategies his therapist must have told him when he was eight.

"Go easier on him for the first few questions," I said into Rudi's ear. He nodded imperceptibly. Priya shot me a look of thanks. I grinned back.

And then Oberoi said, "The answer is Mauna Kea."

I turned and looked at him like he was an idiot. On the screen, Rudi raised his eyebrow.

"The answer is Mauna Kea. Not Everest. That's the highest," said Oberoi. "Tallest is measured from the base, and Mauna Kea is half in the sea."

"Sir," said Priya, pulling her headset from her ears. "Sir, that is a trick. We cannot do that. This is the first question. He'll be a laughingstock."

"He has to learn," said Oberoi. "Think of our ratings. Go on, Ramesh. Tell him what to say."

"The answer is Mauna Kea, Rudi. Everest is the highest," I repeated.

Of course the boy said Everest. He looked so confident, so young, so proud of himself.

And then the studio lights turned red.

"Wrong!" shouted Rudi. "Wrong!" The audience gasped. "He got the first question wrong! The first time ever! It is Mauna Kea. That is the tallest mountain, which is half in the sea. Wrong!"

"Rudi, go easy," I said.

Rudi smiled, ignored me, oh how he loved this, and shouted again, "Wrong! You thought you could come here and make fun of us little Indians? You thought we would roll over and die? You think we're pathetic? *You're* pathetic! You useless duffer." He was shaking with anger. "We'll take a break, then we'll be back with another challenger. Let us hope he is better than this one."

The audience began to laugh.

The boy wept inconsolably. He looked up at the crowd, and his face was covered with tears.

The audience clapped and clapped and clapped.

Priya left the room and hurried into the studio to deal with the weeping and broken child.

NINE

Two months into the show. Our ratings were ticking upward. Washing machines were still being sold. Rudi's life was still a mess.

On Facebook, I saw that Priya's birthday was coming up. Conscientious young man that I am, I wished to buy her a present. But I had never bought anything before for a woman so high-class. What did they like?

I walked around a mall one Saturday in a state of confusion. On WhatsApp I tried to dance around the question. Did she like chocolates? Which clothes stores had she been to recently? What music did she listen to?

I must not have been so subtle, for finally she simply texted, *Ramesh, if you want to buy me a birthday present, I like flowers.*

So I bought flowers.

Then Rudi and I stumbled into another disaster.

We were being investigated.

Just another mess to add to everything else I had to deal with.

How did I hear about it at first? I heard whispers of phone calls to Rudi's old classmates. I received an email from some Central Bureau of Investigation underling asking for my assistance, then an urgent phone call, then a letter, full of stamps, signatures, and angry capitalizations, all of which I ignored.

I thought it was some crank, maybe a journalist, or a scam, or somebody jealous about Rudi's success, trying to get hush money.

It wasn't.

Her name was Inspector Anjali Bhatnagar, and she was a senior investigator at the Central Bureau of Investigation (Education Division). She had seen us on television, had looked up the educational records of one Rudraksh Saxena and been extremely puzzled.

Here was a boy who had formerly been somewhat stupid. Poor tenth-class results, no extracurricular activities, unimpressive pre-examinations record, and here he was, the Topper! How had that happened? I could just imagine her at her computer, Google and administrative records at the ready, rubbing her hands together as the details of Rudi's life came into clearer focus. This was the sort of thing she had gone into public service to stop. Or maybe—I hoped—she just wanted a payoff. The rich and idle and fair-skinned, people like Rudi, had always cheated and paid their way to the top. She must have known that no one woman could stop that.

Next she went to Rudi's parents, and they phoned him, panicked. He didn't care, of course he didn't; they were nothing to him now, just a link to a past he pretended had never existed.

Then she turned up at the studio, in a dark suit instead of the usual khaki uniform, definitely from money, and she demanded—demanded!—to speak to Rudi. She had some official-looking summons that she waved at us. We weren't rich enough yet to laugh in her face. I hovered in the background of his dressing room, trying to look inconspicuous and subaltern. I mumbled out the word "manager" when Bhatnagar glared in my direction.

She was trouble, you could tell straightaway, from the way she held herself, the way she glared at Rudi, no pleasantries, no praise, none of the "I saw your Bournvita advert the other day" we got from everyone else. He was just another spoiled rich boy to her, rather than the fount of all knowledge. She was one of those true believers in the law, one of the Central Bureau people who were totally incorruptible, completely resistant to government pressure—and that was something so unlikely it was like an election without ballot-stuffing. Unbelievable.

She was one of those clever people who didn't realize the law was just what rich people wanted it to be.

Rudi sat in the dressing room, slurping and flicking his way through Frappuccino and Tinder. He was taking the meeting too casually. His brain had become warped by too much money, too much everything, too easily. This woman could destroy him. She presented a greater danger than anything we'd faced. I needed to tell him, signal to him somehow.

"How did you prepare for the All Indias?" she said.

"Worked," said Rudi. I texted him, all capitals. *DON'T FUCK THIS UP, DO YOU KNOW WHAT SHE CAN DO TO US?*

"Who were your tutors?"

"I'm naturally intelligent," he said. He looked up from his phone and mouthed the word "whatever" at me. I would have laughed if I hadn't been so nervous.

"Your parents didn't allow me to see their financials. Is there a reason for that?"

I needed to get Rudi out of there. I was shaking with worry. "You're needed in the studio," I said loudly, but no use. He plunged on.

"They hate you, probably," he said.

At this Anjali Bhatnagar took a deep breath. "My God!" she exclaimed, unable to hold her anger. She was a senior investigator at the Central Bureau of Investigation. You didn't fuck with the CBI. People cried in front of her, spilled their guts. She knew no masters but the Indian people.

"If you wanted a date, all you had to do was ask. I would have said yes," Rudi said, swiping away on his phone.

"Date?" she said. Rudi's smile lit up his face, the first in days. I could not believe he was joking, in front of this woman who had the power to destroy everything we'd built together.

"Ramesh, see what my diary is like next year."

She kept her composure. She tucked free strands of hair behind her ears. "I am going to get you," she said.

"In bed?" Rudi asked.

It wasn't even a good line. That upset me even more. I wanted to scream in his face: this is my future you're destroying, for a stupid, witless joke. I won't lie. I thought of Priya. I thought of a little farmhouse somewhere, with a bunch of kids.

"I got Malhotra. I got Fernandez. I am going to take you down," Bhatnagar said softly. "I will never stop." You could tell she wouldn't.

"Am I supposed to care?" said Rudi, inspecting his fingernails. "Because I don't."

She left without another word.

"Man, what a set of knockers on that one," said Rudi, smirking like a schoolboy. He expected me to smile along, the way everyone else around him did these days.

"What insolence!" I said. I was angry. "You can't treat a woman that way. Your elder, somebody with that much power! Anyone! Rudraksh!"

"Whatever, dude," said Rudi.

I tell you, in this country respecting women is only for temples, and for rich aunts with heart conditions.

Rudi rummaged around in his Armani suit, pulled out a bag of something, white powder, I didn't want to know. He said, "Fuck off." So I did. I should have stayed around. I should have stopped him. But I didn't.

A few days later, we got our official summons, all the forms present and correct. I made our lawyers fire off a holding letter, grease some wheels, delay things, but we couldn't avoid it forever.

Another bloody complication. You think you're just faking exams for rich people, nice and simple, just the standard corruption of the moral values we Indians hold dear to our hearts, and then all this happens.

Priya and I were beginning to have regular lunches, and later that week, over a sandwich in the canteen, she asked me, "Do you know who Anjali Bhatnagar is?"

I opened my mouth and gulped air.

"How did you know about her?" I asked.

"I'm good at my job," she said.

She placed her cell phone in front of me. Page after page of Anjali Bhatnagar, a fan forum, Photoshopped deepfakes on Google Images, Facebook groups, news conferences where she told corrupt politicians she was going to get them and their kids, videos of her discussing anti-corruption initiatives at the Jaipur literary festival, watched by a crowd of adoring whites, interviews where she tore into other guests. India is the only country in the world where you get both sides of an issue, six, eight people, on TV and make them fight each other until their guts are on the floor. It is our great contribution to world culture, that and the bhangra song they play at gora weddings.

"Every second person on the news is the son or cousin or mistress of a neta. You have to be very careful who you mess with," Priya said. "I would not want a woman that tenacious after me."

You don't take out the rich and connected without coming to some harm. I read the articles about Bhatnagar's career, and how she had suffered. She had been passed over for promotions and received death threats. These stories, leaked from inside the CBI, littered the press. Anonymous editorials from government newspapers called for her to be sacked.

She was the last person in the world we wanted after us. She got results. She had taken down rich, connected people, and now I was guessing she was out for blood and her career was on the line, and that really was frightening. Rudi, a fucking Topper, a TV star, would be the catch of a lifetime.

"We're fucked," I said.

Priya looked at me and tilted her head to one side. "Only if you did something wrong," she said.

I couldn't say a word.

We had become closer lately and I often used silence to build a wall between us. Like a parent, or a producer, she tried to use it to get me to talk. But I said nothing.

On, on, on it stretched, that silence, like the timeless eons before the world was created, a primordial cosmic silence, leaking into a canteen serving tandoori paella.

"You can talk to me, you know," she said. "I know you are not like the rest of them."

But I was. Oh, you can convince yourself you've only acted out of poverty and desperation, but only for so long, and so I still couldn't say anything.

"Please, Ramesh," she said, and took my hand. "If something happened, you can say. I won't tell anyone. You can trust me. I understand."

I looked down at her hand in mine.

The bell rang for the end of lunch, and a hundred employees stood up together in a communal groan. I did the thing I least wanted to. I took my hand from hers.

She looked disappointed for a split second, and then quickly began to gather her things. I mumbled some excuse and left. I had not betrayed myself, but I knew I had to make it up to her somehow.

I had to ask myself what I wanted.

I wanted her. I didn't want riches without end, I'd realized. Only real pricks want that stuff—the cars, the cash, the fame. What an un-Indian sentiment, what an Instagrammable sentiment; I was starting to feel more like that every day.

So when I got home from work that evening, I asked her out. By text.

I waited nervously for her reply, like a kid after the All Indias—well, the kids whose parents haven't hired me.

She said yes. Three little letters.

When I met Priya again, the lunch incident had been forgotten.

We met in a mall, on the weekend, like American teenagers courting in a film.

I managed to slip away from Rudi that Saturday, for a few precious hours. An escape from tax forms, legal documents, the recent threat of investigation hanging over us, from the confused mess of his new life, the hangers-on, the money, everything.

I walked into the coffee shop, and there she was, at the far end, in jeans and a knitted sweater. I sat down. I didn't know how to start.

"So," I said.

"So," she said.

I was considering launching into a fascinating discussion about the structure of Rudi's monologues when a girl behind us shouted out, "He is my boyfriend, everyone has them, Daddy." My eyes snapped onto Priya's, and hers onto mine, and then we looked away.

"Everyone has them now," the girl said again, filling the room with her voice. The father harrumphed that it was a Western thing, only low-class Indians did it.

Priya's eyebrows moved up and down as she sipped at her coffee, and I tried not to laugh. The father and daughter fought, shouted, without a care. In America, they would be on camera for the world to see, but here people simply eavesdropped.

Then I started to really shake with laughter and I felt a sharp sensation. I looked down at my thigh, and there was Priya's hand, pinching the flesh above my knee. She winked at me. I winked back. Then I did the same to her. Soon our thighs were stinging with pain and we only stopped when we were both breathless with exertion and a few uncles at the next table started making tutting noises.

So we started talking, about anything and everything. Whatever pretense we had concocted was forgotten.

We talked about our parents.

"Civil servants," she said. "Honest, can you believe? Only a government pension to live on. I have an uncle who was in the police. Honest too. No money. I send them all a little every month."

"Not civil servants," I said. "Just my father. Not honest. No uncles. No one at all. Also no money. I don't send him anything every month. In fact I haven't seen him in seven years."

"What about your mother?" she said. Nobody ever asked about my mother.

"Died giving birth to me," I said. Priya went quiet, replicating my silence this time, and placed her hand over mine. I squeezed it back and broke the silence. "Tell me more about this absurd honest family of yours."

I wondered if I would ever meet them. What would they think of me? Rude, uncultured, north Indian—all synonyms, really. They would be elegant, refined, like their daughter. I was getting ahead of myself, like a mother who sees her son share a two-word conversation with a girl at temple and starts to measure the drapes, calculate the dowry, name the children, and schedule the childminding.

"You know, they built a house, got cheated by developers, and now I give them money every month, and whenever I'm not working I feel guilty. They believed in socialism, that they were building a new India, a better country full of equal people," she said.

"I knew someone like that," I replied.

I was about to tell her about Claire, the whole misery and heartache, but the silence choked me up again, and then my phone rang.

Rudi.

"Forget him for just one day," Priya said, and took the phone from my hand and put it back in my pocket.

We left the café, got into a cab, and went shopping on the other side of Delhi, an hour of comfortable silences, browsing the mall together, our bodies close, our knees touching, our arms brushing against each other as I held open doors, the rose scent of her hair in my nose and the sparkle of her earrings catching my eye.

When it grew dark, I knew I had to get back to Rudi. My phone had a dozen missed calls.

"Oh God, leave me alone for just one day, boss," I said when I called him back.

Rudi went on a rant. A nice stream of insults for me.

I could imagine him, sitting in the dark, his face hollow with lack of sleep. I hung up as quickly as I could.

"I have to get back," I said to Priya. I made a very forward, Western-type move. I took her hand in mine. "This has been wonderful."

Then she made an even more forward, Western-type move.

She got very close to me, moved her hand to the side of my face, pulled me to her, and kissed me.

"We have to do this again soon," she said.

I let go of her with extreme reluctance. As I left, I kept looking over my shoulder at her. She waved me off, and mouthed the words "Hurry, hurry."

She was the best thing that had happened to me for a long, long time.

I felt sorry for Rudi.

We were three months into the show. It was all too easy for him. Three hours of hanging around a studio every night, maybe two ad campaigns a week, two hours each for fifteen lakh. It went to his head.

He stopped going to the studio for production meetings, said he would only turn up a few hours before air, that he was a professional now.

I was his only friend. Who else did he have? But I was trying to spend more time with Priya.

He reconnected with his school friends who had ignored him before, who now went to Delhi University and turned up on Fridays to our flat when they wanted quick entry into a club. They would mill around him like flies on shit, going on and on about Grey Goose vodka and where they wanted to do their master's and the best club nights in Delhi.

One particular Friday, one of his hangers-on, Shivansh, sidled up to me and said, "Who are you?" Then Shalini, she of the kohl eyes and henna tattoos on her inside wrist, said, "How did you meet Rudi? You're his servant, right?"

We had met before, of course, and we would repeat this every Friday. Maybe they were being cruel, maybe the drugs had zapped their brains, maybe they were practicing their barbs for middle-aged married life.

Children.

Rich kids, Instagram kids, Dubai-educated American-accent kids, kids who were rappers, up-and-comers, my-name's-Purana-Killa kids, here's-my-SoundCloud kids, they insulted me when my back was turned, as if I couldn't tell. Imagine all the suffering I had undergone, the work I had done, the money I had made, to be mewled at in half-lit clubs by chutiyas who frequented delis, chocolateries, and pan-European fusion eateries.

We were all the same in the dark anyway—why did it make so much difference?

On these nights in the club, Rudi would saunter back to our booth with two white girls on his arms, the ultimate status symbols, better than the Bollinger that Nigerians pour over their heads. With him back in our presence, everyone would have to be nice to me again.

And then he started ramping up the drugs.

I should have kept an eye on the drugs. At ad shoots, while I sat at the food table (very socialistic, the same food for everyone, just like at the gurdwaras), he would barely be present. Lost, zoning out, ordering alcohol on apps for me to pick up later.

Wandering about the flat at night in a daze.

I really did want to help him, but how could I? People have to want to save themselves.

Ratings were still high, the mothers were still tuning in, I was still making money, temples and convents were still being donated to, but Rudi had to develop a drug problem, didn't he, joy of joys, so as to make the Western rock star parallels even clearer: India is a land of intellectuals, so our pop stars are quiz show hosts.

When did the little shit start doing coke regularly? Who did he get it from?

Maybe he did it because people put him down.

"What is this Rudi nonsense?" husbands read from their newspapers. "What's wrong with the good Vedic name Rudraksh?"

"Does he do anything on this show other than give small amounts of money to orphans and unemployed middle-aged women?"

"What is he hiding?"

Maybe he did it because he had no real friends. Me? I wouldn't have stuck around for free.

I found the envelopes of powder and threw them away. I found others, filled with strange Chinese tablets, and threw those away too. More appeared. I wanted to take him to a doctor, but I didn't.

Why?

I don't know.

I felt guilty. I was carrying on some Romeo romance, and I wanted to go easy on him, but I knew he was a liability.

I tried to make more time for Priya, for our lunches and coffees, but Rudi consumed more and more of me. I could not do without her. It was the first time I had felt like that about anyone.

Soon I had to look after him full-time. We returned to the flat in the early mornings, after nights out, and then I had to babysit, and deal with his life, and worry about mine, and how I was finally going to tell Priya the truth, for I had to, I'd realized. I had to, or she would find out, and she would never forgive me. The thought of losing her made me start to feel distinctly uncharitable toward Rudi in particular, and Indian teenagerdom in general.

I started watching the daytime soap operas while Rudi dribbled in the background, bucket placed delicately, artfully, at just the right location under his wretched maw, at just the right angle to catch the jet of projectile vomit.

In the boredom of daylight, even I began to drink. Just a little, now and then, but it was still too much. The smell of alcohol. Feeling sorry for myself. Being useless and not doing anything about it. I tried hard not to think that I was turning into my father.

Parental supervision was thin on the ground, shall we say.

Rudi's parents had disappeared entirely. They'd Indian-parent-blackmailed him (we have done everything for you, sacrificed holidays and SUVs and our blood pressure for your future, and you do *nothing* for us) into setting them up an expense account, and they were on some Italian lakes vacation, no doubt filled with languorous spa trips, swinging, Dolce & Gabbana–branded everything, and many surgeries and fillers and lipos, and that was just Mr. Saxena.

Before they left, they had actually tried to get rid of me one final time. I'd gone to my old place, which I visited once a month, crossing back into the shit side of Delhi—nice to see you again, Mother Yamuna, still full of chemical foam, are you?—and found an envelope among the mountain of crap in my letter box. Inside, a printed note, in a newspaper-ransom-style font, seriously, like it was the seventies and Pran or Amrish Puri was behind it all. *We know your secret. Leave now. Leave him.* It was so pathetic, I knew it had to be them. They weren't sharks. He was a mid-level accountant and she ran an ethnic designs fashion label. It was just what you would expect.

They gave up entirely after that, on me and the kid.

In our flat, the dishes and the plates and the bottles piled up. Our cleaning woman stopped coming, claiming demons inhabited the place. The landlord knocked on the door in his jogging gear, white hairs creeping out of the neck of his polo shirt, and told us we were being "very bad sports."

We had bricks of money under beds, inside statues of gods, in the fucking fridge, because Rudi had seen it in a gangster movie.

We said yes to anything, any shoot, any ad, any mall opening, we got paid, and life went on. I tried to remove the bags of powder, and said nothing more. Maybe I worked him too hard, but I had to keep him earning money. If the truth came out, if Anjali Bhatnagar got to us, what then? The threat of the CBI was still being held at bay, for now, by our lawyers. If he became unpopular, what then? What would happen to him? What would happen to me? There was nobody waiting to catch us if we fell. I didn't have any family, and, well, Rudi didn't either. We had each other and that was it. I didn't want to think about that at all.

One day, a few weeks later, on the street outside my flat, Sumit approached me.

He looked different. Or maybe it was me who had changed.

At first I thought he was an autograph hunter, or a fan in need of a favor, one more of the thousands who had deluged me and Rudi, who turned his Instagram into a sea of requests for donations.

But no, it was Sumit, coming to me, coming to beg.

"Brother!" he said, his smile a little too manic.

"What's wrong?" I asked, because he'd never been nice before.

"A little trouble," he said. "Nothing big. A client. He's demanding his money back."

"And what can I do?" I said. I moved toward the waiting car, and Sumit tried to look honest and pathetic at the same time, but couldn't. He'd never had to before.

"That was all in the past," he said. "You can help me. I will be forever grateful. The past is the past."

"Is it? I'll always be small, Sumit, no matter the brains I have. I could have all the money in the world, and I'd still be small. Isn't that what you said? No, brother, I cannot help you."

And then I left.

Rudi and I went to TED Talks, because that was where Rudi said all the hot, posh, uninterested girls were—his favorites. Tire-necked ministers interviewed him at after-parties about the secret of his success, and he said, "Always listen to your father and your mother. Work hard, harder than a dog, harder than Hanuman when he moved the mountain to bring that herb back to Ram," and the ministers nodded and said that we were nothing, nothing without culture and tradition, and the newspapers said, "See Rudi's Surprising Secret to Topping," and uncles and aunties in family WhatsApps across the land scolded children for not going to temple enough and then bought ever more products with Rudi's face on them.

Meanwhile, Oberoi was growing fatter on the success of Rudi and *Beat the Brain*, and what did the prick do? He decided to go into politics, and that meant getting into bed with the People's Party.

It started small. Wispy tweets about Vedic traditions, then *bam!* a second later he was appearing on platforms and bowing and screaming about intellectual elites and cosmopolitan vermin, and the title on the TV was calling him a "thought leader."

He dragged us along to one of his functions, because even if he might have hated Rudi, his name opened doors.

We were felicitated. Golf club, south of town, new money, bunting, garlands. One of the pre-Diwali celebrations that stretched earlier and earlier into the year.

The right-wing saffrons were out in force, back-slapping with cube-clinking Johnnie Walker in hand, one-upping each other with offhand comments about the poetry of the Upanishads and the sanctity of the Indian language.

Oberoi made a speech, right up on the platform, with a fat crowd of People's Party ministers sitting behind him. The usual nonsense, "Our country is strong today, stronger than it has ever been, and that is down to one man, the prime minister," and at that everyone clapped. He was so excited with himself. Everyone was watching him. He was in the limelight for once. He couldn't be stopped. He could see his political career stretching out before him. "This is a country going places, this is a country on the up, a country where a humble producer like m—" He had the breath knocked out of him as a huge hand thumped him from behind.

"We should hear from him," said the big man, a government minister, his voice deep and gong-like, drops of sweat on his temples, his collar translucent with perspiration. "Never trust a politician": that was what Claire always used to say, and I never have.

"Who, Mr. Minister, sir?" said Oberoi, as the fear on his face fought with the hatred.

"Rudraksh Saxena. You are very interesting, Mr. Oberoi, but we are here for him tonight."

"Yes, sir," said Oberoi quietly. He sat down on a chair, whiter than a Western panel on racial diversity. I hid my laughter in my drink.

Up went Rudi, unsteady after too much whisky and coke.

"We are the future, I am the future, this man," he said, grasping the minister, whose name he did not know but whose body fat percentage showed importance, "is the future, aren't you?" He started jabbing the man's stomach, and kept repeating, "Aren't you, aren't you?"

Then he jumped off the stage, crying, "Waiter!" Everybody applauded him. Even Oberoi did, with a grimace.

There were more speeches from members of the People's Party. Oberoi stayed onstage and tried to grab the microphone, but was always brushed away by somebody more important, more powerful, more fat. His moment had passed. Speaker after right-wing speaker insulted NGO libtards, saying the titans of postwar Indian history had been too secular, too liberal, too Muslim-friendly. Money had been given generously, by Oberoi, to the prime minister's religious toleration foundation.

For most of the evening, Oberoi stood around looking hopeful and small, hands clasped near his crotch, like a prisoner before delousing. He kept going after people, big people, asking constantly for business cards, introductions to investments. He kept badgering them for selfies. All the money, all the importance he had, and he still wanted more.

I spent my evening shadowing Rudi, making sure he didn't get into any trouble, didn't drink much more, didn't offend people who shouldn't be offended.

All my days were wasted, on the show, and making money for Rudi, and keeping him occupied somehow.

All my nights were wasted too, be they in clubs or restaurants or bars, making sure he didn't get drunk or hurt or worse. Making sure no one saw him behaving in a disorderly manner. Making sure he was never caught out, that the newspapers would never expose anything, so that his fans—India's housewives—could keep buying whatever he was advertising in order to keep our economy going at 7 percent a year.

I should have been with Priya. I should have been living my life. I kept meaning to carve out more time for her, but Rudi was at a critical point. He was on the edge and had become a real risk. We were coming up to the festival of lights, but for Rudi, things seemed only to be getting darker.

I dreamed my idiot dreams, of running away from everything, from free drinks and free money. That never helped.

So I had to have fun somehow. In my own way.

At work and in bars each day, I handled stupid questions from roomfuls of sweaty writers. We'd had to hire them, to keep Rudi's jokes fresh, to make him really shine, to make sure he always had something to say, to make sure he never froze again. There were tens, hundreds of millions of rupees riding on him. He wasn't just a boy. He was a business. He had to be kept in peak condition.

All the writers had idiot names like Siddharth-call-me-Sid and Nikhil-call-me-Nik and idiot Western educations and similarly idiot Western problems like being ghosted by women or receiving the wrong order at a coffee shop. You heard these terrible, terrible rumors about them—that they used *electronic cigarettes*. Indians. Electronic. Can you imagine? What has India become, that all our problems must be sorted by people with American master's degrees?

I would launch into rants, just to fuck with them. "When I was a boy, all we had was carrom boards, with plenty of talcum powder to make them go fast, and if you ran out God help you, and our fingernails bled from it." Sometimes I would tell them that my only friend had been a stick called Pramod.

Priya told me in our calls and texts how Oberoi treated her. At meetings he'd say "fat Gujju bitch," "dhokla eater," all of the usual insults.

He was getting worse, she said. She tried to do everything he wanted, and still it wasn't enough.

I kept my mouth shut and my fists clenched beneath the table. In the India of twenty years ago, I would have punched him and that would have been that. Now we have Western morals and complaints procedures and nothing ever gets done.

How she took it, I'll never know. I learned from her what strength was. Poverty, that you could escape, with luck and brains and insulting everything that dared to move. Being a woman, in this country? You could never outrun that.

All I wanted to do was to spend time with her, and I never got the chance.

PART TWO

PART TWO

TEN

So there we were, Rudi drunk, disheveled, covered in vomit. Me lying by him, a bottle in my hand, miserable, overworked, stressed. Both of us with the world on our shoulders.

We were ten days from Diwali. Rudi was under pressure to be top of the TV rankings at the most profitable advertisement time of the year.

And then we were kidnapped.

Bang! The door burst open, I started to shout out, but I could hardly make myself heard.

I saw that face, the yellow eyes, the bead necklace. I saw the man move over to me, laugh at my useless protest. I tried to reach out for my phone, but he kicked it away. He laid down the pair of folded wheelchairs he carried, and kicked our Diwali gifts, our boxes of free samples and bribes and flowers out of the way.

Bang! A stick smashed into my face. *Bang!* Rudi and I were bundled into the wheelchairs. The man wheeled me out into the corridor, and into the lift, and then he returned with Rudi a minute later. It was as if he had all the time in the world. We were insects he could just pick off at will. It was extremely humiliating.

Then out into the shor sharaba of the street, turmeric-fingered fellows abounding, young men just hanging around doing nothing—we are a country of young men, with the attendant problems. The West is too old and fat for revolution; here we are but a single humiliating loss to Pakistan away.

I screamed uselessly into my surgical mask, gurgling a little blood in my mouth, the sound lost in the noise of paan spitters and autos. A face came down close to mine, those yellow teeth again, the wet buffalo stink of halitosis. "Better keep quiet, or the kid gets it, okay?" He didn't need to do anything to Rudi, he was out of it. He didn't need to be beaten up. He had already done that to himself with the drugs.

This guy was all business, none of the talking like a movie gangster that Rudi did to the writers when he wanted to scare them. "I'll fuck you so hard your children will feel it," that was his favorite, and then it was grandchildren, mothers, fathers, all future progeny, all past ancestors, as he got angrier with the Niks and the Sids, peppering his insults with high-class words, thesaurus words, advanced English vocabulary words, because he was the Topper and he was an intellectual and they were nothing.

We were thrown one by one into a battered Maruti van with some hasty red crosses painted on the side.

I looked at my captor's eyes up close and knew there was going to be trouble.

Eyes like my father's. Hungry eyes. Born-in-the-shit-but-never-going-back eyes.

He smiled and took out a roll of tape, and wound it round and round the top of my head, a few more times around my hands, and over my mouth. "Going to be a bitch to take off," he said. "Might just have to cut all your hair off, like when you were a baby." The smell of his mouth was like a bubbling sewer. The smell, the fear, that was bad enough, but the tape over my eyelids, that was the worst part. Every time I moved my head I was in agony. I tried to stay as still as I could. It did not work.

We moved off with the squeaking of gears, metal on metal. The air around us was thick with noise. I could hear the Audis of bankers' wives, street kids selling plastic-wrapped Paulo Coelho at intersections, people squeaking dirty rags on your car, either blackmail or cleaning, you couldn't tell. It was the perfect time for a kidnap.

The tape started to give me a migraine. My head was on fire. My wrists too. My spine was stiff with the effort of sitting still. I was hot. I couldn't breathe. I felt like I was having a stroke.

We drove on. Swearing came from the front as turns were missed, mashed acceleration, sudden braking, reversing, nothing like Pawan's sleek driving.

The heat made me melt. Driving without AC is hell. How do people do it? You lose half your weight each journey, and a whole bunch of IQ probably. If all Indians had air conditioning everywhere, the gap between have and have-not would disappear. All that ball-scratching and moaning turned into valuable GDP-raising work!

If my mouth hadn't been taped, I would have made conversation.

"Nice breath you have there!"

"Do you do this kidnap stuff freelance, or are you on a long-term contract?"

When he finally woke, Rudi tried money. The driver hadn't taped his mouth. Typical.

"I can get you anything. Money, women, women made of money, money made of women, anything, just let us go." No response. Barely ten minutes later came the cry of every Richie Rich everywhere, "Don't you know who I am?," and then, God help him, "Please, please just let me go. Diwali is coming soon," at which he got a few laughs.

A few hours later, the car stopped. We were dragged out, one by one, and pushed across sandy dirt. You simply had to admire the man, doing this all on his own, a Westerner would say. It was a hot, grimy early evening. If I'd been able to see, maybe I would have seen an endless expanse of earth, the soil out of which we Delhi dwellers all spring. If I'd been a farmhouse owner, maybe I would have enjoyed the country air, the freshness; instead, all I could smell was fear and sweat and my own misery. I felt my feet stumble over earth, stone, marble, my sides bumped against walls and doors and tables. I could hear nothing. That was the worst part. No traffic, no men and women shouting their way through life, no vendors, no sellers, no merchants. Nothing but silence. It was like I was dead. No wonder American suburbanites are on so many medications.

I felt myself pass into a cooler climate, then through a door into a room. I was thrown down, against cold, dusty marble. A minute or two later I felt a mattress next to me explode with air and hiss as Rudi was thrown onto it.

"Stay here. Shut up," said the low rattle of the driver's voice, right by my ear. "Or I'll turn your andas into a fucking omelette and there'll be no kids for you." I felt his hands move onto mine and there was a slight loosening of the tape at my wrists. I took it off quickly, and then the pieces around my mouth, shuddering as the skin on my lips was peeled off. I could not face doing my eyes.

There was no fan. Sweat stained my clothes, made them heavy with its stink.

I groped around. There was a glass-fronted wardrobe on one wall, and some intricately carved wooden doors leading outside. Expensive. Solid when you thunked them. A farmhouse? Some goonda's country lair?

Sometimes I amaze even myself with my powers of deduction.

I felt someone kick me. "What the fuck?"

"Yaar? Man? Dude? Dude?"

"Stop fucking saying dude, Rudraksh."

He kept kicking.

"Jesus, fuck, Rudi, stop," I said. "There's only us here, boss."

I steeled myself. I slowly removed the tape around my head, almost ripping half my hair off, grimaced at the sting of my skin being subjected to a low-tech exfoliation treatment, did lots of swearing, cried unbidden tears and all that stuff, then did Rudi's, who yelped at my every move. I fucking breathed and he yelped. Maybe I was a little rougher than I could have been. As my eyes adjusted to the darkness, I looked around. A dirty marble floor, a high barred window, all sorts of junk scattered around the edges of the room, old clothes, cardboard boxes, carpets. The smell of mothballs in my nostrils.

"It's okay, boss," I soothed him. "Not as if you've been kidnapped, is it? Ha ha."

I shouldn't have done that. The dam broke.

He half talked, half wept. He went on and on about the perils of money, how we should have hired a better bodyguard, my uncountable faults, how we should emigrate to America, my rudeness, the Indian education system, the perils of a rice-based diet, how the British should never have left. In his mind, a great chain of historical fuck-ups had led to this moment. He kept running his hands through his hair, movie star hair, five thousand Gandhis a cut, not the greasy mane he'd once had, the one he'd shared with every moped courier and two-bit tailor from here to Haridwar.

His face was a little bruised around the nose, his skin was pale, either through fright or sleeplessness or drugs, but in volume at least he was unchanged.

"I wish I had never become rich," he cried, and my God, what a phrase for an Indian to say. Even beating couldn't get rid of an attitude like that.

All I had for company was his voice and gora face in the half-darkness, the wardrobe, which I saw was full of textbooks and novels, the mattresses, and the various odds and ends. Imprisonment in a glorified janitor's closet.

I felt around my face for any lasting damage. Nothing but soreness and the taste of blood in my mouth.

"At least Oberoi will be fucked," Rudi said when he had calmed down. "Prick."

"Yes, but Priya—" I said without thinking.

"Priya? All you do is think of her. Whenever I need you, you're thinking of her. Forget her. She's out of your . . . everything," he hissed.

"Don't you think I fucking know?" I shouted. I'd give the kid that. He knew exactly how to hurt me best.

Rudi's eyes grew large. I had never lost my temper so openly, so violently in front of him. Normally I sniped under my breath. He gulped and shut up.

"Keep quiet in there!" came the driver's growl through the door. Rudi nearly jumped out of his skin. There was no mistaking that voice, not after having listened to it swear through traffic for so many hours. "Or I start cutting off things that cannot be uncut!"

I waited a few minutes. I cursed myself. No more shouting from me. I had been so good at avoiding attention for most of my life. Just a little bit more of that, Ramesh.

"I know you like putting me down. I know it makes you feel better. I know you feel alone. I know you're hurt and depressed and alone. I get it, okay?" I whispered, giving him as much psychobabble as I could muster, about communication and mindfulness and all the other stuff I had picked up from daytime TV. "No more getting angry. We need to work together to get out of this alive. Okay?"

He paused for a moment.

"O-bloody-kay," he said finally.

I could have sold him a blender or a knife set. I had picked those skills up too.

Look at us, classes and castes and colors coming together

under dire circumstances, like one of those films about the '71 war, you know the ones, where the noble Sikh and the wiry Dalit die in each other's arms, having blown up a Pakistani tank squadron using little more than a rifle, some pungent daal, and the even more pungent memory of their mothers' undying love.

After we'd made our grand declaration of unity, we realized there was nothing we could not do together.

We talked shit, moved on to the usual tea stall conversation topic, actresses from the nineties. Rudi had a thing for Madhuri Dixit. Me? I was a Manisha Koirala guy.

We did not sleep a wink. Jesus, Rudi could talk, like a little kid sleeping in his parents' bed. "Are we going to be okay?" "What's this going to do for our careers?" "I need a whisky." "What about that Bhatnagar lady?" On and on, like he was on one of those US talk shows where you got randomly picked from the audience and you had a minute to be interesting or you'd never be famous and get to use your Instagram to sell multi-level-marketed massage oils.

And always that word, "dude." When I was half awake, "Dude . . ."; when I was asleep, "Dude . . ." I was having this great dream, me and guess who, running toward each other through Swiss meadows, twirling, when I heard "Dude . . . Dude . . . Dude . . ." Stretched out, whining, when I didn't answer. I didn't know where he'd picked it up from. Maybe it had happened when he'd started the drugs. Another reason to hope he'd get off them.

"I'm not talking to you until you call me Ramesh," I said.

"Is this really the time, yaar?" he asked.

"Yes," I said. "We're under great pressure. This is when relationships change and become stronger, when people realize what they truly mean to one another, when they stop calling each other dude. Think that through. I'm going to sleep, okay?"

Rudi continued to talk. Every time I nearly fell asleep, there he was, groaning away. Nothing to distract him, no phone, no Instagram, no WhatsApp. I'd open my eyes and watch him shivering, sweating, the drugs and the social media moving out of his system. But the noise! My God. It was a blessed relief when, the next morning, the door slammed open.

"Out!" shouted the driver, grasping me by the waist and pulling me up.

As I was pushed out of the room, I willed my morning erection to wilt. They always cut off the conspicuous parts, I thought, these people.

For the first time, I saw where we had been brought. I found myself in a courtyard, green with potted plants, white marble floor, red tile roof, burbling central fountain of naked nymphs in light sandstone. The air was cool and moist. Paradise. A farmhouse, a rich man's place. I had been right.

We were led around the colonnade into a large, beautiful lounge. Dark wooden furniture, soft white sofas, a large flatscreen, like a classier version of Rudi's parents' place. The walls were strung with electric lights for Diwali, and a large framed painting of Lord Ram with movie star muscles jutted out from under recessed lighting.

"Our guests," said one of two men on the sofa. "Namkeen, quickly," and the man next to him, a boy really, clearly his son, got up and left. He gave Rudi a venomous look as he walked away.

Oh shit.

I knew that face. I knew that kid.

It was Abhi, the one we'd humiliated, broken on national television.

The man, Abhi's father, bid us sit. He was as prosperous-looking as the room, with a beautiful sultan's moustache, shining with wax, white chinos and open-necked shirt, a cummerbund girding a fat waistline. He radiated wealth.

He reminded me of the maharaja, the mascot of Air India, our beloved joke of a national airline. Fat and wise and mirthful, though the airline itself was short of money, short of staff, always bottom of the international league tables, another one of our great national shames, like the '62 war and female illiteracy.

"Sit them down," he said to our captor. The driver took a position behind him, eyes scanning the room for potential threats. He gave off a little smile, the smile of a man who has singlehandedly kidnapped you and made you look ineffectual and weak and MBA-having.

"You won't mind if I don't tell you my name," said Abhi's father.

"You'll pay for this," said Rudi, aping some film again, then deflated into silence. The maharaja twiddled his thumbs until his boy came back with a plate of salty treats that he laid in front of us.

"Good work, Abhi," said his father. "Sit down."

The kid looked a combination of deeply embarrassed and deeply, deeply angry. He didn't hold eye contact with anyone. He reached for masala peanuts every few minutes. He had the same prominent nose as his father, the same soft brown eyes, but without the confidence and command. His leg shook. I remembered the last time I'd seen him, looking broken and small, surrounded by hundreds of people laughing at his failure.

So his father had gone to the trouble of kidnapping us just to avenge his son. I wished I had a father who'd done that for me.

"So, gentlemen, down to business," said the maharaja. "You know exactly why you're here. You humiliated my son. So I shall destroy your show. Do you like my plan?" He stretched out to the table and started assembling a plate of biscuits.

"We'll never play along," said Rudi immediately.

"You will. You will. Won't they, Pratap?"

The driver behind him grunted, looking at me with hatred in his eyes. Not Rudi. Just me. Why am I so hated? What have I done, apart from commit many crimes that would shame me in the eyes of the gods?

"And if you don't play along," Abhi's father continued, turning to me, "I will simply tell the world what you did, Mr. Kumar."

"Heh?" I said, braying like abused donkeys do in those charity videos. It was not his knowing my secret that caused the reaction. I was more surprised to be directly addressed. Nobody seemed to do that apart from Priya.

"Ramesh Kumar, Educational Consultant. You didn't even change your name. Fool. You cannot hide from me." The maharaja wagged a golden-ringed finger. He had two rings on each hand, a signet on each pinkie, no wedding band, I noticed.

Oh shit.

I looked at Rudi, and his face made me feel worse, so I stopped.

Was I perturbed? Was I put out? Was I terrified of exposure? Did I flinch from life, for even one moment?

Yes.

My wits couldn't save me now. I couldn't lie or insult my way out. I had no contacts, no schemes, no information. I had been made stupid. I had been made powerless. All I could do was sit and watch, and hope I came out the other side whole.

"It will go like this," the maharaja carried on. "We make a video and put it on the YouTube. You stay here until the money comes through. You go home. Just business. Yes?" His eyes grew darker. "Normally, nobody insults my name, my family, my son and lives. Consider yourselves lucky. Consider it my good deed for Diwali." He took a bite of biscuit and began to smile again.

He looked so very pleased with himself. Tasteful furnishings, tasteful life. Only two things spoiled the impression. The first was the man behind him, eyes burning with hatred. The other was his son, who looked like an old cinema poster in some two-goat town, washed out, pale, but shaking with anger.

"Anything to add, son?" said the maharaja. He even consulted his son. He was real father-of-the-year material, this man.

"I don't care if they live or die," Abhi said.

"Capital, capital." His father beamed, and slapped him on the back. "See, this is what I was saying. This is the first step on your road to success. You will look back on this one day when you are famous and thank me." He looked at us. "Well then, your people have two days to get back to us. After that ... Pratap, what happens after that?"

"Bad things," growled Pratap. A real drama queen.

The kid bit his fingernails and ate some more peanuts.

"Would anyone like any Lagavulin?" asked Abhi's father, clapping his hands.

Nobody did.

We were thrown back into our garret.

A few hours later, the door opened again and we were hauled back to the living room. A camera had been set up on a tripod, and two chairs stood in front of a large white collapsible screen.

"Sit," said the father. "Abhi." He beckoned to his son.

"Yeah," the kid replied, "if Rudi could just say that he's been kidnapped and the ransom is fifty crore, okay?" Fifty crore? Six million dollars? For Rudraksh Saxena? Him? I didn't care how much aspirational electrical equipment he sold. He had gone up in the world since he'd met me.

"You don't ask anyone if it's okay, you tell them," said Abhi's father. His voice grew louder and he pointed at Rudi. "Especially when you're talking to this good-for-nothing, no-brain, haramzada duffer."

Abhi dipped his head. He must have heard plenty of it growing up. At least it was directed at someone else now. "Ah, yep, okay, I mean, yes." He started again, and this time the hate had returned to his eyes, and his words were steady. Who said that children never listened to their parents anymore? "You're going to be saying you've been kidnapped and they have a day to deliver the money. Fifty crore. Get on with it."

"Better," said the maharaja, beaming with pride. "Pay them back for what they did to us."

Rudi dutifully repeated the terms. They'd even bought a newspaper for him to hold up. He tried to look bored, as if nothing could affect him. Unfortunately the act was undone by the look on his face and the shaking of his knees every time he moved. Withdrawal. Better now than never.

Abhi and his father watched the footage on a laptop.

"Doesn't look scared, does he, boy?" his father said. "Not the way he made you feel, no? And it needs some music and effects. It needs to look professional!"

"Music will not do that, Papa. It will look cheesy. I'm telling—"

"They had music and effects when they humiliated you, didn't they, beta?" his father said, and the kid fell silent. "If you want to be a big person, beta, if you want to be a TV star, then that is the way you have to behave."

Abhi looked down. His face, youthful, fresh, handsome, curled into hatred.

They made Rudi do it again, and this time he was totally over the top, lips quivering, nearly fainting with fright. Pratap did not look pleased.

"Want me to beat him?" he asked, but was waved away.

We were led back to our room again.

The next day was long and boring. We did nothing but mope. I tried forcing the door a few times, but I didn't have the muscle for it.

I wondered what the headlines were like. What a story! A sensation. Rudi would always be someone now. Kidnapping is like that. You're not someone until someone tries to kidnap you. What an honor! Better than the Padma Bhushan.

I let myself think about Priya. I had been trying not to, had been trying to keep her in the back of my mind, away from all this, something secret, something precious, just for me.

All I could think about was her face, sick with worry. I felt desolate. Can you imagine?

And of course, now someone knew my secret, and in this country if one person knows something, then everyone soon will.

What would she think when she found out? Then I would be no better than the rest. A liar seducing women with his ill-won wealth. I could not bear for her to think badly of me, and that was the first time I'd thought that about anyone in a long, long time.

Maybe I just wanted to look into someone's eyes and see something other than a business transaction.

The kid, Abhi, brought us food, reeking of hatred. He was, well, pretty. Demure. Thin, with delicate hands and beautiful brown, almost amber eyes. No wonder his father thought he should be famous. No wonder they thought it was his birthright to be on TV. Pratap stood just beyond the open door and scowled.

"You guys are going to hell," Abhi said. What a conversation starter. His accent lapsed into American at the ends of words. He spoke softly, too softly for the sentiments he expressed. "I hope you feel like shit. You should have been nothing, you cheater. I should have been you. I will be you. Once your show loses all its money."

Was this part of the assertiveness training too?

"No, actually, I'm fucking amazing," Rudi said. "Like I've just fucked Aishwarya Rai. You, Ramesh?"

"Er, like I've just become the cricket man who is best. You know, that guy, Australian," I said. Sometimes there can be a distance between my thoughts and my words.

The kid looked down at what he was holding, two plastic plates of roti and sambar, and then dropped them on the floor with a little smile.

"Oh fucking wonderful," said Rudi. "A real fucking drama queen! I tell you what, next time come and tell me about the hidden trauma of losing your mother, yeah?"

"Fuck you!" said the kid softly, and his face began to well up again.

Rudi was doing bad cop, it seemed, so I decided to play nice.

"We can make things better if you talk," I said, in my most obsequious lower-caste voice. "Please, beta, tell us your cares." I could have added, "Live long. Be happy. Jeete raho!"

The kid was about to say something. He looked at me with a strange expression, a growing trust, I could tell. I had broken through to his soft interior.

"I told my father we should have had you killed," he said.

Maybe not.

"Hey," said Pratap, unable to hear our words but knowing they wouldn't be good. The kid scrambled back like we were lepers and slammed the door shut behind him, and thus ended the training session for his ascent to Western corporate life, or was it supervillainy?

"What was that Aishwarya nonsense about?" I asked Rudi, after I'd failed to scrape our food off the floor.

Rudi sat with his back against the wall, eyes closed, sweat beads on his cheeks, world-weary. "Sounded good, didn't it?"

"Sounded strange really, boss."

"Oh," he said, and shrugged his shoulders. "Sometimes I don't know the difference, dude."

Two days passed. We did nothing. Once a day we were led out into the corridor to use a bathroom next door, and then thrown back inside. No showers. The room smelled of terrified young men. Very hygienic.

The drugs continued to move out of Rudi's body. He tried not to let it show, tried to turn his face away from me. I could see the muscles of his jaw clenching, I could see his spine twisting and flexing in pain, I could hear him punching himself and swearing in the middle of the night when he thought I was asleep.

I tried not to worry about him, the situation, about Priya, about the Bhatnagar investigation, but I could do nothing but.

Regular meals, delivered by Abhi. He was still angry. I was too tired, too bastard hot, too worried about Rudi and Priya to try bridge-building.

"Roti again? Don't you have any gluten-free options, you little fuck?" said Rudi.

I started to fret.

Two days. The deadline had passed.

The moneymen hadn't come through. I could imagine Priya, her hair tied up, pen and phone in hand, making principled arguments for paying. I could imagine her calling the uncle she'd told me about, a cop, an honest cop! What a strange family. Far too virtuous to be in-laws to the likes of me.

I could imagine her fighting for me, and I nearly felt good.

I knew that if anything happened, they wouldn't touch Rudi. It would be me on the chopping block. I remembered the look in Pratap's eyes.

It was fair to say that by the night of the second day, I was shitting myself. No news. Nothing. All the production company had to do was pay the damn money. Simple. We'd make them double the ransom in chapati ads alone. They could start a phone-in contest, and the winner could get Rudi's tear-stained shirt, or maybe I could take their kid's exams.

When the door slammed open that second day, near midnight, I hadn't slept at all.

Pratap strolled in, face lit by moonlight, his gaze fixed only on me.

Rudi woke quickly, looked at Pratap's face, and realized something was going to happen to me. A little danger had quickened his instincts. I hand it to him. He grew up in that moment.

He stood up. He squared up to Pratap. He raised his fists. Pratap feinted one way, and punched him in the stomach. Rudi didn't fall immediately. He tried to stand up. He raised his hands again, the fool. His softness was no match for Pratap's wiry, corded muscle.

Another punch, Rudi groaned and collapsed.

"No money," Pratap said. Then he turned to smile at me. "I wanted to do this from the minute I saw you."

It must be my face.

He walked over slowly, slowly. I saw his yellow little teeth, I saw his red eyes grow larger and larger. I couldn't look. My gaze shifted downward, to the prayer beads knotted around his neck. I scrambled backward, hit the wall, started to rise up it, slipped slightly. He punched me in the stomach. I doubled over. He put my arms in a lock, my face pressed to the floor, tongue licking dust.

"Which one?" he said.

"Which one what?"

"Which one shall we cut off?"

I started to shout. Rudi wriggled like a worm, clutching his side. "You touch him, and I'll fuck you harder than I fucked Miss India," he said.

Look at you, Rudi, I thought, look at what you've become. I felt so proud, even though I would have changed the phrasing.

He crawled over to us, over the grimy marble floor, straining every ounce of energy he had to save me from my terrible fate—then Pratap gave him a kick in the groin, and Rudi grunted with pain and stopped.

"No more comedy from you, Brain of Bharat," Pratap said, "or you won't be doing any fucking ever again."

He grabbed my hands. I tried to struggle, but he simply sat on me, driving the air from my lungs like the pollution on the ITO intersection. I saw the glint of something in the corner of my eye.

A knife: not a small one, but long and lethal, one of those half-knife, half-saw things they use to cut tomatoes and aloos when you get a pav bhaji, working-man's knives, razor sharp, cheap, the knives that have won the evolutionary race above all others to be the tools of Delhi's poor for cutting food, for committing crime, for solving all life's problems.

"I think the little one. You won't miss it, will you, boy? My master is being too soft, and that never gets you anywhere, does it?"

And then he cut my bloody pinkie finger off.

It was over in less than a second. I wish my finger had put up more of a fight.

I saw the knife cut through skin. That was bad enough.

Then it went through muscle, then cartilage, then through the curve of my knuckle, and up and out, through muscle and skin.

So simple. One fluid, relentless motion.

Blood spurted out of the hole, thick and alive and finally free of its prison of flesh.

I screamed out in pain. I looked down, and on the floor lay my finger, the nail bruised and jagged, the skin creased from bending and beckoning. It looked pristine, untouched, for most of its length, until you got to the bottom, and out peeked perfect white bone, and around it a pool of blood.

Pratap yelled in triumph, his voice rumbling, thick with pleasure. I felt faint. I saw a blurry image of Rudi vomiting.

I felt wet all over my hands. I saw Pratap grab a cloth from his pocket and wrap it around my fingers. He gave me another kick.

"Better hope they pay up this time," he said.

The next few hours, I was totally gone.

I just about remember Rudi's face. Lots of tears. Very touching. I remember the smell of antiseptic, and a bitter liquid I tried to spit out, tablets and water being forced down me. I screamed my way to sleep.

I woke when it was morning. The floor around me was brown with dried blood.

Rudi lay in a crumpled pile in the corner. My fist was bandaged. Poorly. There was a roll of tape by Rudi's hand.

I counted the fingers.

One. Two. Three. Four. Shit.

I shouted but no sound came out. Mouth fucked, dry, raw, like I'd cried and spat and pissed my body's entire supply of water.

In that moment I thought about Sister Claire, about all the money I'd made, all the pride I'd had, these stupid dreams, trying to make myself a ... What? A businessman? An entrepreneur? A man-about-town? And for what? Where had my dreams brought me? Missing one finger and who knew what else tomorrow. If I got out of this, I'd start a school, I thought in those sickening hours, for orphans or slum kids or American children from Ohio who were addicted to opioids, and never think about Gandhis again. I'd certainly never live in Delhi, or anywhere near it. Me, far away in the south, verdant green, backwater streams, coconut milk in every fucking meal, or abroad, fuck it, me and Priya. I really needed to be serious, to think about our future, where we were going, and God knows, if I was lucky, maybe I'd end up like a Westerner on my knees in a five-star restaurant with a ring and her saying yes yes yes.

Enough of kissing and holding hands and doing all of the actions without saying the words. Enough of coyness, Ramesh! Enough of cowardice! Be a man. Make it official! Tell the world!

No! Leave her out of it. Let her be. Enough! That was my other voice. The one that had only doubts, the one that told me always to run and hide away from the world, the one that said that I was in this game only to make money for myself, and that nothing else mattered, that all this love business was a useless distraction that would get me killed.

Be truthful, for once, Ramesh. What did our future look like if we ended up together? I'd spend the rest of my life hiding the truth, worrying what would happen if she found out about me. I would be lying to her every single day, telling her one cheek was coffee and the other was chocolate. I would be no better than him.

This was all in my head. If you had looked at me, you would have just seen quiet, dry weeping. I gather that most philosophers throughout history have been quite similar.

Everything came to me vividly, like a movie dream sequence. Time slipped away as smoothly as kebabs down the gullets of toothless nawabs.

I thought of a time when I'd been happy, maybe that two-week period in 1998 when I was three and we'd had nukes and the Pakistanis hadn't, and then, fuck, they'd done their own tests and we were back to level pegging.

I thought about all sorts of strange stuff.

Sex and death and history and family.

I thought about the Chor Bazaar, where for centuries all the stolen stuff in Delhi had washed up to be sold, about the Qutb Minar, soaring into the sky like the erection in some amateur scandal video, the ones that got leaked and whole families killed themselves out of shame. I felt myself slipping through history, through all the burnings and riots and empires, the Ghaznavids bringing death from their Turkic abodes, the pleasure gardens of the Mughals burning in 1857, the streets wet with blood after the riots of Partition.

It was some very, very posh shit.

Then I dreamed about my father, how he hadn't turned up. I'd expected him, like a rotten rupee. Must have been dead. Or rich. I tried not to think about that. Otherwise Rudi would definitely have found him and got him on the show, just to see the look on my face. Other people, rich kids in clubs, complained about their parents, their suffocating closeness, that all they did was complain and cut off expense accounts and ask when they were getting married. I was alone.

I started thinking like Rudi, that everything in my life, everything in the soil and the air, had led to this moment. My mind searched backward in my life, went through each turn and twist to find a place where I could have avoided this fate. I wiped out all memory of Priya, and then Rudi and Claire and my father, searched for the point where I could diverge and be saved, but found only darkness and blood.

There was no way out.

I had to save myself.

I got up. Rudi said sorry a few thousand times.

We sat and talked, and pledged eternal loyalty to one another. "I'll clean up," he said. "I have been a mess. You have been my sole friend, my only protector. I have treated you abominably."

He said he'd clean up. That was something, okay?

I found a way out.

The memory of my helpless dream made me search through everything in that room, turn everything inside out.

It was all very metaphorical. Pain had made me extremely high-class.

The solution was in the wardrobe.

It was filled with dozens of mildewed paperbacks. Robert Ludlum. Sidney Sheldon. Wilbur Smith. Textbooks of Vedic mathematics, science, and English. Third-place trophies for school sports days.

I suppose I had also needed something to distract me, anything to stop me looking down at my right hand. I had been throwing books around, stepping on them so much that a parent would have given me the thrashing of a lifetime. Rudi had gotten into it too.

I saw the instrument of our deliverance hidden behind all the crap, wrapped in newspaper. I pulled it out, long and hard and heavy and perfect.

A cricket bat. A cricket bat!

And not just any bat. I looked at the black scrawls on it, names of heroes to every Indian boy and girl, just not me. I whistled to Rudi, who was cheerily ripping book covers in half. "Goatfucker," I said. He turned and looked at the bat. His face broke into a deranged smile.

The pain from my finger made me shake. The bandage was colored with spots of brown-red like it had been invited to some avant-garde, MBA-type, single-color Holi celebration and the rest of me had not.

I handed the bat to Rudi with a wince. He gave it a few swings through the air. We nodded to each other. Nothing else had to be said. The next time someone came in, we'd make them pay.

How exactly, we didn't know. But the ransom clearly wasn't coming. There was nothing to do but act.

We moved to our places on the floor and went back to crying and being pathetic. Rudi hid the bat behind his back and made weird moaning noises.

"You don't actually have to make any noise at all!" I whispered, and the moans quietened to a bizarre fucking meowing. He grinned like an idiot, blind to danger, like a soldier before a battle thinking only of loot and pushing the thought of death out of mind.

There were no words said between us, no grand plan. Maybe we should have made one.

We only had to wait a few hours. Abhi. That stupid idiot.

He came in with the plates piled high, probably wanted to repeat his dropping of the food, maybe more theatrical this time, but one look at the bloodied bandage around my finger and he turned white with disgusted pity.

He laid the daal and chapatis down in front of me, trying not to get too close, nearly bowing as he did it, probably thought he was doing some charitable service, like the stuff kids lie about on CVs to get into Stanford.

"Hey, kid, could you push the plate closer? My hand, my hand. You did this." I started to wail. Overdramatic, yes. Effective, yes. He came closer. He was avoiding looking at my face and that missing finger of mine.

"Closer, beta, closer," I said. He hadn't even come with Pratap. The dumb bastard. He was going to get an education from the Kumar Family School of Educational Abuse.

I saw Rudi rise beside him, gripping the bat.

"Hey, kid," I said. He was close enough to kiss. "Don't move."

He gaped at me. "Why? Can I help you? I'm sorry. I—"

"No, because Rudi's behind you with a fucking cricket bat."

"All right, bhosdike," said Rudi, holding the bat above his head, "out we go. Start shouting. Loud. Put the fear of God into your papa." We needed him to make noise. We needed his father to fear us for the rest of his life. Well, we needed him to give us the car keys. The two were much the same.

Abhi realized he'd been tricked. He gave me a look of sheepish betrayal. Then his eyes turned very cold. I'd made him a man in that moment. He wouldn't be trusting anyone again for a long, long time. I'd made him just like me. Outstanding.

"Help, help," he wailed.

"Louder!" said Rudi, poking him with the willow as we walked out into the opulent greenery of the courtyard. The Americans have it right. Green is the color of wealth.

"Help! Help! They're going to kill me!" the kid said. He looked at us with complete disgust. Rudi nodded, pleased.

The kid seemed more bewildered than angry. His good intentions had backfired spectacularly. He wasn't going to be bringing food to future kidnappees ever again. "Last time, Dad, I promise," I imagine he'd say. I wondered how much he'd get beaten later; maybe not at all, actually, and that really made me sick.

The rooms around the courtyard came to life. I heard doors slam and people swear in confusion.

Our captors came out. Abhi's father was whiter than a funeral shroud. Good. What an idiot. Bringing us to his house.

Letting his son run free. A rich man trying to play a poor man's game.

"Abhi! Leave him alone!" The maharaja's voice was hoarse, his clothes in a state of hastily buttoned disarray. His eyes were wet. Not out of concern for his child, I realized, but because he'd been tricked, he'd been made to look small in his own home, and worst of all, his son, his prize asset, his future TV princeling, was being stolen right from under him.

I held Abhi close with my left hand, gripping his polo shirt by the waist. I held my bandaged right hand to my side.

Pratap was behind his master, wearing a moth-bitten vest. They hissed about something. Pratap moved forward, his sharp little teeth wet with spit.

"Let him go," he said, "or I'll cut something else off." He held a knife, dull and gray, probably another one from his collection. He didn't have to restrain himself now, didn't have to convince his employer about harsh methods. He could do whatever he wanted. He was in heaven.

"Fuck off," Rudi said. "Or the kid is getting brained with this. Which genius decided to keep us in a room with a cricket bat? We're going to take your son for a little ride." See? The plan presented itself.

"No!" shouted Abhi's father. "I'll give you anything. Stop! My boy!"

"Fucking idiot bringing them food alone," said Pratap. He gave his boss a venomous look. Abhi's father looked like he wanted the earth to swallow him whole, Sita style, away from earthly cares into the warm embrace of the earth goddess.

No such luck, my man!

I pushed Abhi over to Rudi, holding him like a shield, and shouted out to the maharaja, "Tell Pratap to put the knife down, madarchod, or I'm giving your sweet rasgulla one in the balls. Or the face, maybe? Don't worry. I've heard they can do wonders with jaw surgery nowadays."

Abhi's father stood paralyzed by anger.

Pratap said nothing, just edged forward, slowly, softly.

"Tell him to put the knife down," I said.

"Put the knife down, Pratap!" said the maharaja.

Pratap shook his head.

"Okay, Rudi," I said, and he understood, swung the bat over his head and into the kid's ribs.

"Aargh!"

Only that wasn't him. That was me. Rudi had hit my bloody hand.

"Bakchod, Rudi!"

"I'm sorry, dude," he said. "Sorry!"

I kept a good grip on Abhi with my left hand, even though he wriggled hard and my injured finger hurt worse than a goat biting my lund off.

"Try to get him properly this time," I spat out. "Five, four—"

"Pratap, put the knife down," said the maharaja. "Immediately!"

Pratap looked at him with hatred, then laid the knife on the floor and kicked it away, his prayer beads falling out of his vest. He would no doubt be going on Amazon later and doing some retail therapy in the Lower Caste Maiming Implements (Blade) section.

"Keys! All of them," I shouted. I looked out of the gate. Three cars outside. The Maruti we'd come in, a jeep, and an SUV.

Abhi's father shouted out for keys, and some bloody servant came hobbling out from somewhere with three sets, tried to avoid my eyes, handed them to me, and scuttled off.

Everyone was keeping quiet throughout the screaming and the kidnapping up to this point, I thought. Just like I would have done.

"Anyone move, the kid fucking gets it, cocksuckers," said Rudi, swinging the bat windmill style like Dhoni, really getting into the violence, drawing on all those years of watching Tarantino films and shouting at TV cricket.

Look at that! Give one kid a very rare cricket bat signed by the entire team of the immortal Eden Gardens victory of 2001, and look what he turns into. Give another kid an education from a French nun, and look what happens to him.

Pratap was edging forward again.

"Rudi, can we swap? This kid is starting to annoy me, and if Pratap comes any closer, I WILL BEAT THIS CHILD," I shouted. Jesus, the pain was killing me, and it was exhausting holding the boy while he struggled, as the blood pounded into my hand. Abhi was sweating, his breath loud and hot in my ear, and my finger, my finger, my finger. His father turned even paler, and started mumbling childhood prayers to himself.

I handed Rudi the kid, who was still crying. Rudi walked backward with him. I waved the bat with my left hand, higher now, just past Abhi's jaw. His father looked like he was having a stroke. His son was an asset, one that a cricket bat across the face would permanently devalue. Pratap looked like a tiger eyeing a memsahib on a palanquin.

"Get in the Maruti," I shouted. There were about ten million of the ratty old things in Delhi. The SUV was tempting, but even in the most arduous of circumstances, you must know who you are and where you came from. I was not born to be an SUV driver. It was not fated.

Rudi threw Abhi into the back and climbed in after him. I jumped into the driver's seat.

I imagined going to Pratap and hitting him a few times, maybe say some filmie dialogue, "I shall piss on your grave when you are dead" kind of thing, but I thought better of it. He might have another knife hidden somewhere; best not to act like a hero and end up dead.

"You tell the police anything," I shouted through the car window, just so they all knew the stakes—I am a great believer in contractual clarity, after all—"and your pretty little son gets it from us. Again. But this time across the face. No more TV for him!"

I turned the key, and off we went. I crunched through the gears. I had some knowledge of clutch control from years of mopeds, and I am a very quick learner.

"That fuck is not going to give up," I said, as the car bounced over dried-up streams and farmers' graves. "Pratap. He's going to kill us or die trying. I know his type."

"We've got very few choices," shouted Rudi. "I say we get to the studio, tell them what happened, file a report with the police—"

"The fucking police aren't going to help us, Rudi. You really want to turn up to Oberoi with this? He'll fuck you over some-how. And whoever Abhi's father is, he's rich and he'll know the police—hey, kid, what's your father's name? Tell us or I'll cut off your finger!" I started laughing. I roared. My hand convulsed with pain. I nearly drove off the road.

Rudi looked at me as if I was crazy.

"No," I added, after I had calmed myself down. "I have contacts. We go to them first. We can't go to Oberoi or the studio yet." Or Priya, I thought. I wanted to go to her right then, take my money and run far, far away, somewhere they had Christmas mass and ate chestnuts straight from the fire and where parents brought their children hot chocolate at night. I had to keep her the hell away from this.

And I couldn't do that to bloody Rudi.

I couldn't let him rot. I liked the little lund, I'd realized.

I tried to hold the wheel with my thumb, tried to keep the vibrations from jarring my wound. I swore repeatedly, at the pain, the road, at farmers to move their cows, at anything.

I drove on through the arschole that is Uttar Pradesh, breeding ground of half the world's murderers, rapists, dickheads, and quiz hosts. I found the main road. *Delhi, 70 miles*. I drove back at a world-record pace.

You want to know who a man truly is? Watch him drive. Watch how he reacts, how he responds to people who cut in, who break rules. Watch his speed, how often he checks his mirrors.

That day the drivers on the Delhi–Agra road must have thought they were driving alongside a madman.

ELEVEN

We went back to my old rented apartment. I stopped the Maruti outside and checked for anyone I knew. Just men, always men, minding their own business, doing the usual midday motherfuckery, keeping their heads down, YouTube-watching, eating, and spitting. My neighborhood was in that sweet spot between rich and poor, the one where people knew not to ask questions, not to look where they shouldn't. To be a busybody, you either need lots of money or none of it.

"Now, kid, are you going to cooperate?" I asked our little princeling. I didn't need to. He looked like one of Krishna's calves, sweet and innocent. He nodded, and then the hatred returned.

"You'd fucking better," said Rudi, who had decided to turn into Arnold Schwarzenegger, only fatter and less threatening. The kid nodded again, his brows knitted together, his gaze moving away from both of us. He hated us. Post-cricket loss-level hated us. I would have to talk to Rudi.

"Okay," I said, opening the door of the van, making sure no one was around—I was in the company of a TV star after all—"on my mark, here—we—go."

At my signal, as soon as the street was empty, we rushed inside, Rudi and I hauling Abhi between us, up the dark stairs, up past the apartments of suicidally depressed accountants and gas board workers and municipal planners who dreamed of killing their colleagues over stolen lunches.

We collapsed back into my little one-room flat. I saw it anew. There was the old bed, the desk, the computer, the life I'd had before Rudi. It all looked so small, so pathetic.

I had an elephant shit pat of junk mail, bills, marriage proposal website ads, and astrologers' predictions that I kicked out of the way like kids do to cats. I threw the boy onto my bed. I took the cricket bat and kissed it. Thank you, Dravid! Thank you, Tendulkar! It was the only time I've ever cared about cricket.

"We'll be okay for a couple of hours here," I said, because it was obvious and it was what film stars said in such situations. With films and nuns as my chief educational influences, it's no wonder I have turned out the way I have.

I knew I must have appeared crazy. Hair wild with sweat, looking like I'd just been kidnapped, because I had. I glanced over at Abhi. "Do not worry, little man, you shall be back with Daddy soon, celebrating Diwali, editing videos, and cutting off hands. No hard feelings about all this, ya?"

"Fuck you," he said, snot running down his face onto his polo shirt.

"What did we do to you?" Rudi asked. I thought it was quite obvious what we had done to him.

"You fucked up my life. You fucked up everything," Abhi said. "Everyone thinks I'm a joke." His ferocity made Rudi fall quiet, his movie star bravado vanished entirely.

"My father thinks I'm a joke," Abhi said finally.

Rudi and I looked at each other at the same time.

Fathers, huh?

"Well," I said sweetly, "we are very sorry. Aren't we, Rudi? We will sort this all out very soon. We will get you back to your father. We will make amends. We went too far, didn't we, Rudi?"

"Yes," he said. He kept giving the kid these strange, gurning looks. I was trying hard to figure it out—oh, it was sympathy. He was growing. He'd become more of an adult. What a silver lining to this whole bloody experience.

"Fuck you both," said Abhi.

"A very understandable response," I said. "But we need information. We can make a deal that keeps everyone's precious family honor intact and whatnot. Then you go back home. Okay?"

The kid grunted. He turned his face to the wall. Bloody upper-middle-class teenagers. If I cannot stand them, why did I choose a life that revolves entirely around them?

"So your papa is . . . ? Huh, beta? Please," I asked in my Claire voice.

"Himanshu Aggarwal," he said finally, while facing the other way. I looked at Rudi. We shook our heads as one. Abhi turned his head. "Himanshu Aggarwal? Construction? HA Builders? 'Take a Rest, HA Is Be—'"

"All right!" I said, stopping him before he recited the entire "About Us" section on his family's corporate website.

People in construction—the worst. They'll do anything. It's putting their stamp on the world, their little pimple on the ass of creation, that attracts the worst sort of person.

Just the sort of people we didn't want as enemies.

I gestured to Rudi and we went into the corner of the room.

"You need to be nicer to the kid," I said. "You humiliated him on national television. Did you not see the GIFs? The reaction videos? The bhangra remix? We need to keep him on side. Please, Rudi."

He looked back to Abhi, who was staring at us like an uncle at a wedding buffet that's run out of butter chicken. Yes, he was *that* angry. Rudi nodded conscientiously, and for the first time in months looked like the eighteen-year-old he was.

"Good, boss. You do that. I have a contact who can help us, but we need to move fast." I had turned my back on Sumit before. That had been a mistake. I'd have to buy him all the Paco Rabanne in Delhi if he helped me out of this one.

"What do we do?" Rudi asked. "What's our angle?" *What's our angle?* Seriously?

"If we give the kid back, his father will back off. Yes, he knows our secret, but you saw him. He's an amateur. An amateur with a pet psychopath underling. A rich man bringing us to his own house. Telling us who he is. We stay out of trouble. We use my middleman Sumit. Maybe we sweeten the deal. You don't really need all those Instagram advertisements, do you, boss? Maybe we give Abhi a little helping hand. And then back to the big time for you and me."

I counted out the steps we'd have to take, with a little masala to make it seem less like something I'd pulled out of my arse. "My contact. Make a deal. Give the kid back. Make our miraculous reappearance, you'll be back selling washing machines on TV in two, three days tops. All right?"

Rudi looked suitably impressed. Or terrified. I have difficulty knowing the difference even after all this time.

"I've been thinking," he said, and he started looking thoughtful and introspective, and God, I knew what that sentence meant, it meant crisis of conscience and I am going to volunteer my medical services in the Congo. "I have been so materialistic. So out of control. I need to get back to basics. I need to reassess what's important in my life."

He looked full of charity and joy and other things that make no money.

"Absolutely," I said. "I agree. I'll sign us up to a Buddhist prayer retreat in Sikkim first thing." Three days of that, vegetarianism and chanting and dead bodies decaying on the hillside and prayer flags fluttering in the fucking wind, and he'd be begging to go back.

"You're my one true friend, Ramesh," he said. "All this money, this false god, it never makes a difference. No one wants me for me. They want me for my fame. We've got to start getting in touch with who we really are. What do we really want out of life? What is happiness?"

I was going to murder whoever made the YouTube videos he'd been watching. Some bhenchod Eastern mystic type, living in fucking California, talking about the evils of materialism from a Malibu beach.

"That is wonderful," I said. "Truly touching. I need to go out."

I was about to leave. I thought of what my life with Rudi had become, even before the kidnapping. Hiding from the world. Now he realized things had gone too far. He was trying to make a change.

I turned back. He was having a crisis, and I had to be his friend. I had to help him. This kidnapping business could be the start of something better, for him and for us.

"Can you please make a start on the kid?" I said. "Make him hate us less. I know you can do it." I gave him a brotherly pat on the shoulder. "You're good at winning people over. Try, all right, boss?"

He nodded, and smiled grimly at me. He wasn't shivering or pale anymore. He looked like a changed man from just a few days before. No more drugs, I thought to myself, I'd make sure there were never any more drugs.

I pulled on a pair of sunglasses and fished out one of my wigs from the old days. I went into the bathroom, stood on a bucket, and pulled out a few thousand rupees from a brick I had hidden in the fan vent, nearly slipping on the marble floor as I climbed down.

"Ah, Ramesh," said Rudi as I left. "Perhaps buy me a phone? Just to check on the n—"

"No!" I said. "You'll give us away in about five seconds. *Let me just check the trending*, then it'll be *let me do a post about being kidnapped*, then it'll be a livestream. No phone. No social media. We need less of that from now on, Rudraksh."

I went out into the street without waiting for the reaction. A few people looked at me. The neighborhood was getting richer, clearly. The local moonshine joint had gone, the tailor, the butcher, you know, the useful things, and in had come flower shops and workout studios.

Unlike Rudi, I could go out easily. My face had never been on the news. I was just the servant, the associate, the underling.

"He was devoted to him," they would say if I turned up headless, if I got any coverage at all. There were no good photos of me to use. No Facebook, no Instagram, nothing. It was as if I didn't exist.

I bought a cheap smartphone at a little electronics place, cash only, no identity cards needed in east Delhi, no sir! Government regulations against Pakistani undercover agents? Against Dubai-dwelling dark money? Ha! We spit in the face of national security when there is money to be made. We live in our premodern world and we defy the state and its grubby claws besmirching our freedoms. For now.

And then I did what I'd been wanting to do from the minute I'd been kidnapped.

I rang Priya.

I felt overwhelmed. I sat in a café and drank coffee, Indian coffee, savoring the burnt, cheap taste of chicory, watching little people live carefree lives around me, eating vast family dosas and slurping down lassi in lower-middle-class contentment. But I wasn't any better than them. I was them and they were me. I'd just gotten a bit richer, and my morals and values were yet to adjust to my newfound wealth.

I could be putting her at risk, her life, her career, her payments to her parents, but I needed to listen to her voice. I needed her to know that I was all right.

I sat there for far too long, listening to the excitement in children's voices as they begged their parents to buy toys, firecrackers, sparklers for Diwali. Maybe I'd be listening to some of my own one day.

I swallowed my fears. I rang her.

I had memorized her number, of course, one of those tricks the rich have forgotten with their smartphones.

"Ramesh?" she said. "Ramesh! My God, you're alive." And then she began laughing, and then sobbing and finally sniffling with relief. "You're alive!" she said.

"Yes," I said. There was a strange lump in my throat, and I found myself unable to say anything else. That's either love or a lack of proper hydration.

"Where are you? I'll come—"

"No!" I said. "You can't. It's complicated. We're safe. We escaped."

"We paid the ransom straightaway," she said, "and then we didn't hear anything. I thought you—"

"What?" So Abhi's father had betrayed us. Cut off my finger. Stolen the ransom.

I breathed out long and hard.

My finger, lost for nothing. For drama, for show, to make a point.

I was capable of many things, but never something like that.

"I'll do anything to help," she continued. "Tell me where you are. I want to help, Ramesh."

"No," I said, even though I wanted to see her more than anything. I wanted her to run to me and tell me it would be all right. I delighted for a moment in the pure selfishness of it. "I'll be in touch tomorrow. I promise. I just wanted you to know I was alive." I hung up.

I didn't tell her what I really wanted to say, the let's-run-away-together-and-never-look-back thing, because of the many-dozens-of-skeletons-hidden-in-my-closet thing.

I didn't tell her I loved her, either. But I wanted to. I would do. Nothing would stop me, when all this was over.

So the ransom had been paid. Oberoi had come through for us after all. Maybe he wasn't so bad. Maybe he'd felt guilty for bringing Abhi on the show in the first place.

I sat and thought about Rudi too. It seemed that kidnap and violence brought out the caring side in me. At the end of the day, I was the kid's only friend.

It was my job. More than that. It was my calling. It was my fulfillment of sanatana dharma, my way out of purgatory, out of the life I'd built for myself, this lonely little meaningless life.

I needed him to be all right.

That was what responsible managers did.

That was what friends did.

It had to be done.

"Sumit? Guess who?" I said when the call went through.

I was taking a chance. The last time I'd seen him, I'd turned him down. I'd cast him away.

Sumit stayed quiet for a long time. "Motherfucker," he finally said, laughing. "I thought I was rid of you. Everyone is looking for Rudraksh. Have you seen that kidnap video with the terrible music?"

I breathed a sigh of relief. "You know those contacts of yours? Mafia dons? Undersecretaries? Samosa wallahs?" I said.

"Do you want my help or do you want to insult me?" he shot back straightaway.

Good question. I knew I was pushing my luck, but I didn't want him to know how much I needed him. I needed to watch some YouTube videos on interpersonal relationships.

"I need to contact a Himanshu Aggarwal. Builder. Big guy. Let him know we have something that belongs to him."

"What have you gotten into?" he asked. "Do you know who that is?"

"Can your people get the message to him?"

"Give me a few hours," he said.

"Thank you, Sumit bhai," I said, and didn't even feel dirty at being so nice. I hung up. Maybe it had been too easy, I thought. I spent the walk back worrying if he was going to fuck me over.

I grabbed a newspaper, and was glad to see that we—well, Rudi—were front page, top center. I was on 10 percent commission, remember. I picked up some Westernized boy-snacks, full of cholesterol and sugar, Gatorade and milk shakes, Maggi noodles from one of a million stalls. Maggi with soy, Maggi with chili, Maggi with egg. A few honest cheap rotis for myself.

It was a different India out here. I'd only been out of it, living the high life, for a few months, but I'd gotten used to the other side, even though it was, what, five miles away?

Air conditioners, drivers, armed guards at storefronts, and gated apartment complexes. The shops were freshly purified heavens, filled to the brim with helpful staff, even sweeter for their total falseness.

This was my India. Foul smells, butchers cutting chicken necks in front of you, the little cluckers squawking as they died, elbowing and scratching your way to counters to be served, unexplained noises after dark, potentially poisonous smells, screams of pleasure and pain.

And this was a nice part, a lower-middle-class striver part of Delhi, on-the-up Delhi, half-filled-metro-hole Delhi, a place I had slaved for three years to rent an apartment in. I wasn't even talking about the really foul parts, where even I'd never been to, where people lived like gnats on a lemur's ballsack, where everyone was missing teeth or organs or legs and nothing got better even as the GDPs and the HDIs were going up, up, up all over United Nations PowerPoint slides.

Rudi and Abhi were trying to talk when I got back to the apartment.

Well, they were sitting and staring at different sides of the room. Rudi kept attempting small talk. "What do you want to do when you're older?," "What's your favorite YouTube video?," "I'm sorry for shaming you in front of hundreds of millions of people." You know, that kind of thing.

At least he was making an effort. I gave him a little thumbs-up.

There was just one thing I had to do first. I had to be hard.

"Abhi," I shouted. "Get up!" He moved without a moment's hesitation. "Up against the wall." His family had tried to fuck me over, and I was going to repay a little of that tender care and attention.

I took out the phone I had bought earlier and opened the camera app.

Abhi started trembling.

"Say what you did," I said. "Say it, or your pretty little face is going to get hurt."

Rudi looked at me with confusion. "Ramesh, what are you doing?"

"Just a little extra insurance. Start talking, Abhi, into the camera, say what you and your father did."

It was over in a matter of minutes. A nice little video file saying exactly who had kidnapped us. I made a copy onto a memory card, just for insurance, and stuffed it into a pocket.

Abhi was silent after that. He sat on the bed and sulked.

Rudi kept on talking to him.

"In all honesty," he said, "I know that what I did was bad. I will make it up to you." He glanced at me, and I winked my approval. "I was not fair. I did it for ratings. I made them hate you."

Abhi kept staring at the wall. I knew that feeling. I too had spent many hours staring at that wall feeling a general animosity toward Rudraksh Saxena. But that was in the past.

"I can give you anything," said Rudi. "You want to be a politician? I can do that. You want to be famous? You want to drink Bollinger? You want the best table at Indian Accent? You want to date starlets? Tell me what you want, dude."

What an authority! How words and opinions rolled off his tongue. He was a seasoned man of the world, a man who could get a table at the best restaurants in town, a man who had access to film stars. Better than being addicted to drugs, but my God, what an annoyance!

But then his voice changed and another Rudi entirely emerged.

"I know you hate me. I want to help you. I fucked up. I am a fuck-up. I'm only famous because someone else took the goddamn exam for me. I know I'm no good. But I have money now, and I can help you. Just let me help, please," he said.

Abhi shifted around to face us. "There isn't enough money for you to fix what happened," he said.

Rudi looked as if he was going to cry. Not good for a kidnapper.

"Food!" I said, because that usually made things better. "Eat. Sleep. Enjoy yourselves, live a little, both of you." I threw the mountain of snacks on the bed. "My contact will call in a few hours." I didn't mention Priya, or the paid ransom.

I logged into the computer and Rudi made one last effort to get the kid talking. We watched videos. I handed out glasses and plates like I was running day care. Twenty-four years old, and this was my life.

It was midafternoon when Sumit rang. The kids were sleeping, the adrenaline having long since abandoned them. Rudi had been talking about Marvel shit. Abhi had answered him only monosyllabically, but at least that was something.

They should have gotten on well. Same age, same complaints about parents and vast childhood emotional abuse, boring, boring, boring. I wished I smoked, had something to take my mind off the sweat and my fatherfucking finger.

"So you kidnapped Himanshu Aggarwal's kid?" Sumit said, over the phone.

"Had to do something."

"Takes balls I didn't know you had." He sighed. "I've set up a meet. I'll take you to the father. You hand the kid back. Everything's good."

"Tell him I know exactly what he did," I said, thinking about the ransom, but unable to say it out loud in case Rudi woke up. I didn't want him to know. He was already under enough pressure as it was. "Tell him no more double-crossing or I'll expose what he did. We've made a video. We'll release it everywhere if he fucks us. Where do I find you?"

"Two hours. Karkardooma metro. Ticket hall."

"We'll be there. You know, Sumit bhai, I was wrong. I could use a go-getter like you in the future. How about it?"

"Sounds like a plan, brother," he said, and hung up.

I woke the boys. Told them to shower. Abhi looked like death.

"Back to Daddy soon," I said. He nodded, still shit-scared, angry, and confused. He deserved a peaceful life, youthful enthusiasms and foreign trips, and then in a few years he'd turn into his dad and hate himself until he died. You know, the normal life cycle of the upper-class Indian male.

After my call with Sumit I went out to the shops once again. I had a genius idea and I knew just where to go to make it happen. "Something for the fuller-bodied lady," I said, shivering with laughter, unable to contain my delight, and I could tell the shopkeeper pitied the wife who was married to this.

The kids had showered and shat by the time I came back.

I threw my package at Rudi.

"Open it," I said, and then went into my wardrobe to look for a woman's wig of long black hair that I'd bought on a whim a few years before. I'd be wearing a man's, medium long, like a seventies film star.

"I am not wearing this," I heard Rudi shout. I reappeared just to see the look of shock on his face.

He was holding a super-value bright pink sari set.

"You're the most famous man in India," I said, and threw the wig at him. "Think of it as a compliment."

Abhi started laughing nervously.

Progress, finally.

TWELVE

We pulled up in a taxi. A huge crowd of harassed-looking office workers was pouring out of Karkardooma metro station into the welcoming embrace of a sea of rickshaw pullers. Bored drivers of battered cars from 2005 awaited their middle-management masters. Men and women rushing this way and that, desperate to make a little more money before the Diwali holidays. It wasn't even rush hour yet, but there were a thousand people coming out of the station. Karkardooma metro station was where Sumit chose to screw me.

The outside of the station was composed of a sheer wall filled with advertisements for catering halls, festivity gardens, elephant rentals, dressmaking—all the paraphernalia of the wedding industry, pumped up even more at that time of year, the industry that single-handedly keeps our economy growing. Weddings for paupers, weddings for billionaires, every day in Delhi a hundred—you could dine for free all year round if you possessed a good suit and the ability to blend in with a crowd.

We walked from the taxi toward the building, past paan spit on the pavement, toy-hawkers eyeing young children, coconut water sellers, diesel fumes, CNG tanks that could explode at any moment. Everyone sweaty. I thought of my father's obsession with crotch rot. He'd have had a bottle of talcum powder out before you could blink.

Rudi was furious, but he looked wonderful, soft and sweet, like your dream daughter-in-law, or Hema Malini in a dance number just before it rains and everything turns transparent.

Inside the metro station was a vast steep pyramid of stairs, endless fucking stairs. I pushed Abhi up the steps, up an escalator, and into the ticket hall. "Not long now," I said. "It will all be over soon, as long as no one does anything stupid."

"That is what I'm worried about," he whispered back, eyeing Rudi and me.

In his polo shirt and slacks, face expressing terror, he looked like he had just accidentally beaten his boss at the golf course. Rudi in his sari, tripping over the dupatta, got many admiring gazes from shortsighted elderly gentlemen. I was in my wig, the fringe settling just above my eyebrows. What a strange group we made, trooping up those stairs to the ticket hall, which was failing to be cooled by giant groaning ACs.

Upstairs, I saw Sumit standing on the far side of the hall, near another set of escalators leading to a platform. He was alone. Where were his armies of followers, dressed like bad copies?

We walked over. I took Abhi by the shoulders and pushed him in front of me. Rudi followed, batting away the hands of strangers trying to graze his waist, pinch a bit of his flesh. "Fuck you, fuck you," I heard him say every few seconds, either to me or the gropers, I knew not which.

"Sumit," I said as we stood in front of him, surrounded by the hubbub of a million gray, wet-armpitted shirt-wearers milling around us.

"Who's the lady?" was the first thing he said. He looked very tired. And very pleased. Too pleased. I saw an expression of victory cross his face. I saw the creases in his shirt, the way it hung off his body. He didn't smell of Paco Rabanne. He smelled of metro station.

He looked hungry. He looked poor. He looked like a young man who was about to make a killing. He was not the Sumit of old. No flunkies, no money, no perfume, just pure desperation.

Oh shit.

He smiled, then pulled out a knife, a little three-inch thing. No one around us noticed. Men shouting, pointing, making threatening gestures? That was just rush hour on the Delhi metro.

What do you do if someone pulls out a knife in public? No clever stuff.

"He's coming with me," said Sumit.

"You ullu ka pattha," I said. "You tees maar khan double-crosser."

Sumit laughed. "Do you know how rich his dad is?" That was the sum total of his explanation. What other reason do you need, really?

"You fucking prick," I said.

That was a mistake. I blame my lack of practice at getting in touch with my emotions.

"After what you did to me, brother?" said Sumit. "The way you turned me down? I had nothing, but now I have this kid. And once his father finds out, I'll make a fortune."

Rudi started to panic, his face pinker than his sari. Abhi started to stutter. Sumit squeezed past me, dodging the rotund bulk of a nearby office worker, keeping the knife to my ribs.

He took Abhi by the hand. He looked at Rudi's face, for just a second too long. He crinkled his eyes, then shook his head.

Imagine if he had recognized him then. Our stupid little plan, destroyed by Sumit, of all people. I never would have gotten over that.

"Better luck next time, Ramesh!" he said. "Now you'll find out how my life has been these few months."

Abhi was weeping again. If he was going to take over his father's business, he'd really have to toughen up. I watched his miserable face as he was led into the crowd and dissolved like sugar in tea.

"What the fuck do we do now?" said Rudi, right in my ear.

My finger throbbed.

Great fucking question.

"Let's see where they're going," I said, squeezing through the crowd. Rudi ran after me, surprising salarymen with his gruff voice and his clunking Adidas trainers squashing their feet.

I heard a wail to my left and saw Abhi waving frantically to us on the escalator. Men were shouting and toppling against each other as Sumit pushed them out of the way.

"Escalator," I shouted, and Rudi and I sprinted through the warren of wet, fat flesh, a maze constructed out of body odor and sweat. My fingers grabbed shoulders, I made a thousand apologies, I smelled stomach acid and bad breath. I had eyes only for the escalator.

We forced our way through, and charged up the ascending, bleating line of people. Abhi had vanished onto the platform. I could hear the high electric whine of a metro train pulling in.

"Get out of my way," Rudi shouted in front of me, slapping people aside and trying to keep his sari together at the same time. It was quite a feat. Out we charged, vaulting over the ticket barriers, onto the platform—just as the metro doors slammed shut. We saw the ghost of a crying, chalk-white face, and off the train went, thirty seconds from stop to start, thank you, Delhi metro, thank you, government, thank you, civilization, fuck fuck fuck.

I bumped into Rudi from behind and he nearly fell onto the electric rail. How ignominious that would have been, how perplexing for the news, Rudraksh Saxena's blackened body in women's clothes, and in east Delhi of all places, what a terrible ending for a multimillionaire.

"Now?" said Rudi. The wig hairs were glued with sweat to his ruddy face.

"There's a very angry construction magnate out there with a twice-kidnapped son and an extremely psychopathic underling. And we've just lost the one thing they care about the most—the one thing that would have saved us from ending up dead and disgraced."

I looked at Rudi.

"Oberoi?" he said.

"Yes," I answered.

We both thought, why not land him in the shit too?

And off we went.

THIRTEEN

I took all the money out of the bathroom: 192,000 Gandhis in crisp, pink two thousands.

We needed to get out of the flat immediately. Rudi was complaining about his clothes. Too hot, too tight, and he was upset about the pinching. I told him the next sari would be the color of his choice.

We hailed an auto on a market corner two streets away, and headed for Gandhi Nagar.

Gandhi Nagar is the sort of place Delhi dwellers go to get lost. That and to do their shopping at the clothes market, one of the last places not filled with white girls buying hippie harem trousers. In the films they go to Paharganj, but now that is sadly rammed full of drug-addicted backpackers looking for material for their novels.

I chose a hotel at random. The Geeta Rest House, the proprietress a middle-aged Sikh lady with an unreadable face.

She looked at my pink-veiled, freshly shaven bride, and I could imagine her thinking: not really a looker, but at least she's paler than him. She took the money for three nights. I handed her a little extra. "No cleaning," I said. She pocketed it without pause. That was how I liked people. Straightforward, rude, and morally flexible.

Behind her, a TV was blaring out something about Pakistan, about terrorism, followed by Shah Rukh and Aishwarya at Cannes, and Oscars and white-man films.

Upstairs, in the room, I made my plan of action. Another one, considering the last one had been forcefully shat on. Rudi jumped on the bed, tore off his wig, and started scratching himself. If a man had owned the hotel, we probably would have been on camera for his future masturbatory needs, and therefore entirely fucked.

"We need to get to Oberoi," I said. "The only way I can see is Pawan. He has our car, he can smuggle us in. We can't just wander into the studio. Aggarwal and Pratap aren't idiots. They'll have someone watching. And once they find out about Abhi, we're done. We have to use Pawan."

Our secret would come out, and then my life would be over. I'd be eternally reviled. No Priya, no fat little children, no future.

The Brain of Bharat took a moment to think. "Why Pawan, though? He was a good driver to us. He could get into trouble."

The kid had a point. I clearly looked unimpressed, because Rudi seemed totally confused by my expression.

"Fine," I said. "We get to the studio. You hide, I pay off the people at the gate. We get to Oberoi. He can bribe whoever has to be bribed. We're back in the money and—" Rudi tried to interject. I put my hand up. "Only for a few months. Then we can become sadhus or yoga instructors or whatever." He gave me an aggrieved glare. "Yes, we'll examine our lives. I promise. No more being kidnapped, no more being kidnappers, no more Bhatnagar investigation. We make our money and then we leave. All right?"

He nodded. "How do we know Oberoi won't fuck us?" he asked.

"Oh there's no danger of that," I laughed. "You're the number one draw on Indian television. You're his career. He won't do anything to you. He just paid a fifty-crore ransom to save you."

"I'm worth double," he said. Didn't miss a beat. Maybe he would be okay after all.

We ate a nice Punjabi dinner downstairs in our disguises: sari and sunglasses. We had mostly ghee, with a side of ghee, washed down with ghee, then went shopping for torches, flashlights, knives, utility knives, chopping knives, saw-type knives—I had a sudden fondness for knives—and another sari for Rudi. We needed to be better prepared. I had no idea how long we were going to spend like this. Better to get him extra clothes while we could.

We also needed some makeup, because while he looked somewhat fetching as a woman, I didn't know how much running and jumping and sweating we'd be doing. The trip to the metro station had been relatively short. I needed the disguise to really work if Rudi was going to spend more time in it.

At the dress shop, I tried to hold Rudi's hand, give the impression we were a young couple out on the town. You know what he did? He slapped my hand away, the shit. I gave a little smile to the elderly owner, a what-can-you-do? one, a big mistake, for he spent the next twenty minutes boring me to death about the flightiness of women while Rudi was changing.

"She's a feisty one, yours, you have to get her under control," he said, tongue anointed with paan residue, clenching his scissors and measuring tape in unsteady hands. I was trying to guess in my mind as to when exactly his wife had left him.

"You don't know how right you are," I said without thinking, and on he went about estrogen-laden fast food and declining sperm counts and how all women nowadays dressed so immodestly and deserved everything they got.

After we got back, I made some excuse and wandered down the street. I nearly rang Priya. I held out. Rudi was right. We had hurt enough people already. *I* had hurt enough people. I would never add her to that number.

Just because you long to hear someone's voice, just because you desperately need someone to tell you they care, doesn't mean you can do whatever you want. What am I? American? This is India. We have duty and honor and all sorts of other things to keep us miserable.

On my walk, I thought of my early business endeavors. Everything had fit together so perfectly, like dance moves on *India's Got Talent*, progressing easily from one client, one lie to the next.

But I had become sucked in. I had lost myself in the world of crookedness.

And I had ended up here. This whole situation was what I had wanted to avoid.

Rudi was right. We should retire.

When I got back in from my walk, the poor kid was clucking aimlessly on our shared bed, arms crossed, giving me dirty looks. It was the longest digital detox he had ever been on.

He eyed my phone. He looked like he would murder me just to touch it.

"No social media," I had to remind him whenever he complained, or gave me a look, or breathed. "No internet. God knows who will be tracking us. Not just Mark Zuckerberg this time, but Mark Rudigetsmurderedberg." He didn't laugh.

Of course I was a hypocrite.

Of course I was a liar.

I'd been lying to everyone since I was seventeen.

I'd bought in samosas for a miserable midnight snack. The year-old vegetable oil melted through newsprint with breathless snapshots of celebrity parties. We ate like dogs, smearing the sheets with grease. Extra fees to be paid at reception, no doubt.

The next morning I called a cab. It came at nine sharp, with a two-horn blast at the front of the building. I did a quick bow to Ms. Geeta in the lobby. A step behind me was my bride, ravishingly made up, avoiding all eyes but her husband's. We walked out.

I let Rudi climb into the car.

"Just a day trip," I shouted back to Ms. Geeta. "Showing my bride my old haunts. Jantar Mantar, Lotus Temple."

She stood in the doorway, smiled her benedictions upon me. "Such a good girl," she said, looking over at Rudi.

"Very well brought up," I said.

We wouldn't be back, of course, so that was an extra night she had been paid for. She'd be even happier with us when she realized.

I climbed into the back of the car and waved to her.

The driver was young, with a miserable little moustache of soft hair.

We drove off and were just about to merge onto the GT Road when I tapped the fellow on the side of the shoulder. "Stop, brother," I said.

"Sir?" he said, pulling up. He had a look of abject fear on his face. I'm just like you, I felt like saying, apart from being able to buy your family a thousand times over.

"I'll give you ten thousand rupees to leave now and give us the car for the—" I started to say.

Rudi gave a little cough and squeezed my arm.

"Fine, twenty thousand," I said. Was that enough? Rudi smiled. I continued, "Go away. Buy a nice Diwali present for your girlfriend. We'll ring you when we're done. You don't tell anyone anything. You make a month's salary. Yes?"

He took the deal in an instant. He thanked us and ran like the wind. He must have really hated his boss. Always check on your employees, I say. Give them psychometric questionnaires. It will save you many tears in the long run.

I moved to the front, adjusted the seat, and eased off into the traffic. I pressed the horn, I swore, I was a little on edge. Rudi sat behind me, complaining.

"How are you doing back there?" I asked twenty minutes of unrestrained driving later.

"It wouldn't be so bad if you could bloody drive properly," he grunted.

Where's Mr. Liberal Charity-wallah when you need him, eh? At least he was only complaining about my driving. See how the rich live! Even the trunks of their cars are more commodious than the highest aspirations of the poor! And still they complain!

We crossed over the Yamuna via the crumbling, rust-ridden Old Iron Bridge—look what the British have left us, idiot laws and broken bridges and marrying for love.

I parked up outside Golden Jubilee Park so we could hide Rudi. He ducked down into the footwell. I spread a thick shawl over him, one I had bought for his feminine transformation. The park was deserted. Weekday morning, no Romeos, no cricket, no homeless people picking up cigarette stubs, no diabetic middle-aged joggers poleaxed by the mixture of freezing fog and building dust. Just male street sellers at the gates lazily shouting out their wares to the drivers piling up at the bridge crossing. After checking Rudi was comfortable, which was most unlike me, I eased back out onto the main road.

It took an hour to get to the studio. The morning rush was usually murder, but the festive season had made it worse. Buses of relatives coming in from all over the country. Trucks full of chickens and goats, ready to be slaughtered. Vans of would-be kidnappers. The air conditioning couldn't hide the smell of acrid smoke. Where it came from, no one knew—a useful conversation starter with the posh people.

I read an article that said we Delhiites lose four inches of height due to pollution. I salute our street urchins whenever we pass, paying the price that every rich man does not, with their German air purifiers chugging away, removing the poison from their every surrounding. Their children will not have ten years of life stolen, their children will not have lungs dyed black. I am one of you, I want to say to the hollow-cheeked young, and we will have our revenge somehow, but for now, I must play my part and watch and wait until the moment is right.

All that wonderful life energy that in the West goes to making muscle-bound athletes and smiling, white-toothed CEOs here goes to combating the dust, the dirt, the whole world trying to send you to your grave. No wonder we are fighters, no wonder we are all little stunted bags of energy, no wonder we never stop. The world has made its mark on us, tried to smother us from our first moments, and one day we will rise and laugh and piss on it all.

The guards at the studio were their usual annoying selves, more facial hair than brain.

I stopped by the gate, and the questioning began.

"Who are you?" one of them said. "What do you want?" said the other. All I could see were their bushy moustaches.

"Are you a Pakistani spy wreaking vengeance upon our glorious reality television industry?" I half expected.

"Just a driver, brother," I said. "Have to collect one of these TV star fellows. You know how they are, annoying, rude, inconsiderate." I heard a grunt from behind me.

"How would ten thousand rupees each be?" I said. I heard the cough again, my bloody mistake. "Twenty thousand, sir? Just let me through. You never saw me."

They looked at each other and nodded.

I pulled out my wallet and handed over the money. Their moustaches twitched with delight. They even gave me a little salute. You had to admire their professionalism.

We got out in an alley behind the canteen. Rudi swore at my driving, at being dressed like a woman, at the whole fucking socio-historical situation.

"Want an Evian, do you, boss?"

"Oh fuck you," he said.

We walked inside as calmly as we could, past uninterested porters watching nautch girl item numbers on phones, all of them ignoring the wigged man escorting a poorly made-up young girl through the bowels of the studio. No one got out of our way, no one showed deference, no one held doors open. We were nothing. A young writer type walked straight into us, some pipsqueak who Rudi would have shat on normally. He gave us a dismissive, 30 Under 30 look and went off. Rudi grunted, but held his tongue. It was good being famous—you could deal with that sort of pissant person, sometimes.

We shuffled through the corridors, heads down, until we reached Oberoi's room, and gave three loud knocks. "What the fuck do you want?" we heard.

Rudi and I shared a look. This was it. I turned the handle. The door opened. We went in.

Oberoi was sitting at his desk. He raised his sunglasses to the top of his head. His face, usually so ruddy, so full of life, so full of whisky, drained of color.

He knew who we were the minute he looked up. So much for the saris, wigs, and sunglasses. Rudi raised his eyebrows at me. I shrugged my shoulders.

Rudi threw off his wig. It lay on the floor, shorn of life, looking like a drunken rat. "Hello, Oberoi," he said. "Pleased to see us?"

Oberoi looked at me, then Rudi, then back to me. He scratched his cheek, scuffed the skin, left deep red welts above the track of his designer stubble.

"You're alive," he said. He tried to compose himself, tried to pull out words, continued to scratch, then opened his arms wide to show how wonderful this all was, that we were back, that we would be welcomed like sons returning without white girlfriends from MIT.

He stood up in shock, opened his mouth a few times, and then fell down again on his chair. It squeaked in protest.

He collected himself for a moment. "What happened?" he said. "Who took you? We have to get you back to the show straightaway. It has been impossible. We have to get a shoot, we can do an ad campaign, have you thought about a charity for disappeared children?"

"He had his finger chopped off," Rudi said. How sweet.

I waved my hand in the air.

"My God. I'll call the police. I know people. We can get this sorted, straightaway," Oberoi said. "How atrocious!"

"We know who it was," said Rudi. "Developer called Aggarwal. The father of that boy that we humiliated."

"Aggarwal, Aggarwal," Oberoi said, with stresses on each syllable, stretching the vowels this way and that, as if some secret of the name might reveal itself. "Never heard of him," he said, as he pulled out his Samsung. It was covered in little false jewels, and shone like a bald man's skull. He dialed and put it to his face. I was dazzled by the light reflecting off the back and nearly raised my arms to my face.

"Sub-Inspector!" he shouted, and got up, his voice rising in volume, like when you had a phone call on the metro you wanted to show off. "You won't believe who's turned up! Yes! Send some men over, would you? We must sort this out, straightaway!"

He put the phone down, and folded his hands across his cotton shirt. "This is fantastic," he said, swiveling in his chair, trying to give the impression of having recovered from his shock. His foot tapped on the carpet. "My life has been hell, honestly. And to make it worse, my wife's on a fast, she says for Navratri, but that is so far away, and she has been a fucking nightmare. Another goddamn juice cleanse. Speaking of which." He reached into a drinks cabinet behind him on the wall, the labels proudly arranged next to a ten-year-old photo of him and his family at some Scottish distillery, and unscrewed a bottle of something expensive.

Rudi had his head in his hands, thanking God the nightmare was over, and that he'd have his precious YouTube again.

Oberoi sat back down in his chair. On the table in front of him was a pile of headshots, children, hundreds of them, with a piece of paper attached to the back of each one.

"You boys, you're going to be fine," he began to blather, and casually started to move the pile off the table with one hand. He was smiling, he was laughing, he was sipping whisky, he was saying how wonderful our lives were going to be now, but still he kept moving the photos, his hand like a claw around them.

"What are those?" I asked.

"Nothing, nothing," he said.

"What are those?" I asked again.

He dropped the tumbler in his hand and it hit the table. I knew immediately that it was something, with that same gut feeling all Indians are born with, it's just that the fat ones have lost it, the air conditioning and drivers and *Economist* subscriptions dulling that innate primordial knowledge.

"Oberoi," I said, in a cool, calculated voice that came from God knows where, "why are there hundreds of pictures of children on this table, and why do those look like casting questionnaires?"

Oberoi shook his head vigorously and tried to cover up the photos as I grabbed at them. Stapled to each one was a profile with the silly little details of each child's life: their favorite book, how frequently their parents beat them, the name of their therapist, and the name of the program—

"*Beat the Brains*?" said Rudi, reading the paperwork.

"It's a spin-off," Oberoi said, but his voice betrayed him. He snatched the paper back from Rudi and grabbed as many photos as he could, clutching them to him, embracing them in his arms like a doting mother. It looked like he was wearing one of those Rio carnival dresses, all the feathers white. I moved past the desk, as did Rudi from the other side. Oberoi was trapped.

Never has there been a worse liar in the history of high-level production executives.

I moved in closer. I could smell his aftershave, like kharbujas rotting in heat. What is it with the men in this country and their hideous perfumes?

"It's a spin-off," he repeated, as he gripped the papers.

I snatched an application from him, and he groaned as if he'd been hit.

"The date on these is two months ago," I said. All the kids had glasses, looked like the children in milk ads, chubbily studious, white teeth, never answered back, your perfect child made into flesh.

And then came the smoking gun.

"'You saw *Beat the Brain*,'" Rudi read quietly from one of the profiles. His other hand gripped Oberoi's collar tight. "'But now meet the next generation, taking over the mantle of the cleverest in the country. Before there was one. Now there are many. *Beat the Brains*. They're the future.' You're behind this, aren't you?" He was whispering. The sari and the makeup made his rage even more terrifying.

We shared a brotherly look of mutual respect. Rudi brought his face close to Oberoi's. Where had he learned all this from?

"No. No," Oberoi moaned.

"Know someone called Pratap?" said Rudi, and Oberoi flinched.

He had worked it out even before me.

I looked around the room. In the corner, Oberoi had installed a new little shrine, to curry favor with any visiting religiously minded dignitaries. I walked over, picked up something called a religious services directory, solid as a phone book, full of saints' days and cut-price priests. I marched back to him, hefting the book in my hands. The pages were saffron-edged and smelled of incense.

"Talk," I said.

"There is nothing to talk about," he said. "I am your friend, your producer, why would—"

I hit him hard across the head with the book. Again and again and again. When I'd finished, his skin was red. It stung. No blood.

"More?" I said.

"It was me," he said.

"We weren't ever meant to come back, were we?" said Rudi. Oberoi kept silent. His sunglasses hung from his ears on a broken frame.

I hit him again, that sweet last one a parent does because the kid doesn't expect it. That one hurts the most. When you hit them, make sure they can't get back up.

Rudi kept his grip on him. Oberoi wriggled like a worm.

"Fuck you, Rudraksh," he said. "You take all the money, and what do I get?"

"Millions," I said. "Not enough?"

"Nowhere near. You make hundreds of millions, and I get a producer credit. That's nothing. My wife, my kids, they all want and want and want. I can't pay for my house. I can't pay for their Diwali presents. They have college and school fees—"

"I could always do their exams," I joked, but the bastard couldn't be stopped. Just had to tell us everything. Couldn't keep his mouth shut.

"I came up with this bloody show. And who got to star in it? The moneymen had to go and pick a fucking cheater. You think I wouldn't find out? Who do you think made the anonymous tip-off to Anjali fucking Bhatnagar? But your lawyers made her stall. I know Himanshu Aggarwal. He's angry, he's vain and thinks his son deserves to be on TV because he's rich and has a nice face. So I told him I'd put the kid on the show, make him a big star, and then you did just what I thought you would. Rudi couldn't help humiliating him. It's easy to manipulate you once you realize how stupid you are. How could anyone believe you could be a Topper?"

Rudi looked as angry as I'd ever seen him. Angry, hurt, and humiliated. But there was no time to lose, for I had just realized we had to make a run for it.

"When you called the sub-inspector, that was actually Pratap, wasn't it?" I said.

"Damn right. Fuck you," said Oberoi.

I hit him again and he was quiet.

Then I joined some more dots and figured out that Shashank Oberoi was double-crossing everyone.

"You kept the ransom for yourself, didn't you?" I said. "Priya said you'd paid it, and here I was thinking Aggarwal had pocketed the money."

"You've been talking to Priya?" said Rudi. "When? I thought we were doing no communication."

"Boss, is this really the time for questions?" I said. "We do not want to be here when Pratap arrives. He might kill us on sight. We might tell him the truth and he might kill this double-dealing prick. Who knows? I do not want to take chances. We take Oberoi now, and we try to survive, okay?"

He could see I was right. He gave up. "Fine," he said, sounding unfine.

"I'm sorry for not telling you."

"Okay, we go," snapped Rudi. Oberoi moaned again. "But you're coming with us." Oberoi began to say something, but Rudi slapped him. "You're going to be our new hostage. We kidnapped Abhi Aggarwal, did you hear about that? But we lost him, and you're his replacement. Only we're not ransoming you. We're going to expose you."

Oberoi gasped like a teenager. He started to twitch his arms and grabbed at things on his desk. Pencils went flying, photo frames of the dead-eyed wife. He could see, clearer than he could see us, his fate: prison, or worse, entombed in concrete in some shopping mall in Noida by a vengeful Himanshu Aggarwal.

Rudi grabbed his wig off the floor. I took one of my knives from my backpack. Oberoi followed its point out of his chair, out of the office, and down the corridor.

In the canteen, we smelled garlic and onions dissolving into oil. Just a few more corridors and we'd be out, and then we could figure out what to do next. We tried to look as inconspicuous as we could. Just skip past a few tables of people eating lunch. What could be easier?

Oberoi was desperate to scream, but the knife pressed into his back made him think again.

We were meters from the door exiting the canteen, meters from freedom, when it opened, and the one person I didn't want to see stood right in front of us.

Pratap had arrived.

Eyes bloodshot, teeth sharp and yellow. Skin a little greasier. Anger problems still evident.

He opened his jacket to reveal a gun.

"You're going to come with me," he said quietly.

"Kill them now," hissed Oberoi. "Now. Do it!"

One or two people pulled their faces out of their lunch and saw Shashank Oberoi shouting at someone. Nothing out of the ordinary. They resumed eating.

Oberoi's face was split with a manic grin. He'd seen his chance. Two bullets and he could run.

"The show paid the ransom," said Rudi quickly. He held out his arm, shielding me. "Oberoi took it. He's double-crossing you."

Pratap gave us a cold, long look. "Where's my boss's son?" he said.

"Ah," said Rudi.

"See, they're lying," said Oberoi, trying to grab my shirt and push me toward a wholly unwanted martyrdom. "Kill them," he hissed.

Pratap raised his gun. I saw his eyes locked on mine. He believed Oberoi.

He began to laugh.

My fingers cramped in pain. He had already cut one off, and his face was not that of a man who had been happy to stop there. I took ahold of Oberoi's shoulder and tried to push him the other way. I did the same with Rudi, hauling him in front of me. That's loyalty.

Unfortunately my grip on Oberoi wasn't as strong as it should have been.

He wriggled free, pushed me to the floor, gave me a victorious smile, and ran as fast as he could.

He ran much more quickly than someone fat and rich should be able to. I gave him credit for that. He was gone before I could do anything, and I was left staring down the barrel of a gun.

Pratap looked dazed.

"See, we weren't lying—" started Rudi.

"Not the time, boss!"

Pratap raised his gun again.

It was time to go. "Gun!" I screamed, and everyone turned their heads. I could be loud when I wanted to.

I hunched down, pulled Rudi down too, and we ran, without looking, between tables of people eating lunch. I heard Rudi swearing next to me.

I heard a gunshot.

I didn't know where it went. Not in me. Not in Rudi. That was enough.

Men began to scream. Plates of sambar and idlis clattered to the floor. I stumbled. Rudi ran past me, trailing sequins and pink.

We fled to the far corridor. It was packed with people, the guards at the front, always the first to run. Their jobs had been passed to them by their fathers, and in time would go to their sons. Death would complicate that inheritance.

We ran as a herd down the corridor.

I heard two, three more shots. One flew above my head and blew up a tube light.

Elbows dug into my sides, nails clawed at me, I heard shrieks of various octaves.

We broke through the doors. Rudi and I used the crowd for cover. They ran in every direction. I moved toward the packs of runners heading to the back of the studio. I jumped across carefully tended lawns and manicured hedges and elderly porters.

I could do nothing but run, so I did.

Men and women clambered over each other, over metal railings and flesh, everyone for himself. I ran around a corner until I reached the car, where Rudi stood, looking white-faced at the chaos around us.

A man sprinted past me to the passenger door and started hammering at the window. I threw him out of the way. "Sorry about that," I said, like a Westerner.

"Where's Oberoi?" Rudi said. He was breathing hard. He looked exhausted and miserable.

"Gone," I said.

"Jesus Christ, Ramesh. He knows everything." But he was too tired to be angry. "I'm fucked. You're fucked. We're fucked. India's fucked. The socio-econom—"

"Let's go, huh, boss?" I said. He grunted. Down he crept into the footwell. I started the car, and we set off as if rocket-powered. The guards at the gate were long gone, no turbaned salutes and stiff-jawed officiousness today. The police wouldn't come for hours.

This kidnapping business was going very well.

FOURTEEN

We stopped outside Golden Jubilee Park again. The radio had mentioned an incident at Delhi International Studios, but nothing about us or Oberoi.

Rudi looked angry with me, yet also very fetching in his polyester sari, with its fine brocading and little pieces of reflective mirror. His hair and makeup were a mess; he had streaks in his foundation and lipstick smeared everywhere. We would soon fix that, never worry.

"What do we do now, huh, genius?" he asked, spitting out the window.

"Only one thing left," I said.

I would have done anything to keep her away from it all.

I was putting her in danger. I was destroying her career. I was using her.

And I didn't want to think about the worst part. Oberoi knew the truth about me and Rudi. She could find out. She would think I was just as bad as everyone else.

"What?" Rudi said. "Ramesh! What?"

"Priya."

"Priya?" Rudi asked.

"Our assistant producer," I said slowly. "Medium height.

About twenty-five. Is largely responsible for the success of your television career."

Rudi's anger turned to a vicious little smile.

"I know who she is, Ramesh," he said slowly, as if I was stupid. "But she's Oberoi's underling. Why would we go to her? She'll betray us, won't she?"

"I know her, she'll help us," I said.

He began to chuckle. "You know her? That's not good enough for me. Is she close to you? Did you have some special relationship? Did you secretly go shopping and drink coffee with her and not tell anyone about it? Were you off having dates, Ramesh? Is there some reason we should trust her?" The little prick was loving it. He had known all along. He wanted me to tell him what she meant to me. He had me right where he wanted me.

He wanted me to say it.

So I said it.

"I like her."

"You like her?" He began to smirk with amusement. "You like her? But that's not enough. There are plenty of people I like who would betray me in an instant. I want more than like, Ramesh. Why should we trust her? She's Oberoi's assistant, after all."

So that was the way it was going to be. He was going to get his revenge. He was going to make me say it. Fuck him. I was going to say it. It was true. I'd never said it about anyone before.

"Because I love her," I said.

"Oh, love!" said Rudi. "Now I understand. Ramesh weds Priya? I truly did not know. How wonderful! My felicitations to the happy couple." He reached over to give me a hug, but I pushed him away.

"You prick," I said.

I pulled my phone out of my pocket and rang her.

"Ramesh? Is that you? My God, you're back! I cannot tell you how happy I am. And Rudraksh too?"

"Yes, him too." The little shit.

"There was a shooting today, at the studio. They've sent us all home. Was that anything to do with you? Oberoi's disappeared. Production's been suspended indefinitely."

Her voice leaked into the car. Rudi started to make kissing noises.

"Oberoi did it. He arranged the kidnapping. He stole the ransom."

"My God," she said. "My God. Ramesh ..." Then she went silent.

"Priya," I said. I would have to do it, I would have to drag her into this. I had no other choice. The whole world was after me. I wasn't being manipulative, I convinced myself. I wasn't Papa. It was the truth.

"Priya, can we come to your place? We have nowhere else to go."

"Of course," she said. Not a moment's hesitation.

She told me her address. "Be safe, get here soon," she added.

"You're too good," I said, because she was. Look how she put me before herself, and so quickly. The man who married her would be a lucky one. Not me, then.

Rudi and I set off. We pretended we were on a day trip again. I pointed out grimy office buildings, pretended they were all

UNESCO World Heritage Sites and called him "darling" in my Khan Market voice.

We didn't want to think about Oberoi. We didn't want to think about exposure. We didn't want to think about prison.

I didn't want to think about telling Priya the truth.

We reached her flat another three-mile, ninety-minute Delhi trip later.

She had phoned ahead to the security guards, and we went straight through the gate, then past three apartment blocks, the balconies all laundry-strewn, until we reached hers. I parked the car in a free space and hoped nobody would impound it. Rudi and I hurried into the lobby, into the lift, first floor, second, third.

There she stood, holding her door open, worry etched across her face.

Priya.

Her mouth gaped open when she saw the way we were dressed.

She beckoned us in. I moved forward. I hugged her.

She smiled at me. I smiled back.

I could be destroying her life. We would have to get Abhi back and Oberoi imprisoned and then keep the truth from coming out. But the kidnapping, the danger, the betrayal, that was not what I was worried about. She would find out. She would definitely find out somehow. Then what would happen? Selfish as usual, Ramesh.

She moved around her flat unsteadily, as if not quite sure what to do. Otherwise she did not betray a hint of nerves.

Indians are great appraisers of property. It is the clearest way of seeing where someone is in the world. What is caste compared to square footage? The best valuers are prospective mothers-in-law, of course, but every one of us has the gene.

There were two bedrooms, one turned into an office, then a small kitchen, a dining room, good neighborhood, Mayur Vihar, very posh, very nice. She was on the up, a junior production executive—and look what I'd done.

And here I am talking about the floor plan.

She looked beautiful. She had joined the very short list of people I was glad to see.

Rudi sat down on the sofa. He clicked on the television. I heard him sigh with relief.

Priya nodded slightly as she watched him, dressed so beautifully in that pink sari, ripping off his wig and throwing it to the floor. "He looks good," she said.

"I picked it myself," I said. I removed my own wig. Finally my forehead was clear of fringe.

She shook her head. She crossed over to me and removed the sunglasses from my face. "There you are."

We stood and looked at each other.

"You'd better close the door if you don't want someone to see," she said.

I went over to shut it. That had been careless of me.

"Ramesh!" she said, pointing at my hand. She came over to me and took me by the shoulder. She was right up close. "What happened?"

"My finger," I sighed. "They cut it off. For the ransom."

Priya held my hand tight in hers and pulled me to her. My face was covered in her hair. I shut my eyes and felt it tickle my cheeks.

"I'm so sorry," she said, again and again.

"No, I am," I said without meaning to. She would see. She'd see how rotten I was inside, and then I'd be saying sorry to her for the rest of my life.

"I'll fix you up," she said, and kissed me on my cheek. I wanted to kiss her properly, but she let go of me and went into her bathroom.

Rudi turned from the couch and gave me a wink.

"Fuck you," I said, quietly enough that Priya wouldn't hear.

When she returned, she had disinfectant, bandages, soap, and a basin of hot water. She snipped away the discolored bandage and gasped at what she saw.

I didn't look, of course.

My eyes were closed. All I could feel were her fingers on mine, quick and deft and soft, the pads of her thumbs, the palms of her hands, the little calluses on her fingertips.

When I opened my eyes, my hand was swaddled in white. Priya led me to the sofa. Rudi tried hard to look engrossed in the program.

"I forgot. Food!" said Priya. "You've not eaten, have you?"

Rudi and I shook our heads like little schoolboys.

"Food!" she said again. "Eat first, then we plan later. Kitchen, come."

"Two bedrooms in this apartment?" I asked as we stood in her kitchen. "Very nice." I had to make conversation. Always ask an Indian about their property, I'd heard, in these sorts of social situations.

"I may get abuse, but I get paid," she said. "I'm Oberoi's perfect idiot. I work hard. I don't undermine him. He thinks women are easier to control. I'm . . . I was good at what I did. I was irreplaceable." She looked at Rudi and me. "I don't think I have a job anymore, do I? Neither do you two."

Rudi and I shook our heads again. Men of the world, knowers of wine and whisky, supposedly, reduced to silence.

There were dozens of photos of her on a thumbtack board on her kitchen wall, Goan beach student trips, young people living carefree lives. What the hell was that like?

She moved to her freezer, and took out some little boxes. "My mother's care packages. At least you'll eat them," she said. "Not eating your ma's home cooking. Isn't that the worst sin any daughter could commit?" She laughed.

I could think of worse. Fucking up the love of your life's future, and just before Diwali too. That was definitely worse than being rude to your mother, no matter what Indian society said.

We explained everything to her while she microwaved the food and delivered it to us, yelping as her hands were burned by volcanically hot plastic.

Well, not everything. Not the exam fraud. I could see Rudi trying to skirt around the edges of it. He could see me trying too. It was our little secret, one we kept together.

"So Abhi Aggarwal has been taken by your friend?" she asked when we'd finished devouring the food. It was hot and it was tasty. "And Oberoi did all this for money?"

"Pretty fucking much," said Rudi. "Said his wife and kids had bled him dry."

"Ha, he would say that. Rudraksh . . . Ramesh," she said. "What have you got yourselves into?"

"We're fucked," Rudi said.

"Rudi, you're a crorepati ten times over," I said. "If that's fucked, then what are the rest of us?"

"Oh, stop complaining. You have her," he said, and pointed at Priya.

"Stop it, Rudi," I said.

"Your life is so simple, Ramesh. All you do is take my money and spend it. You fucking call her, and don't tell me," he said, his voice growing loud and high with self-pity. Clearly his moral evolution was slowing down. "I don't have any friends. Do you understand that? I have no one. Everyone wants me for my money. I only have hangers-on. You. My friends. Even my parents. My own fucking parents, Ramesh, only give a shit about me for my fucking money."

"Can I remind you that MY FINGER HAS BEEN CUT OFF," I shouted. The neighbors and their little Stanford-attending beta could go to hell. I would do lots of incense-lighting and money-donating to whoever the god of neighborly silences was. "Prick. It's like you haven't grown up at all since we met," I continued. He bubbled with anger. Good.

"Boys! We only have one thing we can do," Priya said. I looked at her. You could tell she'd been planning something. I'd just been thinking about food and my finger, and she'd somehow come up with a plan.

"Yes?" said Rudi. "I'm waiting. Any time now," he said, as if he had any clue about what to do. Neither did I. We were just running. We needed someone to do a little thinking for us. Indian men! At least I knew my limitations.

"We have to go to Anjali Bhatnagar," Priya said.

"Her?" shouted Rudi, jumping out of his chair. I laughed. I couldn't help it. The makeup made everything he did funny. I was amazed he hadn't wiped it off yet. Maybe he'd grown used to it on television. Maybe he liked it. "Her?" he said again, made dumb by disbelief.

Priya took a long breath, and then she began.

"She's the only authority who can help you. She's Central Bureau of Investigation. She can get you out of anything. You have to go to her and beg. You beg. You tell her about anything you did wrong, and I know you've done something wrong, the two of you, it's just that you're both too cowardly to tell me. You tell her that whatever you did is way less important than getting Oberoi. He arranged your kidnapping. He stole the ransom money for the Brain of Bharat! That's huge. It'll be the biggest scandal in years. And she'll get all the credit."

I thought she had finished, but she went on, teasing out the words from her mind.

"And she won't be annoying the rich and the powerful. It'll just be one man, one crazy rich man who wanted more money and wanted to fuck over the most loved kid in the country, the one who every mother wishes was their son. Don't you see? He's the perfect criminal. And she gets to catch him. So we go to her, and you boys, you stupid, prideful, idiot boys, you beg Anjali Bhatnagar to help you."

I was impressed.

Rudi was not.

"Beg? Beg?" he shouted. "I know where begging gets you. I begged the whole world. I begged girls. I begged my parents. I begged my friends to be my friends. And no one cared."

"She's our only chance," said Priya.

"My worst fucking enemy, the investigator from the Central Bureau of Investigation, is the only person who can help? She's out for my fucking life. I'm fucked! What a pair of geniuses I'm stuck with. 'Let's go to Priya, she'll know what to do,'" Rudi said, doing the universal uneducated Uttar Pradesh voice, and it was obviously meant to be me, and we all knew, and that was more insulting than the voice itself. "'Oh, I'm in love with her, oh, she's the perfect woman, oh, I want to marry her and have a million retard kids, and then somehow nobody will ever find out what we did and we'll magically avoid prison.' You fucking idiots, no wonder you love each other. I'm going to sleep." Rudi marched off, continuing his tirade as he headed toward the bedroom.

You don't suddenly become a better person. He needed some time. He was a teenager after all.

And I was what? A twenty-four year-old saint? I had no right to judge him.

"I'm sorry about that," I said. I tried not to think about the prison part. I willed her not to ask.

"Did you actually say all that?"

"Not exactly."

"Did you mean it?"

"I like you. You know I do," I said.

I went for it.

Hang the world. Hang danger.

"I love you," I said, and it was worse actually saying the words and having her looking into my eyes just then than this whole situation—not the finger thing, granted, that was quite bad, but worse than being kidnapped and on the run, for sure.

"I love you too," she said, and God, my heart nearly exploded, like a Punjabi at an all-you-can-eat buffet, and I thought she was going to lean over and kiss me, but she pulled back and said, "Is there something you want to tell me? Something about you and Rudi?"

I looked away quickly. That was a mistake. When I looked back, I could see her earrings catching the light.

"About what?"

"How you know each other," she said, and touched my hand. "You know exactly what I mean."

So there it was. Finally. The moment of truth.

I had a choice. A final choice. I could stay silent, as I'd been doing since the day I was born, hiding away from the world. Or I could be honest. I could tell the truth. I could take a risk and trust someone else, trust this person with my secrets, with the truth, with my life.

I chose the second option.

"I ran a business," I said, looking down at my lap, "where I fixed the examinations of rich children and got them into top universities. I did it for Rudi, and then I came top. I don't know how I did, but I did, then I blackmailed his family to make money, and then I got kidnapped and so here we are."

"Oh," she said.

I carried on talking. There was nothing else I could do. I wanted to explain. I wanted her to understand. "I just wanted to make money out of all this, as much as I could. But then you came along. And then everything changed. I wanted more. I wanted you. But I knew if you ever found out, you'd leave, because that," and my voice, very pathetically, cracked, but just for a moment, "that's what everyone does." I was surprised to hear myself say it.

"Oh," she said.

"If you say oh again, Priya, I think I will be sick," I said, and looked up at her face.

She seemed disappointed. "I want you to promise me one thing," she said.

"Anything."

"You always tell me the truth from now on, understand? One more lie, Ramesh, and we are done. I will not stand for lies." There was a wildness in her eyes.

I nodded dumbly.

"Honestly, I figured it was something like that. And now that we can tell each other the truth, I can do this."

And then she moved forward and put her hand on the side of my face, and I knew exactly what she was going to do. My heart was beating like crazy.

She kissed me. Full on the lips.

Our faces moved apart.

"You knew?" I said.

"I knew there was something going on. I just wanted you to say it. I want you to trust me."

"But I'm corrupt," I said. "I'm crooked to the core. I'm a miscreant. I'm trouble."

"Yes," she said. "But you're not going to be doing any of that from now on, are you?"

I shook my head. "So you can only be with me if I'm totally pure and honest?"

She laughed. "No one is pure anymore. And that's not why I like you. I just do."

"Oh," I said.

"Ha, now you're doing it," she tutted. "You bloody men, you think you're all geniuses, all God's gift to womankind. My parents, I love them, but my God, all the time, 'marry, marry, marry, you can't be single when you're thirty,' as if that is the solution to all my problems. You fucking men, each one thinks he's Hrithik Roshan. I cannot stand you sometimes. You are weak and foolish!" She winked, then reached over and pinched my arm playfully.

"We are," I said, and put my hand on hers again. I was getting used to it. "Especially me." The stump of my pinkie finger throbbed, and I winced from the pain.

Priya looked at me with concern.

"Now that we're together, you'd better not get any other parts cut off. I need you whole."

I began to blush.

"So what exactly do we do now?" I exhaled.

"We need to make a plan," she said. "Step by step. What were you thinking?"

"Er," I said.

"You haven't had a plan up to this point?"

"Only in our heads. It changes from minute to minute."

"Not written and pinned down? That doesn't sound like the Ramesh I know. He's always so in control. Contracts, social media, errand-running." Priya smiled. "Come on then," she said. She grabbed my good hand and led me to her spare room.

We messed around. On her laptop, she made a PowerPoint,

and conjured up slide after slide of swooping transitions and GIFs and headings in Comic Sans. We laughed like children. We were drunk on intimacy. We sat close together. She rubbed my hands, held my wrists, kissed me, looked deep into my eyes, laughed at every stupid joke.

Then finally she tied her hair back in a scrunchy, put her glasses on, and stuck her tongue out of the corner of her mouth in concentration. "We need to get serious. God, this is just like when I was studying for my BComm," she said.

"Exactly the same. I'll wake the master," I said. He deserved as much of a say as I did.

I crept into the bedroom. I shook him awake, first slowly, then harder.

Rudi slept like my papa had, all angles and legs, poking into me from every way, kicking at me in the night, even when he was unconscious. It was only after whoring nights, when I'd been allowed back down from the roof, that Papa slept like a dead man, long and straight, like the girls at posture lessons at Sacred Heart, books on heads, catwalk-steady, always in control.

"Aargh, I'm awake, I'm awake," Rudi said, spluttering to life.

"Rudi," I said gently, "I'm sorry. I'm sorry for getting angry with you." Priya had made me very free and open with my emotions.

He held my arm. He was groggy.

"I'm sorry for shouting at you, Ramesh."

"I pushed you too hard," I said. "I didn't think enough about you. We can get away after all this is done. We have enough money. We can do what we want."

I could see his pupils glimmering in the dark.

"All is forgiven," he said.

"Let's go, we have a plan to make," I said.

Rudi was full of ideas. It was amazing what food and rest and the assurance of friendship could do. We all had a laugh. For the first time in days, the two of us were entirely carefree.

Our first step? We were decided. Contact Bhatnagar.

But how exactly?

"We'll kidnap her," said Rudi. I was so proud of him.

"Boys," said Priya quickly. "No. I'll do it. I'll tell her I want to be a whistleblower."

"Priya!" I said.

"No," said Rudi. "This is our mess. We'll solve it."

She gave us both a pitying look. "Why would Bhatnagar ever agree to go along with you? And, boys, your track record in kidnapping has not been so strong. I feel guilty. Oberoi was doing this under my nose and I didn't know. I want to help."

"But this is your career, your life," I said. "I can't do that to you. Rudi's right. We have to keep you out of it. There's a risk you could never work again."

"Then I'll just have to be a kept woman." She smiled and elbowed me in the ribs.

That shut me up.

On we went with the plan.

Get Abhi back. Get Oberoi back. Avoid prison.

We had a good night's sleep. Priya in her bedroom, Rudi and me fighting over the blanket in the study.

Early the next morning, Priya rang Bhatnagar.

She was so convincing on the phone. "They're cruel men, Ms. Bhatnagar. And only I can bring them down. They told me everything. I have documents, tapes, USBs. We have to meet soon, today, now," she said, pacing around the flat, her hair whipping from side to side, her feet dancing across the floor. What an actress. I was a little worried then that she was pretending to like me. But what idiot would do that?

They arranged to meet in a coffee shop in a mall, nice and anonymous. She pumped her fist as she hung up.

As we prepared to leave Priya's apartment, Rudi finished his cup of tea and began to laugh. I asked him what was going on, and he said, "When I was young, my darling mother would appear and give me a spoonful of sugar for good luck. That's the reason I'm so fat, a spoon of sugar every time I left the house. Your mother ever did that to you, Ramesh?"

"For the hundredth time, Rudraksh, I did not have a mother."

"Ah shit, dude," he said. "Sorry." Then, as if to make up, "How's the hand?"

"Never better," I said, and out he went into the corridor.

"I want to thank you," I told Priya as she locked up the apartment. We didn't know when, or if, we would be back. She held a little duffel bag in her hands.

"For what?" she said.

"For all of this. You could have walked away. If Bhatnagar says no, that's it, you're an accomplice. You're sacrificing yourself for me."

"Wouldn't you?" she said.

I nodded.

It was true. After so long, I had someone to destroy myself for. Her.

And Rudi, I supposed. He was growing on me.

She handed me the bag. "The moment I open this, you start taking pictures. Understand?"

"What is it?" I asked.

"Insurance," she said, and smiled.

I kissed her. What else do you do in those situations? I kissed my girlfriend, tossed my backpack over my shoulder, and then we stepped back into the world of knives and kidnappings and long-lost missing fingers.

FIFTEEN

When I was younger, the rich kids at school got a whole new wardrobe for Diwali, the poor ones fresh socks or shirts. I got nothing. Diwali annoyed my father. It meant spending money, on clothes, on sparklers, on whizz-bangs, on presents for ungrateful children, but more important he hated the idea of it. Diwali was far too optimistic for him. Victory for light over darkness, what a load of bullshit! His life had never gotten better. He prayed every morning, yes, but to gods who promised fire and destruction, retribution, heads chopped off.

I was thinking about the prick a lot more recently. It was the kidnapping and the beating up. You think your parents are just a source of shelter and slaps, and then you grow up and find out that you become them, not a perfect copy, but one of those pirated films where you can see people in the theater stand up and go to the toilet. If only I'd had a mother, I wouldn't be like this. I would have been half good, half bad; half monstrous psychopath villain, half educated boring man. An accountant, then.

We booked a cab for the three of us, Rudi, Priya, and myself, the strange family unit we had formed. The driver was being extra attentive, almost pleasant. He and his colleagues were slaves to the algorithm now. He asked no questions, had installed a tablet in the back, and applied the horn with added verve, as if to say, Don't you know what high-class fellows I've got in my cab? Priya saluted every light-bedecked temple, every church, every golden gurdwara as we went past. Very promising.

The mall where we were meeting Bhatnagar was a super-premium flagship affair on the Noida border. Most of the malls, opened in the early 2000s, had become a breeding ground for discount sari stores and cleaners who idly pushed around buckets of disinfectant, but the newest ones, like this one, were still the places to wave hello to the Sharmas from the country club. Portofino Galleria was one of the biggest in Delhi, populated at midday by diabetic retirees shopping for Diwali-discount Ray-Bans and graphite golf clubs.

Priya had arranged to meet Bhatnagar in the food court. Rudi and I followed on, a hundred meters behind.

Bhatnagar was dressed in jeans and a white shirt. She had waves of black hair with amber undertones. She looked like one of our actresses when they are photographed incognito on their summer holidays in London.

Priya sat down at her table and they began to talk. Rudi and I stood, partially hidden by a pillar, as close as we dared.

Bhatnagar listened, then stood up, then shook her head. I ducked farther back in case she saw us, and almost pushed Rudi into a potted plant.

Priya took the duffel bag, laid it on the table, and opened the zip.

I grabbed the phone from Rudi's hand, had a miniature scuffle with that silly screen-addicted millennial, and started taking as many photos as I could.

Priya was holding out a brick of cash. Bhatnagar looked betrayed. Priya said something, and Bhatnagar sat down. Priya began to point back in our direction. That was our cue. We moved forward. Bhatnagar stiffened as we approached, her back straight and still, her eyes watchful for further trouble.

"Rudi!" I hissed under my breath as we approached. "Remember to be humble!"

Rudi shoved past a table full of Romeos with hungry faces sharing a family dosa and scanning the food court for single women. They all smelled of Paco Rabanne, of course. He walked over to Bhatnagar and sat across from her. She did a quick double-take at his dress, but otherwise gave nothing away. Perhaps it was a normal situation for Central Bureau investigators to find themselves in.

I looked down at the cash. I flipped through it. The note at the top was real, but the ones below were demonetized, useless. Not that that would show up in the pictures. Any newspaper would kill for them. Anjali Bhatnagar, Queen of Clean, secretly corrupt. I nodded at Priya. Maybe she wasn't as innocent as I'd thought.

Rudi played his part. He started to beg.

"Ma'am," he said, his voice thick with emotion. "You must save us. Our producer arranged our kidnapping. Then he stole the ransom. He would have got us killed."

"Please, ma'am," I added, in a sort of waiter voice. "Only hope. Please save."

Priya gave me a kick under the table.

She explained the whole sorry situation. "Oberoi did everything he could to get Rudraksh Saxena out of the way. He arranged for an innocent young boy to be humiliated on national television just to set his plot in motion. He is directly responsible for Ramesh getting hurt." I waved my maimed hand.

"I also got hurt, yaar," said Rudi. "I am the number one target of a vast criminal conspiracy. Why does everyone keep forget—" He had to swallow his words as a server approached.

We ordered as if we were out on a shopping day trip, the three girls, and me, their peon. I had filter coffee. The others had ginger mochas, a Western invention with a glaze of Ayurveda that our middle classes had fallen for—what better way to show you were at once modern but also in touch with your roots, your culture? That was the business I should go into when all this was done, I thought.

"Why should I help you?" said Bhatnagar. "You bring me here on false pretenses. Priya here confesses straight out that you have committed academic fraud. You blackmail me. And I should help you?"

"People love to hate people like Oberoi," said Priya. "We've read the news stories about your career. You've made too many enemies. Oberoi is the perfect target. A corrupt, evil rich man trying to harm the Topper. A man you will apprehend single-handed. It'll get the country on your side, don't you see? Then you can get as many rich people for academic corruption as you like. But just not these two. Please. They're good people who made bad decisions."

If I hadn't been in love with Priya already, I would have fallen for her then.

I leaned in. "Also we won't email these blackmail photos to every newspaper in the country, please, ma'am."

"Do we have a deal?" said Priya quietly. "Inspector Bhatnagar? Do we have a deal?"

"Fine," Bhatnagar said and leaned back in her chair. Rudi and I almost gasped in relief.

She looked at us, at our clothes, at Rudi's makeup and wig, and shook her head with complete disbelief.

Then she made some phone calls.

They did not sound so fine. They sounded very much the opposite.

I looked at Priya. She laid her palm on my knee under the table to reassure me that all would be well, and I, very stupidly, felt instantly at ease.

"I'll set you up in a safe house," Bhatnagar finally said. "I can do very little else. I don't have as many friends as I used to. Then we'll deal with this man Sumit. Getting Abhi Aggarwal back will unlock the whole situation. Himanshu Aggarwal. God! He's an enemy you can't afford to make. He was on all the boards my ex wanted to be on, the charities, the golf, the sailing squadron. I always thought he was an idiot. Trust someone like him to be involved in this."

Did these people all know each other? Was that what it was like, being truly rich?

"And I won't get prosecuted?" Rudi asked. "I am not getting fucked," he added in most unladylike language. I gave him a kick, a loving one to remind him to draw less attention to himself in public.

Bhatnagar eyed him, and then me, with significant distaste.

"I promise," she said. "Your assistant producer here is a very persuasive young woman. You need to listen to her more and spend less of your time kidnapping people."

And blackmailing, I thought.

"If this hadn't gone to plan," said Rudi, "I was going to kid—"

"We must get going!" said Priya.

"Where did you come up with that plan?" I asked her as we left.

"A film. You know the one where Shah Rukh romances that girl young enough to be his granddaughter." She smiled. "Actually, that's all of them, isn't it?"

Later that day, when we were back at the apartment, a car ordered by Bhatnagar came to pick us up. It dropped us off at some nondescript flat in south Delhi, her department's safe house, she said. The place was emptier than a politician's promises, dusty from disuse, but, crucially, not full of people who wanted to kill us. The living room had large windows that looked out onto nothing. Little clouds of dirt pillowed up with every movement of our feet. Bhatnagar was there and she made phone calls to God knows who, arguing, shouting, cajoling, making deals with her superiors.

"We have a deal," she said about thirty minutes after her first call. "My bosses have given us time to get Oberoi. We'll have to move fast. You can trust me." She certainly looked impressive, a woman who could do anything, move mountains, make miracles happen. I was still cautious. I knew not to trust those who promised the earth, because they could still deliver very little.

"Are you sure about your people?" I asked. Bhatnagar looked affronted. Her father had probably been Indira Gandhi's ambassador to Indonesia. She was old money. She didn't backstab, she said. She didn't sell out. People had tried, and people had failed, to pay her and her team off. "We are incorruptible," she sniffed. "We're the Central Bureau of Investigation."

That was all we said to one another. If things went wrong, she could run to the West. She'd probably get a book deal for exposing the dark heart of India. We'd be the ones getting fucked. Again.

I sat next to Priya on the sofa. She could see the look of mistrust on my face.

"She's on our side, Ramesh, she will help us," she said.

"Nobody is," I said. "You know my worst client in the educational consulting business? Jatin Bishnoi. The crusading TV journalist? Mr. Social Conscience? He beat me. You know why? The results hadn't come out yet, so it wasn't that. It was because his kid had a nightmare, thought I'd cheated him, in a dream—in a dream, can you believe?—and just like that, I got pulled off the street, because his kid had a bad night's sleep."

I shouldn't have said anything, but it was this whole situation. It was Priya. She was having that effect on me. I was arguing, I was apologizing, I was showing myself to the world.

"I'm so sorry," she said. "But we have to trust her."

Rudi was off watching television. Priya and I sat and talked about trivial things. That seemed to be what you did when the world was after you and your heart had spent the last five days beating in your mouth. She held my hand in hers. All I could think was that I shouldn't have gotten involved in all of this, this education business. I should have become an Uber driver—and what, I thought, received abuse for two hundred rupees an hour, day after day, year after year?

Should I have worked in a call center, left at three every morning, earned five thousand measly Gandhis a month bullshitting Floridians that my name was Dan and there was a fault on their PC?

No, I had gone into exactly the right business. High pay, huge stress, followed by months of complete nothingness. All you had to be was clever, morally flexible, unmemorable, unthreatening, a fucking invisible man. A perfect fit.

And of course, I never would have met her.

She was talking about her family again, the future. Perhaps she might go back to university and do a master's. Maybe we would go abroad. She liked the look of Canada. She had never seen snow. Whatever she wanted was fine by me. I was happy to sit and listen. I willed myself to believe that we would make it.

"Thank you for saving me," I said when she had finished. "Back there. And in general. You're very good at that."

"I know," she said. "And modest too."

That night, Bhatnagar left and Rudi and I fought over the sofa. Priya slept in the bedroom, a blank marble-floored cube, a bed with white sheets, white walls, and unwired plugs.

All she had with her was a backpack, a phone, and a change

of clothes. All I had with me was a few knives, my phone, and the memory card containing Abhi's ransom video.

I couldn't help but feel sick about what I had drawn her into.

When Bhatnagar returned the next morning, she had bad news.

"I can't give you much. My bosses want me to do this alone. Your Oberoi has been making friends with politicians . . ."

"That prick," said Rudi.

". . . and my bosses are nervous. I'll work alone. It's not perfect, but it's something."

Her face was lined with worry, no matter how well she tried to hide it. We sat in the living room and talked against a background of thick gray morning fog pushing against the windows.

"The good news is that Aggarwal wants to help. I made him see sense. He realizes he's been fooled." She laughed. "That moron. Totally in over his head. His father must have been the one with brains. He just inherited the damn company. Oh, my ex worshipped the ground he walked on. 'He's so classy, Anju,' 'He knows everyone, Anju,' 'Flirt with him, Anju,' 'Fuck him, Anju, it'll be good for us.' My God!"

Priya began to snort, and Bhatnagar shrugged her shoulders.

"I thought you two boys were stupid, but this country has been breeding idiots lately!" She whistled. "This Oberoi fellow, another champion fool. Up to his eyeballs in debt. Political aspirations. So he decides to get you kidnapped and steal the ransom. Men!"

"Not all of us," said Rudi, and I thought, have you seen the collected works of Indian mankind, boss?

"We get the boy back, and then my bosses have allowed me a press conference. Oberoi may have political connections, but we have the celebrity Rudraksh Saxena. But we are alone, remember that. One word from the People's Party, and my bosses disown me, and you. Fucking typical," she added, under her breath. "It's all I can do."

Bhatnagar drove a government-issue Qualis to Aggarwal's farmhouse. She maneuvered this way and that, with the standard expensive government car insanity, swearing under her breath at slow-moving duffers, at idiot young men driving motorbikes the wrong way, at carts laden with fruit, the ones heroes always crashed into in the action films. Everyone moved out of her way, fearful of who sat behind those tinted windows, wondering which AK-47-toting Yale-dropout minister's son was out for blood that day.

We pulled up at the farmhouse. Bhatnagar told us to wait, then got out and walked over to the gate. She knocked sharply.

It opened quickly, and out came Himanshu Aggarwal himself.

No servants! No lackeys!

He moved forward to hug her, but Bhatnagar sidestepped his arms.

"So good to see you again, Anju," he said. "The boat club was it, last time?"

Bhatnagar gave him a false smile. She turned and waved at us.

We all went inside.

Himanshu Aggarwal was even more irritating the second time around.

"Boys, boys," he said, clasping us to his moist breast, doing the thing where he faked going to touch your feet in respect, and you stopped him and said, "Please, sir, you are older and wiser than me, there's no need."

"Boys, will you accept my apology?"

Fuck no, I thought, and looked at Rudi, who clearly felt the same.

"Yes, sir," we said in unison.

Then Pratap came into the room. I tried to rise. Rudi let out an involuntary grunt. My finger throbbed with pain. The last time we had seen him, he was trying to shoot us. Now he served us glasses of whisky, bitter, ice-cold, repulsive, unrefusable, well, unless you were Priya.

He looked as angry as ever, but he had to be nice and un-objectionable and wait on us without complaint. It was most enjoyable.

"Oberoi has tricked me. He has betrayed me. He has disap-peared. No one makes a fool of an Aggarwal," said Himanshu Aggarwal. His fingers had even more rings on them this time, retail therapy in action. "I forgive you for taking my boy. The idea seemed so simple when Oberoi explained it to me."

"How do you know him?" said Rudi.

"Socially. You know how it is."

Yes, of course I'll kidnap your star attraction, had a nice round of golf, did you? Standard upper-class behavior, no doubt. I had their level of money, nearly, but I would never have their tastes.

"Oberoi said he had a spot for my son on the show," Aggarwal said. "He said Abhi would surely win. And then Abhi got knocked out on the first question. Oberoi apologized to me a million times. He said the trick question was all your idea. He tried to overrule you."

"I didn't set him up," said Rudi. "I would never do anything like that." Just mocked him viciously and broke him down in front of tens of millions of people, but who cared about that?

"So Oberoi told me that I should abduct you. We would split the ransom. A nice little Diwali present for the both of us."

"Do you often go around arranging kidnap plots with people you barely know?" said Priya.

"He told me you were arrogant, out of control, that you deserved it," said Aggarwal.

"Maybe he was right about that," said Rudi, but Aggarwal carried on.

"He told me where you lived. We took you. It was all so simple. But then the ransom money didn't come. I phoned Oberoi and he said it had been refused. He said that I should cut some body parts off. And then, if still the money did not come, I should get rid of you."

"That shit," said Priya.

"It could happen to anyone, sir," said Bhatnagar, without even a hint of humor in her voice. "Who hasn't wanted to kidnap someone at some point?"

"Exactly, exactly," said Aggarwal, speaking quickly, as if he was trying to brush it under the carpet. "And Pratap is very sorry about the finger business. He had to throw it away. It was stinking up the place. Pratap, you are sorry, aren't you?"

Pratap, standing behind his master, tried to pretend he had not heard.

"Pratap!" Aggarwal said. He was watching Bhatnagar for a reaction. She was looking unimpressed.

Pratap gave me a look of disgust. "Sorry," he said.

That was what money could do, I thought. That was what millennia of social control and economic stratification could get you. A forced apology! Groveling! Such power! It was thrilling.

"Anything else?" Aggarwal asked me.

I wanted revenge. I wanted to hurt Pratap. He was going to get away with it, with hurting me, but as I sat there, knowing how much shit we were in, how much farther we had to go, how much I wanted to run away with Priya, I realized that anything rash I did now would just complicate matters. I let it go. No good would come of me going for revenge.

I shook my head.

Aggarwal howled a little longer about how his family had been taken advantage of. These rich people and their problems, family honor and offshore accounts, they are far too much for me. Give me a little money and the love of a good woman any day.

I honestly, truly, for real this time, had gotten ahead of myself.

It is very easy, when you are listening to an idiot drone on, and sharing secret looks with the woman sitting by your side as you laugh into your drink, and life seems so perfect, to think that everything is going to be all right, that all you have to do is find one psychopath producer and bring him to justice, and that soon all will be well.

It is never that easy.

"We've set up the sting to get your son. He's being held by a man called Sumit Gaikwad," explained Bhatnagar, bringing

Aggarwal's pity session to a close. She had used her contacts and managed to find Sumit's whereabouts in a few hours. "Tomorrow, nine a.m., by Humayun's Tomb. We'll give you a bag of money, Mr. Aggarwal, you drive there alone, and we come in and save you and your son."

"Capital idea, Anju," said Aggarwal, and Bhatnagar seemed to use all her self-control not to shudder. "Capital. Himanshu Aggarwal has never been afraid of a little danger. Pratap, serve our guests some namkeen."

Pratap clanked over to us again, bearing mini samosas and spooning out those awful fluorescent green and red chutneys. He was a very multitalented servant, almost better than me. From tea to torture, he could do it all.

Bhatnagar went off to take a phone call. I strained to listen, and overheard talk of press conferences and manhunts and bartering for more departmental resources.

Aggarwal was like a train. He couldn't be stopped—not an Indian train then, but a Japanese one. We pretended to be interested.

Bhatnagar returned, drank four cups of tea, and tried to look amused. When we heard something egregiously stupid, Priya and I rolled our eyes at each other. It was a better bonding experience than the whole kidnapping-revenge-blackmail thing.

Aggarwal changed the subject every five minutes, whiplashing in different directions. The differences between the castes, the original homeland of the Aryan race, Ayurvedic treatments for cancer and Parkinson's, they all got an airing. He raised his voice when he did so, like he was reading headings from a book.

I watched him. Then I realized what he was doing.

The second that Rudi looked bored, or Priya looked away, Aggarwal changed the subject. He raised his voice to regain our attention, and thus satisfied, off he went on another tangent. He was scared of boring us. Him!

How pathetic!

At the end of it, he was an Aggarwal. It was his name. He was expected to do great things. Your name is always your destiny. You can tell a man's life, his opinions, the contents of his stomach, his future, his very dying day by his name. I am a Kumar. There are twenty million of us. Nothing is expected of us but to shit and die.

The day wore on. We listened to Aggarwal, we sat, we worried about Oberoi and Abhi and everything else. We were waiting for Bhatnagar to organize things, to deal with the Indian bureaucracy. It was a wonder we didn't wait for weeks.

At least we ate like kings. I'm a Delhi boy through and through.

Priya and I drank coffee long past midnight, into the morning hours. She had her faults. A fondness for Bengali food. A love of K-pop. She preferred Aamir Khan to Akshay Kumar. Nothing we couldn't get over in time.

We slept in comfort. Egyptian cotton, four anti-mosquito plug-ins per room, en suite bathrooms, rainwater-effect showers, soft towels. Priya reapplied my bandage and gave it a kiss when she was done.

We slept in the same bed, me and her, for the first time. There was no funny business. We were too exhausted by the constant churn of danger to even think of anything romantic. We just lay twisted together, our limbs and our lives entwined.

It was absurd, me and her. It made no sense. She should have been marrying some arsehole IITian and spending the rest of her life in semi-alcoholic Californian luxury, twenty acres and an almond grove. What was she doing with me?

Of course, as I stroked her hair as she lay on my chest, I was stupid enough to say it. "What do you see in me?" or something like that. I heard her reply, felt the movement of her jaw against my chest.

"What do you like about *me*?" she said.

"What don't I like! You're kind," I said. "Patient, understanding, funny, you're good at everything you do. I feel different when I see you, my day feels better, my heart lifts."

"That's why I like you too," I heard her say.

What a dirty trick! A dirty Western trick!

Well, at least no beatings for me that night, no sir!

SIXTEEN

We were down the highway from Humayun's Tomb. Nice place. Like all these tourist traps, I have never been. God knows Claire gave me enough shit for not caring about the patrimony of my nation, Fatehpur Sikri and the Koh-i-Noor and all that bakwas.

The Muslims are like the Christians. They do monuments to the dead, graves, memorials, and sepulchers. The Hindus have it right, I'd told Claire, once you're burned you're gone, and maybe your relatives or co-workers run an advert in the paper. But the Christians and Muslims, they tend graves, put flowers on them, they ask themselves: Am I visiting enough? Am I thinking the right thoughts? All you do is marinate yourself in the bastard past.

Islam is out of fashion at the moment, with the government, with the people, but that doesn't stop people turning up to the things the Muslims built and claiming them for their own and wasting their children's afternoon while they are doing it.

Everyone knows the water is running out, knows it right in their gaand. Everyone thinks the Pakistan shit is about freedom and religion. Nonsense. It's about water. Culture? Patriotism? Self-determination? Those are Western issues. Give me an honest fight about natural resources any day.

First we fuck Pakistan. Then we'll fuck each other, region against region, city against city, Dravidians against Aryans, the grudge match we've been delaying for five millennia. Every country will do it eventually. We'll just do it first, like how the Vedas invented the nuclear bomb and the computer, and the white man, that laggardly shit, took four millennia and an Enlightenment to catch up.

The tomb sat squat near the river, which was ugly and brown and smelled like death. From our vantage point, it loomed in the background over rusted chemical pipes, large concrete biers, abandoned shipping containers, long-dead fires. In ten years they'd probably build a prestige shopping destination and call it the Babur Arcadia.

It was an easy place to observe: one slip road off and back onto the highway, traffic going only in one direction, a giant trap, Bhatnagar said. We would watch the handover from the Qualis, which was partially hidden behind a motorway arch. The dashboard of the car was festooned with Hindu gods, who looked mildly perturbed by the Islamic desecration of their beloved, holy, filthy River Yamuna.

Bhatnagar sat in the front seat and watched Aggarwal, who'd driven there in his SUV, through a pair of binoculars. She was dressed in her uniform, tan khaki like the police. Pratap sat beside her and said nothing.

"Aggarwal is reaching the handover point," said Bhatnagar.

The air was cold and made us cough. The traffic above us thundered along.

"Just a few more seconds," she breathed.

Priya had her eyes on the foggy horizon, fingers gripped white on mine. We couldn't see a thing out there. Potholes and reeds and massive lumps of abandoned concrete.

"Soon, soon . . . now!" said Bhatnagar.

She applied the accelerator and we gunned out across damp grass and marshy banks, out onto the concrete ramparts that had been built to stop the city sinking into the toxic filth of the river, where broken cranes towered above us and huge warehouses stood open, gutted, the windows blind from breaking.

Bhatnagar had Sumit in handcuffs within seconds. He turned his face away from mine. His eyes were red from lack of sleep, and he looked more pathetic than I did when I was a kid. Pictures were taken, for evidence, for the press conference. You could see Bhatnagar constructing the lies she would need to tell. Chai was consumed from thermoses in big wet gulps.

Rudi hugged Priya.

Priya hugged me.

Abhi hugged his father.

Pratap glowered at me.

Aggarwal wept tears of joy, clutching the bag of ransom money between his son and his chest, probably hoping he could run away with it. He cried with meaty wails, "My boy, my boy," his cummerbunded girth totally overwhelming his kid, along with his many protestations of eternal love. "I'll even donate to Congress now," he said. My God! No need to go that far, man, there's no crime in the world serious enough that its price is giving Rahul Gandhi money!

See what effect I was now having on people's lives? I was bringing on reconciliations and love. Admittedly through terror and violence, but still. I allowed myself a little pride.

Sumit sat on the ground weeping miserably, his sports vest covered in dirt and shit. Under any other circumstances I would have found it funny, but now I felt guilty. He had come to me, he had begged me for help, and I, a man who had made it big, had done nothing.

"This kidnapping is the worst thing I have ever done," he said.

"Why did you do it?" I asked him. Priya was standing beside me and gave him a pitying look.

"I was desperate. Please. We came from the same place. All I needed was a little help. I needed money. I came to you, and what did you do? Nothing."

"Is that true?" Priya said.

"He got rich and mighty," said Sumit, his voice growing even more pathetic. He saw a pretty girl, and he had to put it on. "He forgot about his old friends, the little people. Like me."

"Ramesh," Priya said.

"I'm going to give young Sumit here a job," I said. "I've changed. That was the old me." And quite bizarrely, I seemed to be telling the truth. It didn't even matter that Sumit was smirking out of Priya's sight.

He saw sense. "I am sorry for my earlier insolence, Ramesh bhai," he said. "I should never have betrayed you," and whether he meant it or not—for who really knew with people like that, people like me?—I nodded my head in silent acceptance. Rudi and I picked him up and deposited him in Bhatnagar's jeep.

A fisherman passed by on the river down below, and barely looked at the police truck on the bank. He simply threw his net in the air as if he'd seen enough deals, executions, and double-crosses to last a lifetime.

We thought we were in the clear. We were about to say good-bye to Aggarwal and do all the little pleasantries.

And then, with the door of his SUV jutting open, he said, "Do you think I've forgotten?" He gave us both a venomous look. His rings glinted in the morning light. "Regardless of the double-crossing, you still humiliated my son on national television."

Yes, we did.

The bloody rich.

"What are we going to do about it?" said Aggarwal.

What exactly?

I started to speak. Always me with the answers and the plans and the—

"The video, of course," said Rudi. "Ramesh, do you still have it?"

Where did that come from?

I went over to the car, reached into my backpack, past the knives, and pulled out the memory card. Rudi held out his hand and took it, and then walked over to Aggarwal. He pushed it into his hands and gave a little bow.

"I hope that will be all, Mr. Aggarwal," he said. "Maybe we can have Abhi appear on our show one of these days. A grand reconciliation. I'll have my people talk with yours." Then he turned and gave me a wink. That little shit.

Pratap glared at me. If there was one thing that upset me, it was that I had not been able to establish a rapport with him. We were both men of the world, forced to do things we didn't want to by forces out of our control, so very similar really . . . All right, I'm joking.

"Capital," said Aggarwal. "Your secret will go with me to the grave."

He closed the door of his car, drove off in a cloud of self-obsession.

I watched the men who had beaten and tortured me leave without any punishment at all.

Politics. The greater good. Maturity. I was getting sick of it. Priya gave me a reassuring hug as we walked back to the jeep.

One complication down. Many to go.

"We need to hold the press conference tomorrow," said Bhatnagar. "Get our story out. Start a manhunt for Oberoi, hope we catch him before he's stupid enough to do anything."

We drove back to the safe house. I promised Sumit he'd be developing Rudi's personal fragrance line after all this was over.

"Thank you, bhai," he said. "I knew we would be partners one day."

I slept soundly that night, safe in Priya's arms.

And then the next morning, our lives changed in ways we could never have imagined.

SEVENTEEN

Rudraksh Saxena is Pak agent, says producer.

Fatherfucking unbelievable.

Oberoi was plastered like a windshield-spattered bug all over the TV channels and websites, with giant photographs of him and senior politicians hugging and being garlanded and doing pious namastes in different poses.

We had been back at the safe house, enjoying a nice relaxing morning, congratulating ourselves a little after successfully dealing with Aggarwal. We were breakfasting on coffee, juices, and muffins, like we were in some nineties American sitcom. (Of course I have watched them, you cannot understand half of these Western jokes without them. Is it the last thing holding the West together? When the last memory of *Friends* has gone, will they turn on each other and finally have the civil war they have been itching for?)

We turned on the TV. Just the usual, fifteen people on split screen denouncing some Western actress who had named her cat India.

And then . . .

"New Delhi," shouted the female reporter. She was screaming at a thousand words a minute, so it was either a celebrity's nudes being leaked, Katrina Kaif getting cast in the next James Bond, or something about Pakistan. "Shashank Oberoi, producer of *Beat the Brain*, alleges today that Rudi Saxena is an ISI agent. In league with him is his manager, this man"—insert zoomed in, pixelated, cropped, utterly unrecognizable Instagram image—"Ramesh Kumar, aka Umar Chaudhury, a captain in the subversion division of Pakistani intelligence. We will share more news as we get it."

We sat openmouthed, staring at the television.

"That lund," said Rudi.

So that was where the bastard had gone to. You had to give him credit. Three days, and look what he'd managed.

I looked at Priya. Her face was whitening-cream-advert pale. This was it. I was finally exposed. Our future was gone.

I willed myself to pretend that it was going to be all right.

"It'll be fine," I said. "We'll get through this."

"You're famous now, Ramesh," said Rudi, trying to keep a brave face. "Congratulations."

A news conference followed shortly after the breaking news.

Oberoi, flanked by the usual saffron-garlanded politicians, sat before a gang of photographers grappling for space. White walls, tube lights, linoleum, and wall-hangings celebrating the festive season.

He read out a statement, stopping every sentence for a gulp of water, and giving pathetic, choked-sob stares to each of the eight television cameras, from left to right and back again.

"I was tricked." Sob. "My patriotism was abused." Sob. "Just because I wanted to celebrate"—so you get it, the dramebaaz was in full flow—"the academic excellence of this country. They threatened me every day. I had to speak out. When they realized what was going to happen, the ISI orchestrated a fake kidnap to extract their agents. Then they tried to kill me. Their other controller, Hassana Ali"—no prize for guessing whose picture was held up here; they had to use a shot of her on a night out, for that was the only way a Pakistani agent could ever have tricked us, through glamour and seduction—"who was working as my producer, also tried to turn me into a double agent against the country I love. In this festival of lights, our enemies wished to shroud our country in darkness."

Respectful nods from the politicians. Manly back-slaps. Oberoi continued. He had to; his country needed him to say what had to be said. He smoothed his moustache. His hair had turned streaky with gray, which made him look like he'd undergone the second-act mental collapse that mothers do in films—the ones where their kids have married spunky Punjabi girls and put the family fortune in peril.

"But they figured wrong. I love this country. I could never harm it. Not for all the money they offered, not for the houses or the yachts. My love for nation, for tradition, for community is stronger than any fortune."

He finished. The light went out of his face. He did a half bow to the cameras. The flanking politicians nodded. I wondered if they knew or cared what the truth was. They moved like twins, batting away questions, waving their meaty forearms, their lips sprouting spit and "no comment." They had black hair, distended stomachs, and their four eyes perpetually looked into the middle distance of a glorious Vedic future based on mass conversions and respect for elders on WhatsApp groups.

The horrendous pixelated picture of me floated up on-screen again. Umar Chaudhury. It could have been anyone, the eyes and mouth three dark depths, like the Black Hole of Calcutta. Priya's photo was of her in some bar. She would be the queen of the Pakistanis on Twitter by now, the masturbation material of a hundred thousand horny uncles from Gujranwala to Gwadar, the foxy lady agent who had humiliated the great enemy.

"I need to ring my parents," Priya said, when the broadcast had finished and the invited panelists began jabbering about subversion. Her call seemed to take an eternity to connect, but finally she could say, "Mama, Papa, something terrible has happened. Don't believe what you see. Please go to Uncle's. Don't ask questions. Please just go!"

She wept on my shoulder afterward. I held her as she shook. "I'm so sorry," I said again and again.

I made myself confident again. I made myself play the part. "You should move to Pakistan," I said, when she had stopped and my shirt was sodden. "Hassana, I'm telling you, you've got a hell of a career ahead of you there." She looked up at me, her grim expression turned to a smile for the merest second, and that was more than enough.

I put my thumbs to her eyes and rubbed the tears from them.

I wanted to tell her that I wished I'd never brought her into all of this. That we'd manage it somehow. We'd escape somewhere, somewhere foreign and clean and boring, like Minnesota, and never look back. We'd have three children and nobody would ever hurt us, and we'd go sailing in our boat at the weekends and eat corn dogs by the score.

But I knew that would be a lie.

Bhatnagar returned to the safe house ten minutes later. "This place isn't safe anymore," she said as she came in. "The politicians will be looking for us. We have to assume that my department is compromised. I couldn't get one morning of peace with these people around. In my next life, I promised myself I'd steer clear of the rich. We'll go to my house. It'll give us some time. Let's walk to the nearest market and order a taxi from there," she added.

"Is there anything you can do for my parents?" Rudi said, and quite suddenly he began to cry, standing alone in the middle of the room.

Bhatnagar didn't seem to know what to do. She bit her lip in pity. She slowly crossed over to him, held him, hugged him.

"Where are they?" she said, her hand rubbing his back.

"Norway, I think," he blubbered.

"I can get a message through. They need to stay in Europe for as long as possible."

She pulled out her phone, and made the call. I went to Rudi and put my arm around him.

I really had been wrong about him.

We put on our outfits and wigs, the synthetic hair stiff with dried sweat, Rudi's clothes wrinkled and stained with dirt. At least with Priya's help his makeup looked better than my juvenile but heartfelt attempts.

It was becoming such a part of my life that I almost looked forward to it. Glasses. Wig. Sari for Rudi.

Priya hid under a shawl. Bhatnagar donated a pair of sunglasses. She looked impossibly vain. People would stare, but at least she would be unrecognizable. I said nothing to her.

Anything out of my mouth would be a lie, and what would that make me?

As we left, we squeezed each other's hands, and that was enough.

Outside, there was a riot going on. A full-scale free-for-all. Threats, oaths, everything. And all because of us. They must have been sitting there, these men, women, and children, watching the broadcast in incredulity in coffee shops, in their homes, and burst out onto the street.

There are riots in this country at the drop of a hat. We are primed and ready, and what do you need but a few sticks and rocks, and young men fired by millennia of poverty with no end in sight?

We were in a fairly rich neighborhood, though. There were not meant to be riots. Up and down the main market, a crowd bristling with bats shouted, "Down with Pakistan!" "Down with Islam!" "Down with Saxena!" Placards had appeared with mysterious speed, bearing photos of me and Rudi.

I heard snatches of conversation as we moved through the crowd. "I never trusted him," said an aunty, skin the color of gulab jamun, watching from her auto, stopped both by traffic and because its driver had joined the riot. "He always seemed false to me," said her friend, blotting her face with a sodden handkerchief. When you have lost the aunties, you have lost India.

It was a few days before Diwali, so everyone was primed for a little madness and had bought their fireworks already. I tell you, this country cannot plan space satellite launches or solar energy farms or infant vaccination, but when it comes to festivals, the phooljhadis, the patakas, the food, they are all taken care of many moons in advance with military precision.

Young boys, blind with anger, were lighting rockets and sparklers and letting off flash-bangs. Our lungs filled with saffron and red powder as we tried in vain to find a cab. Dark skin, light skin, young, old, Brahmin and Shudra, united in hatred of us. What socialism and development policy had not done, Ramesh Kumar had accomplished.

Families who usually wouldn't be able to get near the neighborhood were using the riot as an excuse to see how the other half shopped. They went in with upturned noses to the stores that barred their way normally, and the guards let them pass, the threat unsaid that any one of their new visitors might start torching the place if they were denied entry, might shout out to the crowd that a Pakistani owned this place, that they had seen a picture of Imran Khan on the wall or a hot beef samosa behind the sales counter.

We moved away from the market, clearly no place to hail a cab. The street scene would be mirrored throughout Delhi, throughout India, ten thousand times over. That hatred could power the whole country for a century if you could store it somehow.

No one had recognized us. The disguises were still working. At least one of my stupid plans had played out as it should. Rudi straightened his clothes as we moved away from the main strip. "People were fucking groping me, yaar, fucking again," he said, with disgust on his face. "Do all men do that?"

Priya and Bhatnagar nodded.

"Oh," he said.

We moved down toward an enclave or a colony or something posh-sounding, and managed to book a cab. Bhatnagar was hyper-vigilant. Everyone approaching us was a threat, every scowl of every street sweeper, every car that moved too quickly or braked too hard. Her head was twitching like a Parsi finding a hole in his accounts.

When it arrived, the cab could barely move because of the hubbub. The driver had to get out and herd the people out of his way, and we had to listen to his purple-faced complaints about the traffic and how the city seemed to have lost control, all the way to Bhatnagar's place.

Her house was gigantic. If someone had a house in Delhi, you automatically assumed they were rich, but hers was on a different level. Green vines climbed the walls of the courtyard, a forest of plants sat fat and regal in terracotta pots, wooden shutters with intricate designs dotted the walls, three, maybe four floors.

"Aadarsh and I were going for a haveli, with a modern twist," she said.

"I'm sure it was all you. You have such wonderful taste," said Rudi, dragging his sari off to reveal a sodden T-shirt underneath. "Such an oasis," he added with a sour face. "A beautifully curated retreat from the cares and worries of the modern—"

"Can we please see the news?" I said, and Bhatnagar led us through large French doors into a living room, past sweet-smelling tapestries and frantic modern art, maybe even the real deal. Her tasteful furniture no doubt was sourced from the poorest artisans giving traditional Indian designs a modern twist from their roofless shacks in Odisha.

We collapsed in front of the TV. We learned very little. That was usual. People thought I was a demon. That was not.

Much empty discussion was raging. We had become a diplomatic incident. Retired Pakistani generals on blocky Skype calls were disavowing their nation's part in the Saxena affair, Saxgate, #PakExamScandal.

"So we need to kidnap Oberoi, right?" said Rudi after a few minutes. He looked at all of us. "We know that's what's going to happen. Priya will make all sorts of humane, liberal statements. Bhatnagar, you'll talk about the rule of law. But we know what we have to do." He dared us to defy him. We said nothing. "Do you have a computer, Ms. Bhatnagar? In the library? I'm going to go watch some videos. Come and get me when you guys have grown some balls."

"He's right," I said, but only after he left.

"He's not," said Bhatnagar, tapping her fingers against her jeans. "I swore to uphold the constitution of this country. I swore to defend it against its enemies. There's nothing in our laws that makes kidnapping legal."

"I don't think anyone else got that message," I said.

"We have to play dirty," said Priya. "There's nothing else I can see." She and Bhatnagar shared a look. They had been talking while Rudi and I bickered the past few days, while we shot shit about food, about Manchester United, about TV series, about pretty much anything that men will talk about instead of the issue at hand.

"There has to be another way," said Bhatnagar, but Priya shook her head gently, with the sort of insistent reasonableness that overcame all opposition. Our kids ... her kids wouldn't ever be able to say no. She would guilt-trip the shit out of them.

Bhatnagar made calls and tried to figure out which of her men were still trustworthy. The TV blared on. Even the BBC was talking about us, although they made it seem one of those crazy India stories, *What are the bloody brownies doing now?*

Priya leaned against me. She started playing with my hair, which was tangled and wiry from the heat.

"You smell terrible," she said, and snuggled against my arm. I didn't know how or why it had happened, but I accepted it. I had never faked any exams about women.

We had coffee. Her face was hidden behind her mug. Her hand was in mine throughout. I felt very adult then, like a man is supposed to, something I never understood, something to do with aftershave and taxes and doing laundry.

For dinner, we ate Lebanese, and wondered what the hell we were going to do.

EIGHTEEN

It was a simple, suicidal plan. But when a whole country is against you, and you have only one senior civil servant on your side, what else can you do?

We would make our move on a Saturday morning, everyone hungover from Friday's whisky and imported wine.

We would break into the People's Party headquarters.

I would break into the People's Party headquarters.

They were drunk with power right now, everyone was licking their lunds round the clock. They had turned India into what seemed like one mass riot from Kargil to Kanyakumari that they could direct toward the houses of liberal journalists and NGO heads with degrees from Harvard. They would be distracted, signing TV deals and film rights and getting their interns to suck them off. I would take Oberoi, force him to confess on live TV, and everything would be right in the world.

I said it was a simple plan. I didn't say it was a good one.

We were running out of time. Sooner or later someone would notice that Bhatnagar's departmental house had been getting a lot of use in the last few days, far in excess of what any educational investigator usually required. That someone would ask questions, because they wanted to drag her down a caste or two, and she would be exposed, and then we would all be going to prison for the rest of our lives, because once you are in there for one reason, you will be kept in for any. We had to strike first.

On TV, the students were rioting. They were thrilled that Rudi had turned out to be a Pakistani agent. "He has shown the false value we place on education in this country," said a man with rainbow-colored hair and a clipped boarding school accent. The People's Party and their saffron-robed followers had turned up to counter-protest. The students were waving Pakistani flags, and there was punching and screaming and throwing of plastic chairs—pre-Diwali festivities, like I said.

Bhatnagar came back that afternoon and described the layout of the headquarters of the People's Party to me. She had not come up with a better plan than Ramesh Kumar. I blame her limited Brahmin imagination, or maybe the long reign of the Nehru–Gandhi dynasty. They have robbed all these do-gooding types of their initiative.

"Office block, Lutyens Delhi, lots of guards, impossible to get into without capture," she said. "You'll have to be quick, Ramesh."

"You mean Captain Umar Chaudhury, the James Bond of Pakistan," I joked. I wasn't even resigned anymore. This was my life now, stupid, dangerous stuff. What did a little more peril matter?

"She's right. The media has nothing but a blurred photo of you," said Rudi. "You break in, you capture Oberoi, then you either walk out with him or you call Bhatnagar and she can pretend to arrest you if things go wrong."

I should have sworn at him, but I was all class now. I gave a polite, venomous cough. He was not the one who was meant to be coming up with ideas. He was not meant to be taking control of the situation and feeling morally superior about his intelligence. That was my job. How fast they grow up these days!

Bhatnagar outlined exactly how I was going to carry out the plan. It was original, at least, and very cheap. "Then we break into the studio, show the world the truth, and help you avoid prison, Ramesh."

"Just me?" I said.

"You see . . ." she said.

"Why the hell would I be the only one going to prison?" I asked.

"Well, Mr. Kumar," said Bhatnagar, "you were paid money to falsify exam results. You have broken the law."

"So did he!" I said, pointing to Rudi.

"I am just saying," said Bhatnagar, "that you're most in danger. They're not sending the Topper to prison, he can always find a way to get out, but you, they'll get you, on kidnapping, on extortion, on the whole industrial system of academic impersonation that you've been running for the last six years."

"Please, everyone!" said Priya. "Can we get back to the plan? Ramesh, we will all make sure you won't go to prison."

"I am not going to go to prison!" I said.

"You and I will go to the People's Party headquarters, Ramesh," said Bhatnagar. "We will abduct Mr. Oberoi. Priya and Rudi must go to the studio. Their faces are everywhere now. There they will gather your production team and coordinate a very special broadcast of your show. We will bring Mr. Oberoi, and then we will unmask him, live on television."

"But Ramesh gets put in harm's way most," said Priya.

Bhatnagar stayed silent.

"That's not fair," said Priya. "It's not his fault any of this happened."

It was clearly my fault that all of this had happened.

I watched the faces around the room trying to come up with some alternative. But there wasn't one. Priya was wrong. This was all my fault.

"No, Priya," I said. "They are right. I have to see this through. Nobody else can go the places I can go. Nobody can move unseen like I can. I have to do it."

Bhatnagar was visibly relieved.

Rudi and I nodded at each other.

After we finished, I went off with Priya. I held her close to me, and this was almost the most unbelievable part of the whole situation, can you fucking believe it, me and this girl, like I'd ended up with Juhi Chawla, absolutely amazing.

Another kidnapping! I was becoming a pro at it. I was even thinking of writing a guide. It's a difficult business, and even harder to make much profit from. You need transport, reliable, fast, unmemorable; water, food, soundproofing, medical gear; a conveniently located series of hideouts, each with communications facilities; most important, you need a plan. Of course, every kidnap I'd been part of—two so far, and who knew how many more to come—had had none of this, just idiots doing desperate things, but as Bill Gates says, you need to know failure before you can know success. Or maybe that was Adolf Hitler.

Our motivational calendars do not care much for proper attribution or morality.

If only Claire could see me now. All that effort she must have expended, dragging her weak body around, short of breath, knowing she was seriously ill but never telling another soul, her breaking voice begging her friends for work, for a life, for anything for her little boy who had nothing.

I remembered the weight of her body while I supported her over puddles and across streets, the way she brushed the hair out of my eyes when we reached the safety of our rickshaw, willing me to know that it was all going to be all right.

What would she make of the man I had become? In dark evenings at the chapel, on days when Dharam Lal had humiliated her, she would beg forgiveness in a soft voice, light candles, sweep floors. Days would go by where not another soul would talk to her save me. People would move away when she sat at tables. There would always be a gap between her and anyone else, and her soft shuffle would reduce rooms of girls to embarrassed silence.

All because of me.

I had wanted to run away so many times, to save her from me, but had never had the courage to face the world without someone to tell me that I was special and that I mattered and that I was so much better than the circumstances of my birth. Was that so bad?

I still felt like a coward.

What had she suffered and died for?

For this?

She had seen a better future for me, one where I wasn't at the mercy of higher powers, where I didn't have to take what the world threw at me. I had risen far higher than she could have imagined. But this country doesn't like that. There's only so far a boy like me is meant to go.

They would make me pay somehow. I knew it. I went forward all the same.

NINETEEN

The only plausible way to get into the People's Party building was to pretend to be a journalist, and the only way to do that was to pretend to be one who already existed. The saffrons might have been crazy, but they weren't stupid. Some little greaseball was always going to give me the once-over, a search on the internet, a check on Twitter.

How did we find the perfect journalist? Did we scour the newspapers of India for one brave soul committed to truth and justice and win him over to our cause?

No.

We searched for journos who looked like me. Non-liberals, non-commies, of course, just your run-of-the-mill gossip ones who shared an unfortunate resemblance to one Ramesh Kumar. There were more than a few. Me with longer hair, me with a moustache, me with glasses. The one we settled on was called Utsav Mehta, a film columnist with a million shitty pieces about Kangana's latest outburst and Kareena's new post-pregnancy bod.

Then we got Bhatnagar—well, me— to message him on Facebook.

I read your article on 5 Top Celebrity Moms, I wrote. *You are a great up-and-coming Indian journalist. Maybe we can meet to discuss sources and . . . more.*

Mehta bit like a goat on its mother's teat. Two minutes—*ping!*

Wow, so quick, and so handsome too. Hopefully you are not quick at other things! Want to meet up for chat? Priya sat by me and contributed the most ludicrous lines she could think of, driving young Utsav crazy with lust.

Bhatnagar checked in, just to see we weren't doing anything too bad, allowing herself to chuckle after she read a line about what cup size Mehta preferred—coffee, of course. He wanted selfies too, and we wrote that it would be better for him to get them in person.

He turned up thirty minutes later at the gate, our little Romeo, panting with anticipation, glasses rubbed to shining, hair gelled like a lychee, and deodorant applied for the first time in years.

Kidnap!

I tied him up and stuffed him in a second-floor bedroom as soon as he got inside.

I let him marinate for an hour, then went in to tell him what I wanted.

"How much does it pay?" he asked after I'd set out my story. He didn't give a shit about Pakistan.

Straight to business, dick deflated, knew when to give up. Not like me.

"A lakh. All you have to do is stick to a story about being tortured into aiding us."

"Five."

"Deal," I said. I'd been robbed. Five lakh for a day's work, what a world. "Think of the article, huh? What a fucking story."

He nodded. "And I could sell the film rights. You're fucking Umar Chaudhury."

"You'll be rich, bhai."

I took his glasses and his media card and his phone, rang the People's Party and arranged an interview for Saturday. I was squeezed in at eleven. Oberoi was a busy boy.

I was a good captor. Fan in the room, bottled water, TV on the cartoon channel.

Mehta didn't struggle.

I watched over him. Let him talk.

He was so rarely listened to that he went on and on. Nobody ever consulted him. Nobody needed his advice. His life was an endless scraping of Twitter feeds for content. He blathered, he described every detail of his existence, how he was ignored, how he was taken advantage of, for who knew when next someone would talk to him? He needed the contact, did not want it to end. He could not control himself, and his voice grew higher as he spoke with childlike enthusiasm about Marvel, wrestling, and octopus-based anime.

I feel sorry for everyone, that's my fucking problem.

This Mehta fellow worked nonstop, seven days a week, for people who'd replace him in a second. I was giving him a career here. He'd be on cable news every night for a year, speeches and talks and symposia. He might just get a chance with the women then.

I left him.

For the rest of the day, I couldn't think. I couldn't eat. I couldn't speak, but then none of us could. No more jokes, no more laughter. The enormity of what we had to do stopped our tongues. That night, I kept my eyes shut and waited for Priya to fall asleep, and then breathed in every detail of her that I could.

The next day, I said my goodbyes. Rudi and I shook hands.

"See you in a few hours, Ramesh," he said.

"You're a good dude," I said, "at heart, at the end of it, deep down, below all the—"

"Yes, all right, Ramesh."

I hugged Priya. There was too much to say.

I caught a well-battered taxi from the local market. Bhatnagar would follow in her own car. When I told him the destination, the driver, gods aplenty on the dashboard, turned around and said, "Sir, are you trying to get fucked or something?"

"Pretty much," I said, and he drove on.

The journey took an hour. The whole time I could see Bhatnagar in the rearview mirror, trying to keep up.

Outside the building, in a gigantic snake, stood a crowd of pilgrims, supplicants, business owners, license needers, heading straight to the very source of power, Saffron Central. The lobby was designed in the old Raj gymkhana style, with fans lazing overhead. An army of men hung around, busybodies each trying to get their 10 percent. I waited in reception as the crowd of favor-askers marched onward. Finally the journalist liaison presented himself.

"You're from DesiAdda.com? Never heard of it," he said. Barely a teenager.

"Gossip. Anything that gets clicks," I said. "Bollywood. Pakistan. Saris falling off."

"Fine, just as long as you're not one of those liberal elite journalists." He must have had specially bred right-wing high-caste bat senses, for he knew where every obstacle was without ever looking up from his phone. "Where did you do your master's? USA? I did mine at Western Minnesota. It's very prestigious. Come with me, we've had people all day for Mr. Oberoi, it's a big story and I'm in charge. You will put my name in, won't you, my uncle is the Minister for Forestries." Didn't need to say any more, did he, the little bhosdike?

I was led down corridors that smelled of bleach, past people doing nothing at all. Faces being fanned, sweat-soaked handkerchiefs, TVs blaring talk shows.

"You want to connect on LinkedIn, dude?" he said, fingers tapping away on his phone, sliding past secretaries, eyes never moving from his device.

We got to the office, or at least I thought we did. The boy didn't say anything, just grunted at the door.

Here I go again, I thought. Another stupid plan, and me at the heart of it. I steeled myself for what lay beyond. I had to get my part done. Priya and Rudi's lives depended on me.

I stepped inside.

And there he was, in the flesh, Shashank Oberoi himself, looking fat and tanned, plenty of food in him by the evidence of his waistline, his hair back to black, clearly recovered from tough times, a twenty-something girl hovering around him.

"Holy fuck," he said when he noticed me.

The girl screamed, her hair shining like a beetle's shell as it whipped around her face.

"My God," the young man said, finally wide awake. "It's Captain Umar Chaudhury!"

"The James Bond of Pakistan, yes!" I shouted. "You pig-dogs, you beef-avoiders, this is the revenge of the land of the pure!" I was in a somewhat dramatic frame of mind. I grabbed my wig and threw it to the floor. Then I thought better and retrieved it. A good kidnapper never leaves his equipment behind.

Oberoi gave me a look of disgust.

"You, boy," I shouted to the liaison, in control now, oh what fun! "Get inside! No hero stuff, come here." I dragged him in, and pushed him toward the corner of the room, next to the girl. "Stop screaming! Just stay here, and this will all be over soon."

I shrugged off my backpack, reached inside, and pulled out a gun.

Of course it was not a gun. It was a cigarette lighter shaped like a pistol. Very popular with our undersexed young men, no doubt. Thank goodness for Amazon next-day delivery!

"Don't move, or I start shooting. And when Umar Chaudhury shoots, he never misses." I placed the gun in my pocket, then took out a length of rope and some rags and threw them at the boy. "Tie her up," I said, "and then yourself."

Shashank Oberoi didn't wait around. He took his chance. He got up, pushed past me, kneeing me as he did so, and ran into the corridor.

"The terrorist is here!" he shouted. "He has a bomb. Call the police, he has a suicide vest, he is going to blow—" Unfortunately he did not get a chance to finish, as I tackled him into the wall.

In the hallway, secretaries scattered, janitors threw their mops and fled, probably begging Kali for intercession against this circumcised interloper. Oberoi expected me to die in a hail of bullets. Instead, everyone just ran away.

"See," I said, grunting as I wrapped rope around his hands—I was not letting him escape this time—"see how your grand plans never work out? And I must add, this one was especially culturally insensitive. Pakistan is a land of varied delights and cultures. Come on, get up."

We shuffled down the corridor, my hand around Oberoi's neck.

"It's your fault," I said. "If you hadn't wanted money and Rudi and me dead and gone, none of this would have happened. Your damn fault. Stop weeping."

In the reception, papers littered the floor. Everyone had cleared out. I seemed to be having this effect on the many places I went, like a Dalit family moving into Hauz Khas, or a black one into a white American suburb.

A few armed guards were stationed just outside the door, shouting into their walkie-talkies.

"Shoot him!" shouted Oberoi, spittle from his mouth landing on my hands. "He's a suicide bomber, shoot him or he'll blow you all up!"

Unfortunately, he was too persuasive. None of the guards leapt into action. Kids to look after, bribes to be collected, pay too low. No point. They weren't even allowed in the building normally—couldn't have them snooping on you looting the state, could you? They might want a cut! They thought no more. They dropped their guns and fled.

"You really are an idiot, Oberoi," I said.

We walked into chaos. Everyone was running around like chickens in a pit fight, over lawns, across sprinklers, some of them barely aware why they were panicking, with no idea where they were running to.

We walked through without a fuss. Well, Oberoi tried to run, but I kicked him and he thought better of it.

The policemen at the outer gate had no idea what was going on. They carried paper plates of papri chaat, their guns swinging uselessly at their hips, and waddled around trying to impose calm through the heft of their bodies, slapping their chunky forearms into men and women and shouting in shrill voices, "Arrey!" "Hey!" "Ruko!" "Sir!" "Madam!"

Outside the gates, journalists, peons, politicians, street accident aficionados, Twitter like–needers, and wannabe cutpurses ran around like madmen.

Oberoi looked around and shouted to someone, anyone, that he was being kidnapped. Help him! Him! Didn't they know who he was? He was famous! He was on TV. He had two hundred and seventy-four thousand followers on Instagram. He had been all over the news, he had *been* the news, for the last three days. Someone shoot this man holding him! Someone!

Everyone was too busy saving their own hides.

It was quite pathetic. Of course, no one had cared about him. It was Rudi and Pakistan they cared about, and the idea that they had been duped and made to look like fools. Some dumbass TV producer wasn't the story. He never would be. He wasn't big. He wasn't prime time. Some people never are. Like me. But I knew it. I was at peace with it. He wasn't.

And that was the real tragedy of Shashank Oberoi.

That and being a prick.

I pushed him in front of me. We jumped and ducked past janitors and peons until we reached the main mass of the crowd spilling out onto the road.

The crowd whirled around us, pressed into us, made me lose my breath, squeezed my andas, my chest, my everything. One arm was stuck fast around Oberoi. The other was pinned uselessly at my side. I was reminded of Karkardooma, of the sweat, the feeling of being crushed by your fellow man, not emotionally, like in our families, but actually fucking crushed to death by some obese chutiya sweatcloth civil servant with bad breath and erectile dysfunction.

I finally caught sight of Bhatnagar parked up ahead, and pushed Oberoi in the right direction.

Bhatnagar threw me a parental I-knew-you-could-do-it-when-you-were-pushed look, and helped me shove Oberoi into the back of her car.

I heard the crunch of knees breaking, children wailing, rickshaws collapsing, stalls being overturned as people ran, sirens, Bhatnagar trying desperately to move people out of the way.

"Are you okay?" she shouted from the front.

"Very good, Anju! Just drive, please!" Oberoi was kicking at me and screaming. I gave him a few back, and thrust a dirty washcloth into his mouth to stop the noise.

We were soon racing to the studio, our siren clearing the traffic ahead of us. Bhatnagar drove like crazy, mowing through intersections, grazing rickshaw drivers, until she realized what she was doing and slowed, her teeth gritted in concentration, her eyes distant, breathing loud and hard, thumbs dancing with a mad rhythm on the steering wheel.

I kept my head down and prayed that Rudi and Priya were okay.

I had survived so far. How much further was up to the gods.

TWENTY

We got to the TV studio. How, I don't know, but we did.

At the gate, the guards, the very same who a few days before had so failed in their duty, their expressions still much chastened after their lack of success in catching the Pakistani agent, bombarded Bhatnagar with questions.

"I'm a senior investigator from the Central Bureau," she said. "Here to get to the bottom of the matter."

"Ma'am, we have to do a thorough sweep," said a turbaned guard with a wounded expression. "Ma'am, we have had a little trouble—"

"Does it look like I care?" said Bhatnagar in her best American. She had her sunglasses on, and stayed very silent. The guards started to panic, their bravado broke, and they let us through.

My finger stump throbbed with pain and excitement.

"Damn guards," Bhatnagar said from up front. "Like everyone in this country, sticking their noses in your business. My bosses. My family. Everyone."

"Isn't that the truth, ma'am?" I said.

We parked at the back again, next to Bhatnagar's Lexus. Bhatnagar moved ahead and checked the corridors were empty. I pushed Oberoi and he stumbled forward.

"Back home," I told him.

Wasn't it just our luck that the place was entirely empty?

We walked to the broadcast room, where we found Priya at a computer figuring out the details of how exactly we were going to make this go off without getting killed.

She was always the smartest of all of us, always on the case.

I pulled out Oberoi's gag.

"Well," he spat, "all the fucking traitors in the same room. I'm going to get you. All of you, especially you," he said, shouting at Priya's back. "I gave you a chance. You'd be nothing without me."

I grabbed the back of his shirt.

"Fucked her, eh?" he said, his mouth showing too many perfectly capped teeth. "*I* fucked her, the first week. She is very clingy, I warn you."

"You asshole," I said, and without thinking, I punched him with my damaged hand. I swore with pain. I kept going. No one stopped me, not even Priya. Maybe once upon a time she would have objected to violence, but that was before she had had the ill fortune to meet me.

I dealt with Oberoi. I was happy. I was proud of myself.

When I was done, he sobbed. He wept. He crawled across the carpet, trying to hide under a desk. He begged for his life. Did he honestly think I would kill him? Who did he think I was? Him?

What a story he wove.

The old Indian one. He'd done it for his children.

"They will never have a future in this corrupt country. I have to make money to get them out. My salary was nothing. You got hundreds of millions, Rudi, and I got nothing." He spat blood at regular intervals. The makeup women would have to work extra hard to get him ready for his starring role. "All my classmates are crorepatis, and me? I don't have two paise to rub together."

"Your Instagram says otherwise," said Rudi.

"All false, all false! Rented houses, cars, lies! Our backers wanted to fire me. Every day they said, cut your overheads, Shashank, cut your prizes, Shashank. How I fought, how I fought. I gave money to the poor, that was my job. I was not a TV producer, I was a social entrepreneur." He went on. I stopped listening.

Oberoi was one of those men who became less impressive the more you talked to him. Wealth, taste, forcefulness, hair, teeth. But slowly you saw there was nothing there, and one day you were amazed you had ever found anything worthy about him at all and wondered at your own stupidity.

He spent the morning under the desk, chin red with blood, his expression blank, no longer a danger to anyone. We all went out onto the floor of the studio because we couldn't stand being in his sniveling presence.

I walked over to Rudi. He was preparing his lines. He had printed them out and was memorizing them, practicing his gestures, his pauses, the faces he would have to make.

"Broadcast of a lifetime coming up, eh?" I said.

He cleared his throat. "Absolutely, my friend. Maybe you could give what I have written a look, clear up any mistakes," he said, holding out his script.

"No need," I said. "I'm sure you've done a good job, Rudi."

I left him with a touch on the shoulder.

Priya spent the afternoon working on Oberoi's computer in his office. She printed out screenshots of everything incriminating. She'd found a bunch of burner phones, all unlocked, in his desk.

"He didn't even try to hide anything," she said. "He just thought he could fuck you and no one would realize."

"Well, if it had not been for my quick thinking and charm . . ." I said, and kissed her.

We brought Oberoi out from his home under the desk. It was a shame. It suited him. We put him to work, hunched over a telephone in the control room, ringing all the staff we'd need for our impromptu broadcast. He pretended he had important news, that he was starting production of a new show. They should have known he was lying—his voice was so pleasant, so many gilded and honeyed pleases and thank-yous.

He was just getting them in for a few hours, their jobs were going to be renewed, it was all going to be okay. They hadn't seen him for a few days? What was this about Pakistani agents? Nothing! All would be explained when they turned up at five.

We would be on air at seven.

All we had to do was hijack the broadcast.

Four technicians, one room, one door. Bhatnagar would do the barricading. We might get ten minutes if we were lucky, before someone at the channel's main production building in central Delhi figured out how to take our pirate broadcast down.

Our show would look like shit, but we didn't need music or lights or an audience, we just needed to get our message out and hope that India stopped rioting, stopped stuffing their mouths with chole bhature and saffron horseshit, and believed us.

"We are putting these people, your colleagues, in some danger," said Bhatnagar before we began, a general in jeans, "so our first priority will be their safety, and to get them out in case of any emergencies. They come first."

We nodded. We were all serious, for the first time ever, it felt.

They started coming in at five, our hapless guests, a parade of boredom turned to surprise when Bhatnagar and I grabbed them one by one and led them into Rudi's dressing room to be told what was going to happen. Rudi handed out food and drink, tried to explain the situation, and confiscated their phones.

Call-me-Nik and call-me-Sid looked like stunned sheep, spit leaking out of their mouths.

"Really?" they breathed. "Really? Really, dude?" they asked.

"Yes, dude," said Rudi.

We had ten of them, cameramen, video people, one harassed makeup lady who kept weeping about her children. "They deserve to grow up with a mother. You are bad people, very bad people," she wailed. "I cannot believe I gave you my home-made murukku."

Rudi walked between them, attempting to give them pep talks. He looked exhausted, nervous, upset.

"Everyone really hates me," he said quietly when I turned up to the control room an hour later with snacks from the vending machine. I had been guarding the door between our section of the studio and the rest of it. The place was mostly deserted, apart from Bhatnagar out in the satellite room. "They were all just pretending to be nice because I was the boss."

"Arrey, boss," I said. "Pretend is such a cruel word."

"Shit," he said, "if we don't get viciously murdered in the next few days, I am going to have to be nicer to people." He gave a vigorous thumbs-up to the passing call-me-Sid.

It was all going well. Thirty minutes to the broadcast. Priya was busy scanning documents into the computer. Call-me-Nik was making graphics on Photoshop and weeping about how he should have applied to law school in North Carolina instead of coming back to the godforsaken mother country.

On the news channels, there was nothing about Delhi International Studios. We might be able to pull it off.

At five minutes to seven, we were all in position. On our monitors, the announcer said a repeat of *Children Dance Dhamaka* was about to start, then the screen went to black and he apologized for the technical difficulties.

Bhatnagar had managed to stop the repeat. My phone rang. "Ready to go," she said. I tapped a grim-faced technician in front of me, who flipped a switch. The monitor went white, and suddenly Rudi appeared on it, standing in front of a green screen.

"People of India," he said seriously, "I have been a victim of a conspiracy enacted by our former producer, Shashank Oberoi, to kidnap us for money. These lies about fraud and Pakistani spies are just that, lies! I will now tell you the truth."

On the green screen flashed graphics, overlays, graphs. Pretty professional for two hours' work at lathi-point.

Rudi was great. He radiated sincerity, and that old housewife-melting charm. His face a little gaunt, the softness around the edges gone. He looked good. A perfect little son in the shit, begging his mother for help. Women probably sat weeping in their living rooms, calling their friends to tell them to get their husbands to switch off the cricket and start watching channel 114. That kid was on it, Rudi, and he was telling the craziest story you'd ever heard, that little sweetheart, didn't you just want to smother him to death, Maneka?

Real honesty bores people, but honesty that's just on the line between truth and falsehood? The world is built on it.

Rudi laid out our case beautifully. He stuttered a bit, and his hands shook, but he said everything that needed to be said. He was good.

We were so close. He was about to really turn on the emotion for the final push, and I was shouting, "Nearly there, boss, nearly there, perfect" at the monitor.

Unfortunately, the show came to an end after six minutes.

"Ladies and gentlemen of India, I, Rudraksh Saxena, the Brain of Bharat, beg you to believe me. I have always told the truth. I have done the best I could with my limited tal—"

And then the channel feed went dark.

Our transmission had been blocked.

"Do something!" I heard in my ear as Bhatnagar shouted at the technicians. Priya was a blur of action, scrolling through the computers, leafing through technical manuals, rooting through servers and code, looking for a way to restore the broadcast.

"Just one more minute," said Rudi, sighing in front of the cameras. "That's all I needed. I had them. I had them."

There was nothing we could do.

It was all over.

Rudi sat on the floor. He was empty. Priya shut her computer and placed her hands in mine.

"I have no idea what comes next," she said.

Then we heard the loudspeakers.

I raced out to the studio's reception.

Guns. Riot gear. Batons. Lazily smoked cigarettes. Delhi's finest stood behind a row of sandbags positioned fifty feet away from the studio door.

Oh shit.

It was a siege. I saw the helicopters buzz overhead, churning the evening smog with their blades.

How had they gotten here before the broadcast ended?

I ran back to the studio, to Rudi, who was flapping around like a pair of testicles. I looked at the crew.

Then I saw him. A cameraman, looking shifty, avoiding my gaze. I have a sixth sense for shiftiness. A suspicious shape in his pocket. It was clear what had happened. I walked over to him and held out my hand. The lund didn't bother any further. He handed me his phone.

"Sorry, brother," he said.

I took it as quickly as I could, and tried to hide it in my jeans.

"Oh fuck," said Rudi behind me.

Too slow.

"I didn't confiscate his phone. Oh God, this is all my fault."

He looked around, eyes goggling. He put his hands to his face to hide his tears.

"It's my first time conducting a hostage situation," he said. "I was busy, I was tired, I don't know what I'm fucking doing." He

302

started shouting, "I don't fucking know," and began crying. He was just a kid, I realized again. I went over to him and hugged him, metro-tight. "Okay, boss, okay, boss," I said, and I told him how proud I was of him, how he had gone through something no eighteen-year-old should, how well he had done in the broadcast.

Outside the police shouted insults and cricket scores through their megaphones.

"Give up, your mad plot is over," bellowed a voice. "You will never win."

What could I do? What could I do? I looked around, searching for something. My gaze alighted on Oberoi.

"Fuck this," I said, and dragged him to the door before anyone could stop me. He was extremely cooperative.

Priya followed me out. "I'm coming with you," she said.

Just beyond the reception doors stood dozens of police officers behind the sandbag fortifications.

I crept over to the doors, pushing Oberoi along, and opened them. "Let us go," I shouted. "Don't come in. We have a hostage! I have a gun." I pulled out the cigarette lighter pistol from my pocket and waved it around. Priya knelt a few feet behind me, too exhausted to do anything. I found myself full of energy and excitement, or maybe I was pretending, acting out a devil-may-care police officer routine, three days from retirement, that sort of thing, from some film I'd watched.

"No further," I said, "or we'll kill Shashank Oberoi!"

"Who is that?" shouted a disembodied voice.

The look on Oberoi's face was quite something. I almost took a picture of it, but the memory of it was enough. His lips did that upward snarl just before you cry. Wonderful.

"We'll shoot him, so you'd better let us pass, right now! And then the death of Shashank Oberoi will be on your hands!"

"Sir, we do not know who that is! You enemies of the people! Surrender! Come out with your hands up!"

We did not.

"We have guns!" I said again, just to make sure they understood. Nobody tried to come inside. Who knew what sort of further weaponry the Pakistanis had at their disposal?

The French call it an impasse.

We let our former colleagues go. That would kill us in the press. Rudi stood in the reception and praised them as they left. "Well done," he said to someone. "Excellent broadcast" to another. "You were a pleasure to kidnap. Give my best to your wife." As he left, call-me-Sid told Rudi to go fuck himself, as did call-me-Nik, pleasant as always.

At the end of it, there was just us left, Priya, Rudi, Bhatnagar, me, and Oberoi, who looked like one of those animals lying burst on the side of the road with its guts spilled out. Which species it had been in life you couldn't even tell, dog or cat or calf—all you could say was that its legs were curled up, its eyes were like glass, and its belly was full of madly humping flies impregnating it with larvae.

We sat in the reception, surrounded by plants and plastic-weave carpet that we had turned into makeshift defenses. The hours stretched on into the morning.

The police clearly did not want to come in. We saw the officers in charge interviewed on TV. Bhatnagar rolled her eyes at each one. "Corrupt," she spat out, or "Lazy," or mostly, "Fat."

The police were in the middle of the biggest story of their lives. This positive PR opportunity allowed them to display a sense of law and order, after they had failed to contain the riots across the country. Maybe one of them would write a book called *Days in Hell: My Part in the Studio Siege*, or conduct TV interviews to finance a new kitchen, or move to Saket, where the people who count live.

The student protesters arrived in the afternoon, when they had finally woken up. The police let it happen, and did nothing but conduct interviews of extreme self-importance and belly-slapping gravitas.

The students cheered us on, telling us to stay inside for as long as we could. They told us we were heroes and would never give in to base needs such as hunger and showers and not being riddled by bullets.

The police very helpfully allowed them to position themselves between the barricade and us. Let all the crazies be on one side, so the TV viewers could make better sense of it all.

What a mess! We raided the vending machines, paying for each item, no vandalism on Anjali Bhatnagar's watch, no sir, and helped ourselves to tinned chanas from the commissary kitchen, which we guessed were a hundred Gandhis each.

Bhatnagar spent her time conducting long, serious arguments on her phone in the back corridors while Priya and I crouched behind the sofas, saying what we had to out in the open, waving once in a while to the cameras, and laughing as lip-reading experts said we were discussing our plans to hijack helicopters to Pakistan.

"I'm never going to work again, am I?" said Priya.

"Not likely," I said.

"Eh, big man, you're meant to console me and tell me the offers will surely come flooding in. What kind of future husband are you?"

"The offers will surely come flooding in, darling," I said.

"Thank you, darling," she said. We held hands and thought about a future that might never exist.

On TV, the police officers grew visibly happier as more students flooded in, knowing it would look better when they finally had to make their move—a few dozen brave officers, a thin brown line against a tide of marijuana-infested, bedbug-ridden, greasy-haired young adults. The photographers readied their slow-motion cameras for shots of bones breaking and screams of rage.

Oberoi was totally broken. I had never seen him like that before. We stopped taking it out on him. That was how bad he looked.

Two days later, we ran out of food.

Rudi must have gone mad with hunger, for that night he decided to end things himself. "This is all my fault," he declared, and tried to break out. "I must pay for what I've done," he shouted. I had to wrestle him away from the doors.

Two days after that, lips cracked with thirst, brains broken by boredom, we managed to leave.

It was Bhatnagar. She'd worked out some sort of deal. I could hear her arguing late into the night, and by the fifth day, she had managed to arrange something. She stood in front of us, explained that the situation was becoming an embarrassment to her superiors, and told us to follow her.

We left. We believed her. We just walked out. We breathed fresh air. The protesters looked strangely at us as we came out. We marched straight past them. They didn't know what to do.

We reached the line of sandbags and still hadn't been shot. That counted as a victory.

A police inspector shook his head, shouted to an underling, "Tell the television to go away for five minutes," and walked over to us.

"What's going on?" he said. "You are all terrorists. Go back inside or we will shoot."

"I am a senior investigator," said Bhatnagar. "I have been talking to my bosses. This is over. We are walking out. You may take us into custody. Stop performing for the cameras."

She started shouting at him about water and food.

"You want to fight? You want a big drama for the cameras?" she said. "It's two days before Diwali, you fool. The new Shah Rukh movie is coming out today. Who is going to be paying attention to this? Who is going to be watching on TV? Take us into custody. Make the students go home. Phone your senior officers. We are done here."

She crossed her arms and stared the inspector down. He walked away shaking his head. He wasn't used to this new type of Indian woman.

We stood in the shade of a police van, manure brown.

We were all exhausted. We slouched on the tarmac, drank water like camels, and hoped that Bhatnagar was right.

Oberoi couldn't have looked more terrified. He was vibrating like a municipal building built on foundations of sand. He slurped water, watched every officer intently, hid in the middle of us, and made panicked phone calls where all I could hear was "Please, sir, you must help me, I have been abducted by Pakistani spies."

The police officers grunted at him. Nobody took much notice.

A few minutes later, the inspector returned.

"Arrest them," he said. "No beatings!"

Bhatnagar nodded with satisfaction. She had done her part.

We held up our hands so the cuffs could be applied.

No one said a word.

Then we went to jail.

TWENTY-ONE

The court case was a real nightmare. I couldn't follow it at all. There were about twelve different parties suing each other for damages, each trying to get their piece of the action; the state was on us too, for breaking the peace, for all the kidnapping, beating, taking over a TV studio, you know, the cool filmie stuff.

It was like we had become Americans, litigious and deskbound, instead of solving things in our time-honored and effective fashion of death threats, eternal curses, and immolating each other's family members.

The personal court cases are still going, perennially on the docket in some municipal courthouse, making lots of money for my lawyers. I get thick letters forwarded to me every few months, with bills and arraignments and demands for devices to be handed over.

The charges of Pakistani spying disappeared magically. It turned out the People's Party had stopped believing the bedtime stories of some disgraced TV producer. They just pretended it had never happened, and *boom!* away it went, the media more than happy to send it to oblivion.

Was any saffron-garbed politician embarrassed? Did anyone

suffer political blowback? Did people remember they had once spent a few days in a riot over some spy plot?

You bloody guessed it.

Oberoi was simply let go. He vanished. I imagined him somewhere out in the world, buying expensive sunglasses, pitching quiz shows to anyone who'd listen, and avoiding people called Rudraksh.

Now, I could have been stupid.

I could have said all sorts of things about Oberoi, his politician friends, the relations between the classes. But I was mature and responsible. The past was the past. I had a fiancée. I was doing my part for international relations and my future ability to continue living.

I let myself dream.

Never do it, my friends! Never think of your future. Take each day as it comes, according to the principles of dharma and double-entry accounting. There is always someone waiting to fuck you, and never in the nice way.

I was on bail. I thought I was going to get away with everything. I had moved into Priya's, was planning to go to Ahmedabad to meet her parents, and was thinking about restarting the TV show.

So when the police came to arrest me for academic impersonation, ripped me from the arms of the woman I loved, who looked like a dumbass then?

It was midmorning when they turned up, a fortnight after the end of the siege. I thought the inspector was there to catch up and drink tea, and then he held up the summons and my world fell apart.

I was taken to the station, hauled into an airless room filled with policemen. The charge was read out to me.

Ramesh Kumar. Educational fraud. Maximum sentence, five years.

Bhatnagar didn't let me down. She defended me for four days in a stuffy office in front of lawyers, underlings, and scribes writing down every mosquito buzz.

She was all business. Her uniform was ironed sharp and not a hair was out of place.

Four days of defense. Worthless. It was obvious I was going to go to prison. They had clients ready and willing to talk. Phone logs. Email exchanges.

When we had finished on the last day, and everyone had packed up, Bhatnagar and I looked at each other, eye to eye, as the room began to empty.

"I'm sorry I could not help you, Ramesh," she said finally, as the last ogling sub-inspector left. "My bosses. Somebody had to take the blame. I tried to make them see sense. You were the perfect candidate."

The story of my life, I thought to myself.

If it had been a movie, Priya would have been there, and she would have shouted, "They can't do this! They can't! He helped you," and Bhatnagar would have charged out to change her superiors' minds, and a Spanish guitar would have started to play and then there would have been a choir of children.

But no.

At the trial, I had great lawyers, paid for by Rudi.

I can't complain about him. His parents had turned up safe and sound, fragrant and tanned, hadn't even heard about any

Pakistan stuff in Norway, and had told him to let me rot, but he hadn't. He'd come to me in my holding cell and promised me he'd do whatever it took.

My lawyers were English-accented and brown-skinned and looked like they'd commit genocide to get me off.

But it wasn't enough.

Bhatnagar's bosses destroyed me. Bhatnagar tried her best. There was nothing she could do.

So I went to prison. The judge, a gray-haired man who had exhausted his reasonableness by screaming at the press to keep quiet, his voice hoarse and cracked, delivered the final blow.

"I sentence you, Ramesh Kumar, for the multiple frauds you committed, to one year in jail." He banged the gavel. The cameras flashed like lightning. My lawyers shook my hand for some Western reason, and sat down to write checks for their new holiday homes, leaving me to stand alone. The guards led me away.

As I left, somebody in the audience began to wail, an old woman. She kept looking around the court for someone to notice her. Finally a reporter wandered over, and she collapsed into him. I wondered which distant relative she'd pretend to be.

I went to prison. No one else did. Ha ha ha!

Somewhere Claire was eating pastries and laughing to herself. "The wages of sin, *jeune homme*, the wages of sin."

The People's Party got me. The country got me. The system got me. I made too many people look bad, and they got me.

Rudi wasn't touched. He hadn't done a thing wrong, of course.

I wasn't involved in his being Topper, how could I be? Surely some urchin type could not come top in the exalted All Indias, the greatest exam in all the world. Surely Rudraksh Saxena had merely been hoodwinked by some unsavory lower-caste middleman type who had promised him riches. What innocent Brahmin boy could tell who these people truly were?

He was only guilty of the crime of being too trusting.

He could go back to selling microwaves and daal and liposuction as soon as he wanted.

My whole life would be a small subsection on his Wikipedia page.

Prison, that was a real experience, I will tell you. Rudi had to pay a fortune to get the gangsters off me. I might have been a nobody, but they knew I was Rudraksh Saxena's manager. I was ripe for some physical extortion.

Thankfully I didn't have to forfeit any of my own money. I got sued, a lot. The parents of every kid who'd fucked up their All Indias in the last ten years wanted a piece of me. Rudi got the cases dismissed. It cost him a lot, but he'd made so much money that he didn't have to worry.

Priya came a few times.

We said nothing much the first few visits.

The last time she came, she said, "I'll wait for you," but who was she kidding? She loved her parents. They'd never let her marry someone like me. She was modern and independent, but they were her blood and they mattered more than me, and they were never going to have a criminal in the family.

I told her then to stop coming, told her we'd been stressed and that anyone could fall in love under pressure, that it wasn't real, just us searching for some small human connection in impossible circumstances.

Maybe it was even true. She cried a lot.

That last time I looked into her eyes, across the table, I saw the most terrible thing in the world. I saw unending love. She'd never leave. She would destroy herself, her name, her family, her future.

So I told a little lie.

"Bhatnagar said her bosses are going after my associates. They'll never stop, Priya. You think this is the end? If we carry on, they'll get you next, and your parents, and everyone you've ever known."

She shook her head. "You're lying," she said.

"I promised I would never lie, remember? The day I told you I first loved you. One lie and we were done."

"I remember," she said.

"You can't destroy yourself for me, Priya. See sense. See the way it must be."

I went over and held her for the last time. I'd bribe the guards later. I felt her tears land on the side of my face.

She said she'd return, she said she'd fight, but her smile was worn, her eyes were dull. She sent letters, which I never answered. I was glad when they stopped.

I pined for her. There were many moments when I wanted to write to her and profess my love, and say that we would run away, hang her parents, hang tradition. If they wanted to see their grandkids they'd better change their attitude.

But I'd told my lie. The perfect lie. I'd destroyed us forever. Aren't I clever?

I had a lot of close calls in prison. The usual, in showers that suddenly emptied, in kitchens where boiling vats bubbled, in exercise yards where anyone could get knifed in the churn of the crowd. I was a celebrity. I was a spy. I was someone.

Rudi had paid good money so that there would only be two of us in the cell, and not the usual fifteen. Then he had to pay more because I was attacked for being spoiled and Western. Only two to a cell! It was against all the Vedic principles.

Normally people say they read a lot in prison and transformed their lives through ancient books of philosophy and religion. I tried mostly not to get stabbed. I had a shower once a day. I ate oily chapatis and watery daal.

One day I had a visit. "Some fellow from Charity Chai to see you," said the guard.

It was my bloody father.

He looked ten years younger than the time I'd last seen him. A man followed him in, clutching a camera by his side.

"Ramesh," said my father. His fingers still stuck in that claw of his, but there was a contentment, a roundness to the rest of him.

"Charity Chai?" I said. Seven years, and those were my first words to my father.

He gave me a little rat-smile and sat next to me on my bed. "The alliteration makes it easier for the whites to remember. Everyone knows Charity Chai," he said. "What a story! He slaved hard at his tea stall to get his son into convent school, but then his son disappeared, so now he does the same for all the children of Old De—"

"Who's that?" I said, pointing at his companion. Papa was far too self-congratulatory and far too full of devious schemes.

"He's from some American streaming service. They want

more feel-good ethnic films, like that sushi fellow. Prakash bhai, turn the camera off. This is a deleted scene," he said, and his body hacked with laughter.

"Nothing feel-good about this," I said.

"What an ending, no? He saved the poor boys of Delhi, but now he has to save his own long-lost son."

"Could have saved me six months ago, Papa."

"I had not signed the television deal then," he said.

I folded my arms and looked at the floor.

"I want to help," he said, and touched my shoulder, and I did my very, very hardest not to flinch, as once I would have. "We can spin them a tale. You did this all for money. I came and saved you. You will be someone again." He saw that I wanted nothing to do with him, even though I hadn't seen him in seven years.

We stared at each other a little longer. He didn't seem to want to leave.

"Papa, can we talk about our feelings?" I said.

That did it. Off he went.

"Call me when you get out," were his last words.

I did not.

I wasn't going to lie anymore. I wasn't going to tell half-truths. I deserved punishment. I was going to take it like a man.

I got out within six months.

They handed me a piece of paper on the way out saying I was to be a productive member of society and that they hoped I would not be back. I had money, but I had nothing else. It was like being born again.

At the gates, I was met by Rudi's car.

There were no journalists. I had been ordered to be forgotten.

I holed up back in the flat. Whenever I passed the landlord on the stairs to pick up fast-food deliveries, he would mutter insults under his breath.

Beat the Brain was still a hit, bigger than ever before. Priya was the producer now. Rudi asked me if I wanted to see her. I didn't even answer him.

I stayed in the flat all day and hoped the world would forget about me.

For a while, I wanted to do the romantic thing, the old dream, set up a school for kids like me. We would harvest rainwater and I would say in assemblies, "I'm not teaching you children how to learn, but how to live," but nah, yaar, that's something for when you're forty. Who the hell wants to live in the arsehole of somewhere with a bunch of whiny kids when you're twenty-five? I thought also that I might be a little too self-centered to make it work.

Rudi was like a changed man. No drugs. No partying. No nonsense.

He got a girlfriend and suddenly I wasn't necessary anymore. She was nice. She wanted me to stay. But I could tell that he needed to be with her.

I left without even saying goodbye.

It was staring me in the face all along.

I was a pariah in India—nobody fucks with the exam system like that and gets away with it. But what do Indians love more than anything? The West. And what does the West like more than anything? A rise-and-fall-and-rise-again story. Redemption. Forgiveness. All that Christian stuff. I admit that Papa had also given me ideas.

To get India to love me, I would need to leave it.

The religion angle had been staring me in the face for a long time.

Temples and mosques, my father, Claire.

I got a business visa to the US. They didn't generally let criminals in, but a little money to their Indian consulate staff cleared up any problems.

I bought twenty-four acres of land two hundred kilometers north of Houston, with good airport links and the interstate a few miles away. I had a main house with three bedrooms and an outhouse with six more, small cell rooms barely big enough for a bed and a desk in each. I bought a van, put up a website, and hired a Mexican housekeeper I'd found in a convenience store whose wages I immediately doubled. I got tamales from her three times a week.

Business was slow at first. The website was uninformative. I had no reviews. There had been a program about Indian cults on Netflix and the Brooklynites were wary.

Then people came flooding in.

A retiree couple. A German tourist driving around the south. A mattress company executive who'd had a mental breakdown. We would all sit around a fire eating vegetarian chili under the stars and talk about the ways our lives had turned out. The days were for quiet contemplation and walking around the acreage, mending fences and doing light physical work.

I bought some cows and let them graze, and a few horses. It was very Vedic.

In Texas they all eat barbecue and shoot guns and drive jeeps, like some parody of America. I was friendly to the local Christians, who came to make sure that I wasn't drugging teenage girls to be sex slaves. They even tried to convert me afterward.

After a year, I was fully booked.

News spread quickly about the strange nine-fingered young Indian who was running a retreat in rural Texas and, miraculously, not drugging anyone while doing it.

Go and find out what's going on, Olivia, Hannah, Rachel, get me some dirt, said the editors.

I was notorious. I looked too good to be true. But I convinced them all. I was open about my past. I had hurt people. I was mending my ways.

The magazines, the internet sites for racially conscious white millennials, the national TV shows, they all descended on me like vultures. I gave free weekends to influencers.

I ran a tight ship. No fucking around. Just talking and walking and working and fasting.

I grew my hair. I started wearing orange, like the saffrons. I put the prices up, first to five hundred dollars a week, then a thousand, with a few free rooms for stragglers and wastrels and drop-ins. I constructed some tents away from the house, with solar heaters and rainwater showers. Our hikes lasted three hours. We replenished ourselves with sacrificially purified mineral water. I confiscated phones. We talked of forgiveness and being true to our better selves.

Instagram, Facebook, Twitter—I was all over them, but I stayed mysterious. I took artful shots of hands meeting in the dust, of footprints on sand and embers in the dusk. I let the media do the selling. I took my guests, my executives and managers, and made them something better. By the end of the week, they shone with gratitude and hard work and inner peace. I made them clear scrubland and put up more tents. For dinner we served them vegan burritos and allowed them a few joints of faux-Himalayan weed in our nightly talks.

I made a lot of money.

I don't know why everyone brown isn't in this business. The whites are begging for it.

I don't even try to be mystical. People just tell me things without me asking. If they call me Guru-ji, I get very annoyed. Just Ramesh, I say. All these rich Americans are guilty about everything, and they desperately need to be forgiven. I tell them how we are all looking for forgiveness, not just them, but me too, and we hug in the pink dawn light.

The whites tell you everything. It's strange how they hide their true thoughts away for most of their lives, but when they finally open up, you know everything about them. Kids, sex, mental problems, incest, rape, drugs, child abuse. We all listen and we cry and we forgive.

The Indian press started covering me soon enough, and sent shifty-looking men and women, Sharmas and Patels. The old accent made my ears burn.

Out came the profiles in India. I had Wi-Fi, of course, even if the renunciants didn't. Forgiveness was coming. You could sense it, but I had stopped caring.

I found myself not thinking about India at all, not even craving its silent acceptance, until my original idea felt like the most pointless thing in the world.

Who cares about being someone there?

In the mornings I bow to my guests, and they to me, and we say "Om!" and let it ring out across the plains, and then I serve them Josefina's bean soup before we sweat out our sins.

It is unbelievably boring.

This place is hotter than a bhosdike. Out on the plain with the cows and the watering holes and the buffel grass, you can let yourself think you are in India a hundred years from now, when everything is at peace and the uteruses have stopped pumping out kids and everyone has moved on from trying to kill each other.

Maybe not a hundred years then.

There are Indians here with strange, mixed-up nasal voices (that even mine is turning into, I fear), who wear cowboy boots and hats with broad brims, who eat beef and vote Republican. They come to the shop I have set up, to buy crystals and Ganesha statues and Dehradun rice, drawn to my celebrity. They have daughters in medical school with colored hair who look straight into your eyes and take no bullshit from anyone.

Even Rudi's going to come down, he says, with his wife. He wants to bring a TV crew. A grand reunion. The housewives will dehydrate themselves through crying.

Thank you, Papa. Thank you, Claire. Thank you, Rudi. Thank you, Anju and Abhi and Priya.

I guess I made it after all.

ACKNOWLEDGMENTS

To my family, who support me in all things. Thank you for tolerating me. I am poorer without you. To my grandparents, who gave me the gift of knowledge. To my teachers, LP, LF, JO, and AM, who told me I'd do this someday. Big mistake.

To Sam Copeland, first reader. Thank you for this all. This is the part where I'm contractually obliged to call you handsome. To everyone at Rogers, Coleridge, and White for sending this book around the world.

To Ailah Ahmed, who makes everything better, and whose faith in this book has been a source of joy. To everyone at Little, Brown, who gave this book a home. To Emily Griffin, who always asks the right questions. To their assistants, for answering midnight emails.

To all the writers I've met, who have cajoled, motivated, pestered, and supported me. To the children of Delhi, many of whom found their way into this book. You deserve the world.

To CB, who lit the fire. CH, AQ, and RG, who gave me time. DH, DR, CL, and TM, who know where the bodies are buried. JG, PR, AS, AN, and SH, whom I should have told about this book. To DL, JI, PS, and FR, the murderers' row. To CN and ZA for always listening, especially when they shouldn't have. To RM, never forgotten, who left us far too soon.

ABOUT THE AUTHOR

Rahul Raina divides his time between Oxford and Delhi, where he was born. He is twenty-eight years old and splits his time between running his own consultancy in Britain and working for charities benefiting street children and teaching English in India. *How to Kidnap the Rich*, his first novel, was written in the forty degree-plus heat of Delhi.